A Long Walk Home

[redacted]

Book Two of The Sand Dollar Series

A Long Walk Home

Barbara Andrews

Tate Publishing & *Enterprises*

A Long Walk Home

Published by Tate Publishing & Enterprises, LLC
127 E. Trade Center Terrace | Mustang, Oklahoma 73064 USA
1.888.361.9473 | www.tatepublishing.com

Tate Publishing is committed to excellence in the publishing industry. The company reflects the philosophy established by the founders, based on Psalm 68:11,
"The Lord gave the word and great was the company of those who published it."

Cover and Interior design by Scott Parrish

Published in the United States of America

ISBN: 978-1-61663-347-9

1. Fiction, Christian, Romance
2. Fiction, Christian, Historical
10.08.18

DEDICATION

To Lauren…
I love you! See you when I get there…

ACKNOWLEDGMENTS

I probably would not have written, *much less published,* this book without the unwavering support and encouragement from my mother. For every bit of self-doubt I experienced, Mom had twice the amount of confidence in me. For all the times that the demands of life pushed writing lower on my priority list, Mom lovingly pushed me to attend to my dreams. Everyone needs a loyal fan in her life, and if one is fortunate to have that kind of unconditional love and support, she is truly blessed. *Mom, I love you. Thanks for believing in me.*

Oh no! I just had a clear vision of Dad's face right now. He is wearing that sad, little puppy-dog expression, wondering where all the attention went! But if he happens to look closely, he will read about some of the sweetest memories I still treasure from our past together…

I want to also say "thank you" to all my girls, special friends who have continued to encourage me, challenge me, and believe in me.

I

The bloody nose wasn't so bad. It would clean right up with the swipe of a shirttail or back of the hand. The real problem was the nice little shiner starting to spread from the corner of her eye to her cheekbone. That kind of thing wasn't as easy to hide. To make matters worse, riotous blond curls, now tangled with leaves and streaked with dirt, were whipping around her face. Once the curls escaped from her barrette and bobby pins, they refused to be retamed. She sat amidst the pile of swirling leaves, skinny legs outspread and hands planted firmly on the ground holding her diminutive body erect. Her books were scattered wildly, her satchel torn, and she watched with some consternation as the last of her English paper swirled and danced away on the crisp, October wind.

"Good grief!" she muttered angrily, wiping her hand across her nose and wincing at the tenderness of her cheek. She studied her scraped knuckles, and a crooked grin turned up the corners of full, pink lips. Well, at least there was some consolation when she thought about the satisfying thud her right upper cut landed on the ugly mug of Danny Tyler. *What a waste of good oxygen,* she thought. That bully had about as much brains as she could pour into Mama's sewing thimble. She'd done her best these last couple of years to follow Pop's advice and ignore the creep—especially now that she was "older." She had even ignored the name-callin' and vicious pranks for which she always seemed to be the target. She couldn't help her tiny stature, but she *could* do something about her Goliath-sized attitude,

Pop always said. It was that heart of a lion inside the body of a mouse that had earned her the nickname "Irony." She was a champion of the underdog, being one herself. She figured that sometimes in life, you came upon situations that demanded no less than a reckoning. Danny had one comin' for a long time, and it looked like she was the one to deliver it.

Oh, she could have held back had *she* been the target this time. Heaven knows she'd had enough practice clenching her teeth and digging her nails into her tightly curled fists that just itched to take a swing. The images of Pop's disappointed eyes and the scornful sneer on her perfect sister's face usually kept those small fists locked into place at her side. No ... she could have turned and walked away had it been *her* bony little chest that dirty finger kept jabbing into, *her* face his nasty spittle landed on, *her* ears ringing from the cruel taunts and insults. She could have pushed his hands aside and walked away with nothing more than a haughty, superior look on her face. And truthfully, she really did start to walk past the excited group of young teens beginning to form a tight circle around ugly Danny Tyler. It was not her business. She had promised Mama she'd be home right after school to help bake and decorate a cake. It was the twentieth birthday of her sister, Kathryn, and Mama wanted this to be a special day since it'd be the last birthday Kathryn would spend as a single woman in her childhood home. In six months, she'd be *Mrs.* Rodney Caulfield, achieving her one and only goal for the last thirteen years. It remained a mystery to Berdine. How could you be standing at the very precipice of life's adventure only to step across and become the *property* of another person? Didn't make a lick of sense. Besides that, Dr. Caulfield was *old.* He was almost as old as Pop... Well, she amended, twenty-eight *seemed* as old as Pop! But Kathryn didn't seem to mind. She just floated around the house, humming and acting like a besotted idiot. She once told Kathryn, "If you *ever* see me acting like a lovesick calf, just pinch me real hard!" Kathryn obviously believed forewarned is forearmed because she took the opportunity right then and there to squeeze the biggest pinch she could manage. From then on, it seemed prudent to just ignore her sister's terminal lovesickness.

The bottom line, to her way of thinking, was that she and her sister were as different as night and day. The only thing it seemed they shared were the honey-colored curls... even then, Kathryn made sure there was a distinction between them. Kathryn spent *forever* in front of the mirror flat ironing, teasing, then twisting her hair up so that she would look "mature." But to *her*, that time was better spent searching for the perfect barrette to tame her badly behaved curls so she didn't have to even think about her hair! As of her fifteenth birthday this year, the perfect barrette had not yet been invented. And though Pop was understanding about most things, he wasn't about to let his girls cut their curls.

The wind gusted, tossing Berdine's unruly locks into her face. Sighing heavily, she pushed it out of her eyes, playing the conversation with her father over in her head.

"Irony, baby, why would you want to cut off all that silky gold? You didn't even have a single strand till you were three years old!" Pop would run a calloused hand over the top of her head, smiling indulgently when she crossed her skinny arms over her chest.

"Pop! It's just in the way! Besides it's too much for my little bird face. Probably why you named me *Bird*-ine ... You knew I'd look just like one! I wish I were a boy! Then I could just get a buzz cut like the one Michael had two summers ago." Berdine stamped her foot in frustration.

"If you didn't have your long hair, Berdine, people would think you *were* a boy!" Kathryn smirked, tugging at a curl as she passed Pop's chair. "Lord knows you sure act like one!"

She remembered how Pop had frowned and shaken his head lightly at Kathryn as she sashayed through the den. Berdine had retorted, "Oh, *shut up*, Kathryn. Just go sit on a shelf somewhere and look pretty. It's what you do best."

"Girls, girls ... try to act like ladies." Pop sighed heavily. He spent a lot of time running interference.

"Ha! Well, at least one of us can manage that!" Kathryn always liked getting in the parting shot as she made her dramatic exits.

Which brought Berdine back to the humiliating truth of her sister's words. Here she was, sitting on the ground, her face bloodied and bruised. Her hair was a tangled mess and, as far as she could see, no hope in the near future that the mysterious and elusive feminine side of her was going to emerge. Mama had made such an embarrassing fuss when she had turned thirteen two years ago and got her period as an unwanted birthday gift. "Oh! My baby Berdie is a woman now!" But where were the curves? Where was the china-doll skin her sister had? Where were those shy, lingering smiles from the guys who'd rather go tree climbing with her than ask her on a date?

She got cheated. Plain and simple. All the womanly genes went to Kathryn, and all that was left over was just enough to give her cramps. She sighed heavily, rubbing her sore cheek. The lingering sting she felt was not so much from the bruise on her face as the humiliation she felt now as she replayed the whole sorry incident in her mind.

II

It all began with Michael . . . seems like things usually did.

He was her best friend—much better than a girl ever could have been. *He* didn't blab her secrets. He didn't laugh when she told him something embarrassing, and up until recently, he was her greatest fan. They used to love racing through the park and down to the creek bed, where they'd fish for hours. He loved the fact that she never backed down from a dare and she pulled her weight when they worked for hours on their secret tree house. In fact, she was the one who designed and directed the whole project. He used to tell her with the solemn wisdom of one six months older than she, "I may be the muscles of this project, Berdie . . . but you're the brains." Berdine remembered dropping her hammer in playful shock as she reached out and squeezed his scrawny arm. "What muscles?" She had laughed playfully and then gasped in startled surprise when he pushed her into the icy, cold creek. She came up sputtering and then launched an attack on the skinny boy, not much taller than herself. They tussled and rolled until both lay breathing hard, flat on their backs in the waning rays of the hot August sun. It was a great summer, she remembered. Exploring the creek during the long hot afternoons, eating picnic lunches in their secret hideaway, catching fireflies in the park after dark . . . they were inseparable.

Mount Holly was a sleepy little town in Berkley County, South Carolina—just northeast of Charleston. Nothing very exciting nor extraordinary ever happened there. Summer meant lots of unsupervised time to pursue whatever adventure hatched in the creative little mind of Berdine. The only obstacle to their complete freedom was that Berdine's parents were a lot more watchful than Michael's dad was. They had an annoying habit of ringing a bell for her to come in at night just after the stars popped out. Just when firefly hunting started getting good . . . *ding-a-ling-a-ling!*

"*Coming!*" Berdine would call out. She'd grimace in frustration at Michael. He cuffed her lightly on the shoulder and grinned.

"Go on . . . I won't catch *all* the fireflies tonight. I'll save one or two for you for tomorrow night."

Berdine stuck her tongue out and then sighed with disgust. "How come you get to stay out as long as you want?"

Michael shrugged his skinny shoulders and brushed back the flop of black hair from his sweaty forehead. "I can think of at least three good reasons: One, I'm older. Two, I'm a guy. And three, my dad's never home by dark anyway. He works the night shift at the mill."

Berdine sighed again. "You are *so* lucky. And summer's way too short. A kid oughta be able to stay out as late as she wants when there's no school!"

Michael nodded his head with the empathy she'd come to count on. He patted her shoulder and said, "Aw, don't feel so bad. Least you got a mom and dad inside and a warm dinner on the table."

Berdine looked startled then lifted stricken eyes to her best friend. "Gosh, Michael. I wasn't tryin' to make you feel bad. You know Mama and Pop would let you come have a plate too. Why don't you come on up with me?"

Michael shook his head then grinned broadly. "And miss my chance to get ahead of you in the firefly count? No way."

Berdine punched him lightly in the stomach. "You are such a pest, Michael Caraway!" They laughed together easily, with the innocence and carelessness only found in that short time of preadolescence.

When she heard the insistent ringing of the bell for the third or fourth time, Berdine knew she better fly. A ring past that would surely constitute a grounding, and Berdine wasn't about to forfeit one minute of her summer freedom.

"See ya!" she called out with a parting wave as she took off in a run toward 311 Apple Grove Lane. She didn't slow down till she was in the front door, leaning back against it, gasping for breath. Mama came around the corner wiping her hands on a dishtowel. She took in the sweaty-faced, flush-cheeked little firecracker grinning back at her and just shook her head and pointed a finger up the stairs.

"Wash up?" Berdine asked hopefully.

"Bathe!" Mama commanded. "Then come down and have some dinner."

"Aw, Mama... can't I just wash my hands and take a bath *after* dinner?" Berdine pleaded.

"You stink like sweat, Berdine!" Her sister passed by, holding her nose and giving Berdine a wide berth.

"Shush, Kathryn. I'll be the mother in this situation, thank you very much." Mama had her hands on her hips and her mouth compressed into that straight line that silenced all arguments... from either girl.

Berdine had decided at that point to cut her losses and turned to trudge up the stairs. Under her breath, she muttered, "I bet no one makes Michael take a bath!"

Kathryn stuck her head around the top of the staircase, delighted for another parting shot. "Michael stinks too!" she hissed. Berdine shook her head, feeling sorry for Kathryn's future victim.

III

Berdine sighed, letting the memory fade, and attempted to untangle some of the knots in her hair. Every time she made progress, a gust of wind would toss the locks back into tangles. She lifted her chin and decided she had sat on the dirty ground long enough.

This time when she arrived home, she would head straight for the bath without Mama even telling her to. Part of the motivation, she thought honestly, was to prolong the moment Pop got a good look at her face. She pushed herself up, her muscles protesting the movement. Amazing… barely fifteen years old and already feeling fifty (or at least what she thought it must feel like). She brushed off the knees of her jeans and then bent to gather up her books and papers. She sighed wearily as she stuffed them into the torn satchel. Funny how when the excitement's over not a soul is around to help you up!

Her heart burned a little when she remembered the horrified look on Michael's face. What in the world had possessed her to step into a fight that wasn't her business? She just couldn't help it. Where

Michael was concerned . . . it *was* her business. Oh, she knew the distance between them had been growing for a while now, and it made her heart ache. It just didn't make sense that, after all those perfect summers when they were inseparable, things slowly started to change between them. Berdine blamed it on "the curse." Ever since that uncomfortable afternoon shortly after her thirteenth birthday, Michael had seemed to start pulling away.

Berdine scowled as she remembered begging Mama to let her stay home from school. Her cramps were horrible that day, and her mood was even worse. Michael had stopped by as he always did to walk her to school, but that morning, she was silent and sullen on the way there. Michael did all the things he knew to cheer her up, but nothing seemed to work. By the time they had journeyed the fifteen minutes it took to reach the school grounds, Michael was growing desperate. When he passed her in the hall during the day, he would search her face, anxiously hoping to solve the mystery of her bad mood. After the final bell rung, Michael saw that Berdine had already taken off down the path—without even waiting for him! He hurried to catch up with her. He almost had to trot to match her determined stride.

"Berdine, *what the heck* is wrong with you? Are you mad or something? You've never gone a whole day not speaking to me! Did I do something?" Michael asked pleadingly.

"You wouldn't understand, Michael!" Berdine grumbled and hastened on.

Michael scratched his head in consternation, studying her expression as if the answers to this puzzle would appear. About the time they neared the creek and their secret tree house, Michael made an impulsive decision. He pulled her arm sharply over toward their tree.

"Michael, stop it! What are you doing?" Berdine shrieked.

"C'mon, Berdine, we're not going home until we talk about why you're mad." Michael tugged her to the ladder. "Now get on up there. I mean it."

"I'm not mad . . . " Berdine mumbled, but she headed up the tree house ladder. Within moments they were sitting across from each other, staring and not speaking. Berdine felt a blush starting at her collar and working its way up her neck and face.

"Okay. Spill it. I thought we were friends. We've been mad at each other before, but we always either duked it out or talked it out. So which is it gonna be?" Michael leveled a challenging stare at the flustered little blond sitting across from him with her arms wrapped tightly around her middle.

"I already told you I wasn't mad at you. I'm not mad at anyone. I don't know *what's* wrong with me. I think I might be sad. Well, maybe with a little mad mixed in there too ..." Berdine rambled, and Michael looked even more confused. Finally he reached out and took her hand.

"You're not making any sense, Berdine ..."

"Oh, Michael!" She suddenly wailed. "I got my period, and now *nothing* is ever gonna be the same again. I'm such a freak!"

She dissolved into deep, hiccupping sobs and threw herself into Michael's arms. If she had seen Michael's expression, she might have slugged his arm, rolled her eyes, and finished off the whole crazy scene with laughter. But her head was nestled against his young chest, tears wetting his T-shirt, and her arms wrapped in a death grip around his waist. She was sitting half across his lap, and her sobs were starting to slow. Michael's eyebrows had shot to the top of his forehead, and at first he held his arms out apart from the shaking, diminutive body. Then, slowly, awkwardly he wrapped his arms around her and patted her shoulder.

In a few moments, Berdine quieted, and reason returned to her like the roaring of a freight engine. She became aware of Michael's tightened grip around her shoulders and how she was huddled against him in his lap. Embarrassment washed over her. She timidly lifted her face and started to speak. In that same moment, Michael's face came down in a sudden, determined movement and mashed his lips against hers. It was an awkward moment, yet heat rose from their bodies like a rushing forest fire. Berdine gasped and then jumped away from Michael as if he had seared her flesh. Michael jumped at the same time, knocking his head against the branch above him.

"Oww!" He yelped, moving as far away from Berdine as he could manage in the small space.

"What did you do *that* for?" Berdine accused, wiping her lips with the back of her hand.

"I thought you wanted me to! You were wrapped all around me like a pretzel!" Michael's embarrassment turned to sharp anger.

Berdine's face burned red, and she couldn't seem to think of any of the snappy comebacks she usually had in her arsenal.

"That's a buncha bullcorn! Don't touch me again, Michael Caraway!" Berdine huffed, and she turned to climb down the tree house ladder. She leapt to the ground and glared up at the flustered boy. "If you want to go around kissin' people, go kiss Jennie Martin. She'll kiss *anybody!*"

Before Michael could get in a retort, Berdine was already running toward home. When she was far enough away, she dropped to her knees, covered her face with her hands and wept like a baby. She wept out of embarrassment and confusion, yearning for the way things used to be. She wept, somehow knowing instinctively that the simplicity of summers past was over.

IV

The road through adolescence to young adulthood is rocky at best and downright agonizing at its worst. Over the next two years, Berdine and Michael experienced the confusion of unfamiliar feelings, bewildering physical changes, and undefined rules in their relationship. As a result, the chasm between them widened. Berdine watched Michael longingly from a distance, wishing they could return to the uncomplicated camaraderie of their childhood. Michael, too, missed the companionship of his one true friend, but pride and the adolescent sting of rejection gradually hardened his heart. Reacting to the loneliness, Michael searched for an identity that would build a defensive wall around himself.

People had always whispered about him, calling him a "wild child." Now, he just figured he'd turn all those rumors into truth. He began to go looking for trouble. He started hanging out with "the bad kids" and smoking with them in the parking lot before school. No one ever pinned it on him, but any minor vandalism incident always seemed to have his name attached to it. He earned the reputation of "a tough guy," and it suited him just fine. Gone were the days of a buzz cut. Instead, the longer his hair grew, the better he liked it. His wiry, awkward body was starting to fill out in all the right places. The girls at school began to notice him, and his "bad reputation" merely heightened his growing mystique.

And all the while, Berdine quietly watched from a distance, her heart grieving the loss of his friendship. Though he was making himself over in a way that fooled everyone else, Berdine was not deceived for a moment. All she had to do was catch his gaze when they passed in the hallway to see the boy she knew hidden behind those dark, angry eyes. She had tried several times to approach him, but his pride and hurt were so thick, he rejected all of her attempts to make amends.

Apparently, he had decided to follow her impulsive suggestion and had taken up with Jennie Martin. Many times, as Berdine passed him and Jennie in the hall, Michael would suddenly pull Jennie into a dramatic embrace against the lockers, kissing her with movie star passion. Berdine rolled her eyes in disgust and passed by quickly, missing the way Michael's eyes followed her over the shoulder of Jennie Martin.

"*Seriously,* Berdie, you can just *tell* Michael still likes you," her girlfriends would say.

"He watches you all the time!" Then they would sigh and shake their heads, wishing *they* were the ones attracting those dark, heated looks.

"Ha! Like I believe *that!* Every time he sees me in the hall, he grabs Jennie for another make-out session!" Berdine huffed angrily.

"Aww, Berdie, you know he just does that to make you jealous! Remember how you two used to go everywhere together? And you didn't even give us the time of day! What happened between you two?" The girls would huddle around, hoping for some juicy tidbits. Berdine just shrugged, unwilling to cast aspersions on the friend who still held her heart.

"That was then. This is now. We just grew up, I guess." She would sigh softly, her eyes fixed on some distant scene.

Things *might* have eventually gotten better. In fact, they were starting to head in that direction. Berdine heard through the grapevine that Michael had broken up with Jennie, *and* he had even smiled at her when she passed him on the way to algebra. And today! Today had started out with hope on the horizon. She had just gotten to school and was running late. Since she didn't have time to go to her locker, she was toting four heavy books, only two of which fit into her satchel. She was attempting to shift the two in her arm to the other side and swing the satchel over the opposite shoulder. She was looking down, so she didn't see the body directly in her path. Wham! She smacked right into a solid wall of flesh; books and satchel flying in opposite directions.

"*Gosh,* I am *so* sorry! I was in a hurry, and I didn't see ..." Berdine looked up and was pinned by the searching gaze in Michael's eyes. "You." She swallowed hard and dropped her eyes, going to her knees to gather up books. Michael went down to his knees as well, and that familiar, crooked grin slashed across his face.

He chuckled. "Still packs a punch. Tiny as a firecracker, but just as dangerous." He shook his head as if remembering a private joke.

Berdine couldn't think of anything intelligent to say in return. She just grinned and allowed him to help her gather her stuff.

"Well! Sorry again. I guess we're both late to class now. Um ... thanks for your help ..." Berdine scrambled to her feet, her heart soaring. She hurried off down the hall then couldn't resist a quick peek back over her shoulder. There he stood, both hands on his hips in sort of a James Dean kind of pose, a thoughtful smile on his face.

"*Oh, help!*" Berdine breathed and then hurried on around the corner.

V

They were on the mend. She just *knew* it! The ice was broken. Surely it wouldn't be much longer before they resumed the friendship she'd missed so badly. She had left school that day with a secret smile on her face, her satchel swinging at her side and a tingle playing around her heart. She was headed home the way she always walked, kicking the leaves as they danced around her bobby socks and turned-up cuffed jeans. She was remembering that summer four years ago when they built the tree house together. Michael had let her be the boss, hammering where she told him to. She always tended to have definite opinions about things, so he was content to let her call the shots. He was nearly always game for any of her wild schemes. They fit together, she thought. Just like the boards they had measured and fitted together. She smiled inwardly, wondering if he'd ever gone back to the tree house in those following three years. *She* certainly had, if only to remember the fun they'd had that summer.

Berdine was lost in thought and almost didn't hear the angry taunts and encouraging cheers from the circle of kids until she was upon them. She sized up the group and knew immediately that a fight was either in the making or underway. She slowed down, straining her neck to peer through the crowd. So many kids had gathered, closing in the circle, and it was hard to see who was involved.

Several kids shifted excitedly, hoping to get a better view. In the sudden, small opening, Berdine was able to squeeze up to the front. She shivered with disgust at the spit flying from Danny Tyler's lips and the red angry flush on his face. He was jabbing his finger against someone's chest and spouting insults.

"An' we all know your daddy is a drunk and your mama is trash. Fact is you probably don't even know who your *real* daddy is. That drunk you live with is probably just the last one your mama took up with." Danny leaned in closer, adrenaline masking his cowardice. Several in the crowd gasped, and it grew deadly silent. Even Danny took a step back when he realized the filth that had bubbled and spewed out of his mouth. All heads turned in unison to the frozen statue across from Danny. Berdine's head turned too, and all her breath whooshed out of her. Her face grew ashen as she gasped at the silent pain on Michael's face. His fists were clenched at his sides, and the only movement she could detect was the steady pulse on the side of his neck.

The first mistake she made was believing that Michael's lack of retaliation was fear of engaging in what was sure to be an unfair fight. Michael might be "wild," "tough," and "mysterious" according to her friends, but Danny was a bully with a chip on his shoulder and mallet-like fists … and right now they were twitching.

The second and more serious mistake she made was failing to restrain her impulsive temper and protective lion's heart. Without a rational thought in her head, she sprang forward from the crowd with a battle cry. With a mighty effort, she swung her book bag over her head and into the stomach of unsuspecting Danny Tyler. He folded in half as the breath left him. From that point on, the whole scene seemed to play out in slow motion.

The kids cheered this strange "David and Goliath" performance. The rushing in Berdine's ears prevented her from hearing both Michael's "What *the heck* do you think you're doing?" and Danny's weakened but mocking taunt: "Looks like Mikey's brought his little girlfriend along to fight for him." All she thought about was wiping that sneer off Danny Tyler's ugly mug. She doubled up her fist, and with all the power in her compact, little body, she thrust upward and caught him on the chin. He spun around once, pulling his fist behind him. It caught her on her cheekbone and across her nose. Then he hit the ground, and all the kids broke into wild cheering. It was pandemonium. She was a hero. Danny slunk away in humiliation while the kids continued to laugh and chatter. She wasn't sure how or when *she'd* landed on the ground, but as the crowd slowly dispersed and she started to look around for Michael, she felt her heart nearly stop. Disappearing over the hill was the rigid, angry form of Michael Caraway stalking away in what appeared to be equal amounts of humiliation and rage.

Her chin dropped to rest on her chest, despair washing over her. What had she done? At first, she tried to justify her interference. Good grief! What was so wrong about standing up for a friend? She would have been *grateful* had the tables been turned! In fact, there had been times over the last three years that she *had* been in Michael's place facing down that toad! And Michael stood right beside her, ready to defend her with his life! What's the big difference? Though she couldn't quite work it all out, she knew she'd somehow crossed a boundary and wasn't sure how to work herself back across.

VI

Berdine did her best to pull her hair back into a ponytail and then headed off down the path. She sighed heavily, wondering if the fragile bridge she was beginning to build with Michael had just now crashed and burned. Story of her life, she thought. She was just rounding the corner onto Apple Grove Lane, when she saw two cars out in front of her house. One, she recognized as Dr. Caulfield's car, but the other was unfamiliar. How late was she? Mama was gonna kill her for "dilly-dallying" on the way home from school. She started up the front walk and could hear music and laughter drifting out through the front windows. Maybe a grand entrance through the front door wasn't such a great idea. She eyed her bedroom window up on the second floor and weighed her chances for getting up there without notice. She made up her mind when she heard her sister's high-pitched giggle and Dr. Caulfield's low rumble of laughter very close to the front window. Scrambling quickly for the low branch on the tree, she swung herself up and began to shimmy higher into the branches that just brushed the outside of her bedroom window.

She had just stretched one leg out to the windowsill, with one still wrapped around the branch, when the front door flew open and several young adults spilled out onto the front lawn.

Dr. Caulfield was pulling Kathryn by the arm and saying, "Come here, sweetheart, I want to give you your wedding gift." He bent down to kiss her noisily just to the right of her lips. She giggled again and pressed her hand to his chest.

"Oh, Rodney! Our wedding is still six months away."

"All right . . . then a birthday gift!"

She danced around Dr. Caulfield with excitement and in that moment, something burned in Berdine's heart. Kathryn really did look happy . . . yeah . . . and beautiful too. It annoyed her a bit to admit it. And if she were truthful, Dr. Caulfield wasn't *that* old—just eight years older. Berdine swallowed hard. Clawing fingers of envy crawled up her throat. She didn't like that feeling. Kathryn was only older than Berdine by five years, yet *she* looked like a *woman—in love.* Would it ever happen to her? A brief vision of Michael's face flashed through her mind but faded instantly. Ha! She doubted *that* face would ever even look her way again!

It was while she was caught up in daydreams, still suspended between the house and tree, that she suddenly noticed how quiet it was. Horrified, she looked down and saw four young adults and both her parents standing down in the front yard staring up at her with a mixture of expressions—shocked concern from her parents and amused curiosity from the others.

"*Berdine Elizabeth Williams!* What are you doing up there?" Her mother's voice rose in equal proportion to the compression of her lips. "Is that a bruise on your cheek? Come down from that tree this instant. You've almost missed your sister's birthday!"

Kathryn cupped the side of her mouth and spoke in a loud, stage whisper. "That's our little tomboy. Her real name is Trouble."

Her friends laughed in amusement, and Berdine's face burned. Pop and Dr. Caulfield merely smiled. Her limbs felt frozen as she willed them to move. How humiliating for six adults to watch her slow, clumsy descent from the top of the tree down to the ground. Pop walked over to her and brushed a heavy hand down her hair. He tipped her chin so he could get a good look at the shiner. The compassion on his face and the rueful shake of his head were nearly her undoing. She bit her lip hard in an effort to stem the tears that threatened to erupt. Dr. Caulfield had come to stand beside Pop, his warm eyes studying the tiny, bruised face before him. He reached out and traced her little nose and cheekbone. She winced as they brushed across her cheek.

Pop quirked a smile and spoke, "Well, Doc? What's the diagnosis? Think she needs surgery?"

Dr. Caulfield squatted down and lifted the bruised and scraped knuckles of her right hand. "Hmm. Doesn't seem to be too much damage. Although I can't be as sure about the one on the receiving end!"

Pop chuckled, and Berdine pulled her hand from Dr. Caulfield's, hiding it behind her back. She ducked her head, and Pop relented. "Go on inside and clean up, Berdine. We'll talk about this later."

Berdine hardly waited for him to finish, eager to escape the questioning expressions. The adults quickly turned their attention to the sporty, red convertible sitting out in front of her house. As she rushed into the house, she could hear her sister gush, "*Oh, Rodney!* You bought me a *car?* I just can't *believe* it! It's too much!"

Berdine hurried up the stairs and into the bathroom, locking the door behind her. For a moment, she leaned wearily against it. She moved slowly to the tub and turned on the hot water, filling it nearly to the brim. She peeled off her dirty, sweaty clothes and sank with relief into the steaming water. Sighing, she closed her eyes and let the warm water heal the aches and bruises on both her body and her heart.

The water had grown tepid by the time Berdine dunked her head and washed her hair. She climbed out, wrapping herself in a towel and caught her image in the mirror. She frowned at the purple shadow outlining one of her stormy, gray eyes. She knew from experience that it would grow darker before it ever started to fade. Not only would the rumors abound at school on Monday, but she'd be wearing a constant reminder of the fight every time anyone glanced her way. She combed out the long, wet strands that reached to the middle of her back. Of course, when it dried, the curls would bounce up and settle just below her shoulders. If she weren't so impatient, she'd probably try out her sister's flat iron. Berdine shrugged and shook out the honey, golden mane of wet hair, knowing she'd never take the time. She studied herself with a critical eye, seeing a young girl sadly lacking in the looks department. When she complained to Mama about her deficiencies, Mama just smiled a secret smile, cocked her head to the side, and tapped a finger against her chin. "Hmmm..." she'd say. "Just you wait, Berdie-girl. You're what they call a late-bloomer. When those pixie features of yours soften and your figure rounds out a little, your daddy's gonna turn gray worrying about the boys who'll come around." Berdine would shake her head in disagreement, knowing Mama only wanted to spare her feelings. She already knew she'd only top five feet one—and that was if she wore heels. And no matter how much "bloomin" she did, she'd never have a curvy figure like Kathryn's.

Berdine shrugged off her self-pity, never really having much use for that sort of thing. Besides, from *her* observations... looks just got in the way of real friendship. Not that her lack of looks were helping much either! She thought again of Michael. Would he speak to her on Monday? Would he let her apologize for interfering? It made her a little sad to realize that she no longer could predict Michael's response.

Berdine dressed and then slowly trudged down the stairs. The house had grown quiet. Her parents, Kathryn, and Dr. Caulfield were in the kitchen, eating cake and sipping coffee. Berdine hesitated at the door, peering in.

Pop caught sight of her and motioned her in. "C'mon in, Irony. Have some of this chocolate cake. It'll cure what ails you."

Pop must have spoken words of warning to the others because none of them turned to stare at her as she tiptoed in. They just continued on with their conversation, as though nothing had happened. Mama got down a plate and sliced off a thick piece of cake, handing it to Berdine with a gentle smile.

Berdine leaned forward and whispered, "I'm sorry, Mama. I told you'd I'd be here to help bake the cake..." Her words trailed off, and Mama just hugged the forlorn girl tightly.

She responded softly, "It's okay, Berdie... You just might want to tell your sister you're sorry for missing her birthday. And later, you need to have a talk with your daddy about what happened."

Berdine groaned, wishing to avoid both interactions. She looked over at her sister, who was studying her with interest. She stirred cream into her coffee and took a slow slip. Berdine stared back, searching for signs of spite but could find none. She took her piece of cake and pulled up a chair across the table. Mama set a glass of milk down in front of her, and Berdine hurriedly lifted it for a long, deep swallow. Feeling as fortified as she'd ever be, she spoke in a rush of words.

"Kathryn, I'm sorry I wasn't here in time. It was wrong of me to miss your birthday. I think your car is really great, and I'm sure you'll turn everyone's head when you drive around town in it. I wish I could stay out of trouble and mind my own business, but I can't ever let a bully pick a fight with someone I love, so I guess I'll always be missing things I should be around for as long as there are stupid, ugly bullies like Danny Tyler . . ."

Her voice trailed off, only because she ran out of breath. Her parents and Dr. Caulfield all shared matching expressions of amazement at the breathless tirade that had just spilled out of Berdine's mouth. Kathryn leaned forward, looking like she might impale Berdine with one of her sharp retorts. Instead, in a rare show of sensitivity, a little smile turned up the corners of her mouth. She reached out her long, slender fingers to close over her sister's small hand and squeezed lightly.

"All I can say," she drawled softly, "is that I hope you made Danny Tyler *pay* for keeping you from my birthday!"

"Kathryn!" their mother gasped, "don't encourage that kind of behavior!"

Her father and Dr. Caulfield just smiled. The moment was soon forgotten, and animated conversation resumed around the kitchen table. Kathryn pulled out her latest brides' magazine, and soon the three women had their heads together, making plans for the coming March wedding.

VII

It was hours later, after Mama and Kathryn had already gone up to bed, that Berdine stole quietly into the kitchen to pour herself another glass of milk. She tiptoed back through the den, hoping to duck past Pop's chair and make it unnoticed to the stairs. She'd just put her foot on the first step when she heard Pop stir and say, "Irony, girl? Come in here a minute. We still need to talk."

"*Oh, Pop*... Why do you still call me that? I'm too old for that now." Berdine turned reluctantly and made her way back into the den. She tucked her feet under her as she knelt at the foot of Pop's easy chair. He looked over the top of his paper and then folded it slowly into his lap.

"Let's see... are you still my little scrap of a girl getting into scraps that are bigger than you are?" His eyes twinkled as he looked at Berdine fondly.

"I can't help it, Pop. I've done like you say mostly... I walk away when *I'm* the one getting picked on. But I can't stand it when it's someone else. How can I just stand by and not help? Is that what you *want* me to do?"

"Who did you rescue this time, my little lion?" Pop asked, gently amused.

"I didn't even stop to think! I guess if I'd taken the time to weigh it all out, I might have hung back. But that Danny Tyler was spoutin' off, and before I even knew it, I was right there in the middle of the circle, ready to make him pay for those ugly things he was saying." Berdine sighed heavily, remembering the agony she had seen on Michael's face.

"Oh, Pop!" Berdine covered her face with her hands. "He'll *never* forgive me. You should have seen his face as he walked away!" She shuddered at the memory.

"Who, Berdie?" Pop spoke in that calm, soothing voice—the one that always seemed to break down the walls.

"*Michael!*" she wailed. She wrapped her arms tightly around her knees, her face buried. Caught up in her own misery, she didn't see the weary struggle playing across her father's face. Her father closed his eyes a moment, trying to gather the words he knew would probably wound his little lion. He sighed heavily, and Berdine lifted her head.

In a quiet voice, he spoke, "Berdine, I know you've cared for Michael for a long time. I think maybe you've always seen him as someone who needs rescuing, and there's a part of you that just can't resist that. Now, don't misunderstand me ... it's a noble thing to be someone's champion. I can't think of a person I know more fiercely loyal than you, but Michael is growing up ... and you are too. He needs to fight his own battles. Lord knows he hasn't had an easy go of things. He hasn't had a mama and papa to guide him and protect him like you have. He's walking down a different path than you."

Berdine stared at her father, a look of confusion and sadness clouding her eyes. "Pop, I'm not trying to *rescue* Michael or ... or ... just be his *protector.* I *love* him. We're meant for each other—like Kathryn was meant for Dr. Caulfield."

Her father chuckled lightly, smoothing a hand over Berdine's head. Trying not to wound the young girl struggling to be an adult, he said, "Berdine, you're only fifteen years old. You haven't even begun to experience life and all of its twists and turns. I know you believe with all your heart that you love Michael, but neither of you is ready to understand what that really means. Just be his friend and let time take care of things."

Berdine's eyes hardened, and her father could see an invisible shutter coming down over her face. "*You* don't know what's in my heart, Pop. But *I* know. I can't just change how I feel."

Berdine's father saw the steel in his youngest daughter's eyes. He felt a twinge of regret, but his words were firm. "I know you don't want to hear these words, Berdine, but I wouldn't be the kind of father I need to be if I didn't speak them." He took a deep breath, pausing to rearrange the words in his head. "Michael is *not* for you. He has no solid family support. He spends most of his time unsupervised. You know those factors have contributed to the problems he's had in school. He's an angry young man who strikes out like a wounded animal when he's cornered." Her father shook his head ruefully. "The road *he's* headed down is not the one we want *you* on."

Berdine jumped to her feet. "How can you know what *'road'* he's on? Just because he's had a hard time, doesn't mean he's going to end up bad. Why are you judging him like that?" Berdine's voice started to quiver.

Her father held up a placating hand, shaking his head, "Now, Berdine, I'm not saying he's going to end up bad. But you know as well as I do that trouble has followed him these last couple of years. Maybe he hasn't been the source of all of it, but he's sure been a part of it a lot of the time. Your mother and I don't want you getting pulled into that."

Berdine's expression turned mutinous. "I'm not getting pulled into *anything*." She crossed her arms and scowled. She suspected that she was very close to her father's tolerated limit of defiance and dared not go any further.

He sighed and put his big hand on her shoulder. Then he slowly turned her so they were both facing the foyer mirror across the room.

He spoke in a gentle voice, "I see a shiner on the face of someone who's *already* been 'pulled in.'"

Berdine stared at her own reflection, stubborn and flushed. Then she lifted her eyes to her father's face. It was calm and steady, and little lines were etched into the corners of his eyes. It was a face she respected and didn't want to disappoint. Her heart dropped with the weight of the conflict warring within her.

She dipped her head and mumbled softly, "I need to think about things, Pop."

Her father turned her back around and gave her a hug. "I know you do, Berdine. Your mom and I love you, and we want what's best for you. We're just trying to protect you from getting hurt."

Berdine nodded slowly and headed for the stairs. Her expression was serious, and her father knew she needed time to process their conversation. *She's a reasonable girl,* he thought. She would surely see the wisdom of his counsel.

He watched her trudge slowly to the top of the stairs, and a lump rose in his throat. He could see a shadow of the mature, young woman she would become. He was proud of his girls. They were as different as night and day—yet both seemed to embrace life with their whole being. He stood still, thinking about a time when they were both very young. Kathryn had always been his little romantic. She was forever turning every playtime into a wedding ceremony. He chuckled, remembering her coming down the stairs in one of her mother's white nightgowns with an old eyelet kitchen curtain wrapped around her head. She clutched some dandelions in her tight fist as she made her way down to the last step. The only dark cloud over the "ceremony" was a belligerent-faced younger sister who refused to play the part of the adoring groom. It made him laugh to remember the cajoling and bargaining he heard as the deal was struck. Twenty minutes later, he'd found his youngest daughter perched on the front porch step, her mouth smeared with chocolate and strawberry sauce, eating the biggest banana split he'd ever seen.

Now, his little Berdine was cut from a different cloth. He could always count on a scraped knee, a rash of poison ivy, or a cup full of earth worms at the end of the day. She was a born adventurer. She tackled life as a puzzle to be solved, and she had little patience with those who felt they needed to cautiously "test the waters" before jumping into the creek, so to speak. She had the heart of an idealist and an unshakeable belief in the potential for good. She didn't tolerate whiners. Her philosophy was that if you just worked hard enough and hoped even harder, things would turn out all right. Her father smiled sadly with the wisdom of one who knew that, sooner or later, life couldn't or wouldn't fit into those tidy parameters. Disappointment sometimes had a way of finding you, even when you did your best. His greatest fear for Berdine was a disillusioned heart. Even a *broken* heart would mend, but a heart that was betrayed bore scars forever. His dilemma as a father was finding a safe balance between protecting her and encouraging her to embrace each new experience with her own natural sense of adventure. He sighed as he returned to his easy chair. Shaking his head in consternation, he thought to himself, *Some days, parenting feels just like a blind walk in the dark!*

VIII

It seemed she had just laid her head on the pillow when Berdine awoke with a start. She lay tangled in her blankets, listening to the hum of the space heater. Dawn was just beginning to cast a gray haze through the slats of her blinds. It was still silent in the house, so she knew without turning to look at her clock that it was still early. A sense of heaviness hung over her, and she couldn't seem to remember why. Yawning widely, she rolled to her side, waiting for conscious thought to catch up. Suddenly, with perfect clarity, the image of an angry Michael Caraway flashed through her mind. Berdine groaned and pulled the sheet up over her head. For a fleeting moment, the temptation to play sick and stay home from school almost won. But Berdine was not the sort to hide from her troubles. Gathering her resolve, she got up to get ready for school. As she washed her face and twined her hair into a loose braid down her back, she planned her strategy. It wouldn't do to wait until she happened to run into Michael at school. It was early enough that she would have time to meet him at his house and catch him before he headed off for school. She just had to figure out what she was going to say to him when she got there. This was the only way it would work. Once they got around other people at school, she knew Michael would avoid her. The only thing that gave her pause was what she was going to say to her parents when they asked why she was leaving so early. She knew Pop wouldn't approve, especially after their talk last night. She looked at herself in the mirror one last time, taking in the bruised cheekbone, and whispered stubbornly, "I've *got* to make you understand, Michael Caraway!"

She crept quietly down the stairs, peering around the corner at the bottom. As luck would have it, no light appeared in the kitchen, and Berdine decided she'd rather slip out unnoticed and explain later than face a possible delay now.

The late October morning was foggy and gray. The air was chilly, and she wished she had thought of pulling on a sweatshirt before she left the house. But since Michael's house was at least a fifteen-minute hike, she didn't dare go back for one. She kept her head down and walked with a determined stride. All the while, words tumbled through her mind. She didn't take time to enjoy the colors of the leaves that still clung tenaciously to the branches above her head. She never heard the distant barking of neighborhood dogs or noticed the few fat raindrops that landed on her face. Her pace quickened, compelled by a sudden sense of urgency. She looked up and saw Michael's house through the patch of woods, standing apart from the few other houses on the gravel road. His "neighborhood" was on the very edge of the town. Michael told her his dad had said one time that he "liked it that way. It's close enough to town if you need something and far enough away for folks to stay outta your business." Berdine suspected that even if the little house were smack dab in the middle of town square, folks would still keep their distance. She never really understood how the Caraways got the reputation of being loners. But knowing small towns, it was probably because they *did* mind their own business. It vexed Berdine to learn that if you weren't part of the gossipers, you usually *became* the gossip.

A few more raindrops fell on Berdine's face, and she looked up at the morning sky starting to darken, even as daylight emerged. She cut through the trees and headed up the gravel path to the cracked stone steps leading to a sloping porch. The screen door had a tear close to the frame, and the wood was chipped and a little crooked. She pulled the screen door open just enough to knock on the dingy, gray door in front of it. She waited for a beat then leaned in to knock a little more loudly. The house sat silently—shuttered and closed off from her. Uncertainty filled Berdine's mind. She slowly let the screen door rest back in its frame. Berdine stared down at the dry, dead grass on either side of the porch steps, trying to decide what to do next. A distant rumble of thunder registered in her mind, and she saw the darkening clouds gathering above her. As she stood weighing her options, a movement caught her eye off to the left of the house. She looked up and saw a flash of blue moving under the old carport.

"Michael?" she called out softly, unsure. When no one answered, she stepped off the porch and crossed the yard, shuffling through the ankle-deep leaves. "Michael? Is that you?"

The grim face of Michael's father suddenly peered around the dented truck door.

"Oh! Mr. Caraway! I thought you were Michael. I was hoping to talk to him before school."

Mr. Caraway studied Berdine's face carefully. His eyes lighted on the purple shadow, and his expression seemed to darken with a mixture of anger and regret. "Was Michael a part of that too?" He gestured gruffly toward the bruise on Berdine's face.

"What?" Berdine was caught off guard. She stepped back a bit, lifting her hand to her cheek. The tenderness of her cheekbone registered his meaning. "No ... no, sir. This was my own fault. Michael had nothing to do with it."

Mr. Caraway continued to stare at Berdine, as though weighing her words against his own belief. In that moment of uncomfortable silence, as Mr. Caraway took her measure, Berdine stiffened her chin and held his stare. He shook his head, almost in apology, and rubbed the back of his neck with a careworn hand. He was not a big man, about five foot nine, and very lean for a mill worker. Michael had already passed him in height and build three years earlier. The faded, red cap he wore had seen better days, and it looked like it had a permanent resting place atop his head. He appeared in need of a haircut and a shave. His eyes were weary but clear. Frayed, worn jeans covered the top of leather work boots with deep nicks in the toes. Mr. Caraway studied those boots now with interest. Shoving calloused hands into his pockets, he took a deep breath. He lifted his head, studying the waiting expression on the young girl's face.

"I've sent Michael away, Berdine. It's for his own good. He needs someone who's around a little more to look out for him."

He watched Berdine struggle to hold herself very still. The only sign that his words had registered was the deliberate blinking of her eyes. Her chest rose and fell rapidly as her breathing became shallow. Color drained from her face, causing the bruise on her cheek to stand out starkly against her pale skin. She stared blankly at Mr. Caraway and struggled to formulate a question.

"*Where?* Where did you send him? *Why* would you send him away? That fight wasn't even his fault!" Berdine held out her shaking hands in a plea.

"It's not just about the fight, Berdine. It's a whole series of things that have been building up in that boy. He needs guidance and discipline. It's for the best." Mr. Caraway shifted his weight uncomfortably and rubbed a hand over weary eyes. Berdine could tell he had just come in from the night shift at the mill and was badly in need of sleep. But she was not yet ready to let the matter drop.

"Why do parents always make decisions without even asking how we feel about it? Michael didn't even get to say what he wanted! How do you know things will be any better where he is? How do you know he won't be even *more* angry now?!" Berdine's voice trembled with resentment.

Michael's father leveled a quiet look at the agitated young lady quivering before him. He didn't bother to defend himself. Sighing tiredly, he said, "Michael wanted to do this. It was his decision."

IX

Berdine's jaw dropped as she digested the quiet words. A little pain shot through her heart and then spread throughout her body. Slowly, her hands dropped, and her shoulders sagged in defeat. So many questions rose to her lips, but all she could manage was "Where did he go?"

Mr. Caraway took in the dejected stance of the girl before him, and he felt a similar regret. "He's going to be living on the marine training base on Parris Island. My sister is married to a military man, and they agreed to take him in. He'll finish out school, and … then … we'll go from there."

Berdine just stared back, tears filling her eyes. "Might as well be a million miles away," she murmured. She slowly lowered her pain-filled gaze to the ground, long eyelashes glistened with unshed moisture. She spoke in a whisper. "I didn't get to say good-bye … "

Both of them stood, unmoving, sharing a sense of loss. Rain started to spatter, and the thunder rumbled a little closer now. A flash of light split the clouds above them, and Berdine knew the sky was about to open up. At that moment, she couldn't have cared less. In fact, she welcomed the sensation of the cold, stinging rain against her numbed flesh. She was startled to find that she could feel it at all.

Mr. Caraway noticed the threatening storm as well. "Want me to drive you back to school?" He pushed the cap up on his head, a little worried at the blank look on Berdine's face.

"No, thank you. I'll just walk back the way I came. I'll be fine." Berdine turned woodenly and began putting one foot in front of the other. She didn't even pick up the pace as the rain started to fall more steadily. Mr. Caraway watched, unsure if he should let her go. He started to call out through the rain, but he saw that she was already crossing the patch of woods.

The rain had now soaked through her T-shirt and jeans, and her shoes squished with each step. Her wet braid lay sodden against her back. Berdine just kept her chin to her chest and walked steadily on, not really conscious of her direction. School would already have started by now. But there would be no Michael in the halls today. There would be no apology spoken. A small part of her was angry. He had robbed her of the chance to say she was sorry! They had made it an unspoken pact a long time ago never to run from their problems. Well, she guessed that pact had weakened over time, and it had all started with that ill-timed kiss in the tree house two years ago. Still, she'd always held out hope that the pact would continue to survive. Even though they'd grown apart for a while, she'd never doubted they'd find that solid connection again. Now he'd gone and run out on her. Didn't even stick around to hear her side of things! Maybe all along *she* was the only one who believed in their forever fate.

Berdine stopped, letting the rain continue its steady, chilling assault against her skin. Thoughts whirled inside her head, and she closed her eyes because even the stormy daylight seemed offensive to her. A sob rose in her throat, and her knees started to buckle. She reached out a hand blindly, connecting with the scratchy bark of a tall, oak tree. Confused, she looked up through the rain. She stood at the base of the tree house, and she didn't even know how or why she had taken the detour to this place. The sense of familiarity settled over her shoulders like a childhood blanket, and she leaned her forehead against the solid pillar. Soon, the sound of her weeping mixed with the steady drum of the rain and rolling thunder. Her knees sagged, and she leaned heavily against the tree, pouring her young heart out with abandon. Eventually, her tears were spent, and though the rain had lessened, a chill in the air had risen. The wind had picked up, and her flesh prickled under the wet clothes. Berdine felt a hundred years old. Without even thinking, she began to climb up the nailed-in footholds. The weariness in her heart spread over her limbs, and she was exhausted by the time she made it into the close confines of the tree house. It was all she could do just to curl up in a ball against the solid wall of the fortress. Her eyelids grew heavy. As the tree house creaked on the gentle sway of the branches, Berdine fell asleep.

She was disoriented when she woke. Her eyes burned, and her throat felt as if it were on fire. She squinted up at the sky, trying to determine what time it was. But whether one hour had passed or five, she knew she'd have to answer for her absence at school. She sat up slowly, her head pounding and body aching. She waited, head in her hands, for the pounding to stop. It was still chilly out, and the sun had made only a feeble attempt to peek through the clouds. Berdine coughed and her chest ached.

"Great…just great…" she muttered. "Not only will I get in trouble for skipping school, but now I'm coming down with a cold on top of that!"

She sat in misery for several more minutes, realizing there was nothing else to do but head home. As she rose wearily to climb down the ladder, a wave of dizziness assailed her. She clamped her jaw tightly and descended to the ground. The walk home was miserable, and Berdine was exhausted by the time she reached her front door. Still not having any idea what time it was, she entered quietly. She could hear her mother in the kitchen rattling pots and pans. Berdine stood forlornly in the doorway waiting for her mother to notice her.

"Berdine! What are you doing here? School isn't over for two more hours! You look flushed! Did the nurse send you home?" Her mother rushed toward Berdine, lifting a cool hand to her daughter's forehead. "You are burning up! Let's get you upstairs to bed."

She put her arm around Berdine and led her to her room. When she tried to speak, her mother just shushed her, fussing over her like a mother hen. Before she knew it, Berdine was in pajamas with the covers pulled up to her neck and a thermometer sticking out of her mouth.

"One hundred and two! I *thought* you looked feverish. This is cold and flu season, you know. I'm sure you won't be the only student sent home from school!" Her mother smoothed a hand over Berdine's forehead.

"Mama..." Berdine croaked, her throat aching and scratchy. "Mom, listen. I've been trying to tell you. I didn't *go* to school today. I...I...went to Michael's house." A tear leaked out of the corner of Berdine's eye and dripped down her flushed cheek. "He wasn't there, Mama. He's moved away. Just like that. He didn't say good-bye or anything. He's going to finish school on the military base on Parris Island!"

Though her heart still ached, most of her tears were already spent. She looked at her mother with an empty, hollow expression on her face. Fully expecting a well-deserved lecture, Berdine was surprised when her mother only sighed and kissed her forehead.

"Oh, Berdie, we've tried to warn you about this crush you have on Michael. You're too young to focus all your attention on this boy. We want you to concentrate on your school work, enjoy your homecoming and prom, plan what you want to do after high school... so many things."

Berdine knew her mother meant well, but it was clear that neither of her parents had any inkling of the jumble of feelings swirling inside of her. And if she weren't feeling sicker by the moment, she would have protested vehemently. As it was, her head was beginning to pound, and her throat burned when she swallowed. It felt as though the bedroom light was shooting glass shards through her eyelids. In a weak voice, Berdine whispered, "I think I just want to go to sleep for a while, Mama."

Berdine's mother laid a cool cloth over her head. She tucked her daughter in up to her chin and lowered the lights. With a soft kiss on her head, she quietly left the room.

X

The several weeks that followed were almost a shadowy dream to Berdine. She remembered awakening, her fever raging, and misery wrapping its fiery tentacles around her body. There were vague memories of people coming in and out. She caught snatches of conversations between her parents and what must have been their family doctor... something about moving her to the hospital if the fever didn't abate. At times, she felt so cold that the blankets piled on top of her couldn't touch the iciness inside of her. Other times, she struggled to free herself from the hot, stifling weight of the covers. Through it all, her most conscious thoughts were of Michael. *Where was he? Was he happy with his decision? Would she ever see him again?*

As Berdine slowly got better, she kept waiting for her parents to ask her about the day she had missed school. Oddly, the topic was never broached, nor was there ever any mention of Michael being the reason. It would have been comforting for her to vent her feelings, but she could tell by the closed expressions on her family's faces that they wanted to avoid talk of Michael altogether. She concluded that they must have believed the whole painful incident would disappear more quickly if they ignored it. As a result, Berdine held her thoughts inside and pretended that her sadness had healed along with her body. But what no one could see—not even Berdine herself—was the slow, insidious growth of that first, thin layer of a hard shell around her heart.

When Berdine had finally recovered enough to return to school, it was a blessed relief that every hour of her day was crammed with making up missed assignments. And with so little time left before Christmas break and finals, she had no energy to focus on anything other than her schoolwork. Berdine had always been an average student, but with homework now her catharsis, she excelled in her subjects. Her teachers took notice of the transformation and praised her for her increased focus. Berdine's parents, however, saw their bold, optimistic daughter fading slowly into a silent shadow of her former self. Even Kathryn noticed her withdrawal and cornered her mother in the kitchen one afternoon.

"Mama! We've got to do something about Berdine. She's just not herself. She won't even argue with me when I do my best to bait her!" Kathryn twisted her engagement ring around and around her finger.

Her mother quirked an eyebrow at that last comment but then sighed softly. "She'll come around, I think… eventually. Don't you remember your first love, Kathryn? And how hard it was to get over that broken heart? We just need to give her time. I think she's already turned the corner. She doesn't even mention him anymore." Kathryn and her mother stared at each other, neither believing the half-hearted claim.

"Why don't you see if you can encourage her to go to the winter dance in a couple of weeks? It would do her good to spend a little more time with her friends. She's gotten so serious about her school work!"

The corner of Kathryn's mouth lifted, a twinkle appearing in her eyes. "Now *that's* ironic: you want her to go have *more* fun and spend *less* time studying!"

Her mother looked a little flustered, and Kathryn took pity, leaning over to kiss her cheek. "Just teasing you, Mama. I know exactly what you mean. It's been a while since I've seen a real smile from her. I'll talk to her about the dance."

It was several days before Kathryn was able to catch Berdine alone, without her nose in a textbook. Kathryn was heading into the kitchen to make a cup of hot cocoa, and she saw Berdine sitting motionless in Pop's big easy chair. She was staring into the fire that crackled and jumped in the grate.

"I'm making some hot cocoa, Berdine. Do you want a cup?" Kathryn called out casually. Berdine never turned her head.

She just answered quietly, "Sure. Thanks."

Kathryn frowned to herself at her sister's monotone voice. "Okay . . . be right there."

She returned with two steaming cups of cocoa and handed one to Berdine. She took a seat on the sofa beside the silent girl and tucked her feet up under her. She blew softly on the hot liquid before taking a sip. Surreptitiously, she glanced at Berdine over the rim of her cup. Berdine still cradled her mug with both hands.

"You've been so quiet lately. What are you thinking about?" Kathryn began.

"Not too much. Just taking a break from formulas and word problems." Berdine turned and gave her sister a small smile.

Kathryn studied the faint shadows and tired lines under her younger sister's eyes, and it bothered her to see apathy there. An unexpected surge of protective anger began to rumble inside of Kathryn. It was one thing for *her* to antagonize and irritate her sister; it was quite another for someone else to come along and wound her. Her frustration mounted as she found herself wanting to both comfort and shake some sense into the younger girl. She took a deep breath, trying to calm down.

"You know, I saw in the paper this morning that the school is having the winter dance this year in the Crawford's barn instead of the school gym. Wonder what that's all about?"

Berdine shrugged vaguely. "I heard Mrs. Johnson wanted to decorate it all up and host the dance there while it was still new, before her husband started filling it up with hay and horses. It's not real close though. Some of the parents are complaining about having to drive their kids out there and then pick them back up when the dance ends at midnight."

Kathryn nodded. "But at least there'll be plenty of room. All of the four years I went to the winter dance, we crammed into the school gym, and it was pretty miserable. It got so stuffy! And no matter how much they decorated and cleaned, it still smelled like dirty socks to me."

Kathryn screwed up her nose, and it made Berdine smile. Some of her old spunk slipped out as she teased her older sister. "Well, I'm sure with the amount of perfume *you* usually wear, no one noticed any other smell!"

"I'll have you know that the boys simply *flocked* to ask me to dance, just so they could get a whiff of my Chanel No. 5!" Kathryn winked, and Berdine rolled her eyes.

"Oh, no doubt . . . Although I'm sure they got more than just a whiff of it in that little gym!"

"You know," Kathryn began, tapping a finger against her chin, "I *could* let you borrow it. I think there really might be some kind of secret chemical that attracts boys. It always worked for me!"

Berdine rolled her eyes again and glanced sideways at her sister. "And now don't you feel guilty just thinking about all those hearts you crushed when you accepted Dr. Caulfield's proposal?"

Kathryn grinned at Berdine. "Why, I do believe my baby sister just paid me a compliment! I might need to record this in my diary."

Berdine just shook her head and took another sip of her chocolate. They sat in companionable silence for a moment. It was a rare experience for both girls, and Kathryn was reluctant to risk changing the mood.

"If you wanted, Rodney and I could take and pick you up from the dance. We wouldn't even need to bother Mama and Pop about it. I've got some dresses you could wear too. I bet Mama could do any altering they needed. My dark green silk would be perfect for you. I'll even straighten your hair if you want." Kathryn's words sped up when she saw Berdine shaking her head after the first sentence. "*Why not, Berdine?*"

Berdine didn't say anything for a moment. She just continued sipping her cocoa. Her expression was resolute, and Kathryn had seen that look many times before. When the shutters came down like that, she knew she was battling a lost cause. It made her huff in frustration, and her impatience rose a couple of notches. Finally, she just couldn't stand it any longer.

She blurted out, "He's not *worth* it, Berdine. No guy should have this much power over you. Just the fact that he took off without giving you a second thought, should tell you he's no good—at least not for *you.* Besides, you and Michael are both only halfway through high school—*children,* really!"

Kathryn's words were darts into Berdine's heart, and the hard shell grew several more layers. Berdine turned her head to pin her sister with a stony glare. Kathryn's eyes widened at the adultlike coldness she saw there. She knew she had overstepped her bounds. Before Kathryn could even formulate the words to salvage the moment, Berdine rose stiffly from the chair and headed toward the kitchen with her cup. When she spoke, her words were icy and formal.

"Thank you for the hot chocolate." She left Kathryn sitting on the couch without a backward glance.

XI

In the ensuing months, a subtle gap began to widen in Berdine's relationship with the rest of her family—especially with her sister. Though she wasn't rude or outwardly angry, neither did she make any effort to breach the growing chasm between them. It was not difficult to make herself invisible with all the plans for Kathryn's wedding intensifying. The focus was understandably on the happy couple, and Berdine liked it that way. She got so good at blending into the background that she learned how to do it at school as well. While her friends were beginning to develop a keen interest in the opposite sex, Berdine held herself apart. As far as she was concerned, it was a waste of time and energy to invest in something that would only break your heart in the long run.

Unbeknownst to Berdine, her lack of participation in the typical "spring fever behavior" landed her with the reputation of being a snob. She had no idea she had become one of the hottest locker room topics. Her aloofness, coupled now with a surprising metamorphosis in her looks over the past six months, caused more than a few male conversations on the topic of the "new and improved" Berdine. She had a noted lack of interest in social activity, and it created very different reactions. Some of the girls began to gossip and turn their backs on Berdine. They reasoned Berdine must be playing on the advantage of her newly blossomed figure and "contrived" disinterest to lure the boys' attention. After all, *no* one could purposely be *that* unaware of the stir they were causing!

The boys' reaction was altogether different and only served to fuel the peevish envy among the girls. It became somewhat of a challenge among the boys to see who might be the one to gain Berdine's attention. All the while, Berdine continued her quiet, studious habits—unaware of the growing undercurrents.

It was a mere two weeks before Kathryn's wedding, and the Williamses' household was buzzing. It seemed to Berdine that there was never a private moment in their home. Phones ringing; deliveries at the door; lists created, checked off, and replaced with more lists; and people, always people, coming in and out at random. Berdine felt a little guilty, but she couldn't wait for the whole thing to be over. Her sister, on the other hand, was in her element. Kathryn relished the activity. In fact, the more chaotic things got around the house, the more animated and happy she grew. The rift between the girls had never fully mended, but Berdine was not so small-minded that she begrudged her sister any measure of happiness. She could honestly say that, even though her own young heart was in shambles, she was glad that Kathryn was floating along on her personal cloud of joy. Berdine did her best to help out when needed and stay out of the way the rest of the time.

Mount Holly boasted a beautiful, historical park on the east side of town square, a perfect place for escape. Berdine discovered that the often empty swing set provided a quiet respite from all the wedding activity. It was in the solitary moments Berdine spent swaying gently on the swing that she allowed her mind to wander to normally closed-off thoughts of Michael. It was hard for her to reconcile who she had thought Michael to be, with his obvious lack of interest he had in contacting her. Was she mistaken in believing they had been best friends? Had she really only deceived herself into believing she had meant as much to him as he did to her? Maybe there wasn't such a thing as a soul mate after all. Maybe that was really only a fairy tale fantasy she'd fallen for. Still, she was unwilling to budge in her steadfast loyalty to him. She often wondered how he was adjusting to what must be a very different lifestyle.

Berdine knew from Michael that his uncle was a no-nonsense, career marine who drilled new recruits each semester. But he was also a man who walked with the Lord. He lived his life according to the motto under which he served: *Semper Fidelis*—always faithful. However little Berdine knew personally about the character of the man, she did know that he was exactly that—always faithful—to his family, his God, and his country. Michael had spoken of him more than a few times in the past. Although careful not to sound disloyal to his own father, the ring of pride and the shine in his eyes when he talked about his uncle was unmistakable. *I'm going to be like him, Berdie… One of these days, I'll wear that uniform, and I'll defend our country. I'll be somebody… I'll make a life for my dad and me. He won't have to work so hard at the mill all the time. And he'll have a son he can be proud of.*

It made Berdine's heart ache a little to remember the earnest longing on Michael's face. She knew beyond a shadow of a doubt he would never have let anyone but her see that vulnerable side of him. And now he was another step closer to his dream. She imagined that Michael's aunt and uncle would make it a priority to ensure that high school graduation was the first order of business. Michael's uncle was fair, but he was also solidly tough. In a way, Michael was probably experiencing a little bit of his own personal boot camp. It was doubtful they allowed other distractions to surface, once that goal was laid out and agreed upon. She wondered, sadly, if the reason she hadn't heard from Michael was because *she* was one of those distractions.

Berdine leaned against the swing, turning her face toward the warming sun. It promised to be beautiful weather for Kathryn's wedding. Then her sister and new husband were off for their honeymoon. It was going to be strange not having to share the upstairs with Kathryn anymore. Not a *bad* sort of strange, though. Berdine grinned to herself. It would be a relief not to feel those penetrating stares boring into her back. She knew it probably took a lot of restraint on her sister's part to bite back what she wanted to say to Berdine. She always looked like it was on the tip of her tongue to let the words spill out. And when Berdine would suddenly meet her sister's eyes, there was almost a look of guilt on Kathryn's face. *Good!* Berdine frowned. Kathryn *should* feel guilty. It made her seethe when she thought about how her family misjudged Michael. She *expected* some of the people in town to believe the gossip that was actually more rumor than it was fact. But it cut her to the quick that her parents and sister had bought into those unfounded rumors. Good grief, hadn't they smiled indulgently in those earlier years when Berdine had spent every free moment with her best pal? Hadn't they thought it was *so sweet* the way they did everything together? She remembered those very words from her mother's lips in response to her father's grumbling one evening at the dinner table. He had expressed a growing concern that "maybe it wasn't a good idea for these two to spend so much time together." It just didn't make sense to her why her family had changed their minds. Hadn't Pop always said, "Don't judge a book by its cover"? When did that stop applying to Michael? Berdine shook her head, stumped by the seeming hypocrisy of the matter. At least the wedding planning helped to turn the focus away from her and gave her time to work through it all in her mind.

That sudden thought of wedding planning caused Berdine to jump up from the swing. She remembered, belatedly, that she had promised Mama she'd stop by the bakery and drop off Kathryn's specifications for her wedding cakes. She hurried away from the swing set toward the park entrance. By now, the late afternoon sun was casting shadows on the tall hedges lining the wrought iron gates leading out of the park. She guessed it was closing in on dinnertime, if her calculations were correct. She hated to imagine the trouble she'd be in if she'd dallied the afternoon away and didn't make it to the bakery by the time they closed. She hastened on, deciding to cut through down by the creek in order to shave off some time. It wasn't the easiest route because of the overgrown brush and thick trees, but it would definitely give her a fighting chance to make it in time.

Presently, Berdine became aware of the growing volume of voices. She couldn't yet see the source, but it sounded like a group of kids just beyond the cluster of trees up ahead. It wouldn't have aroused her curiosity if it hadn't come from the vicinity of the tree house she and Michael had built. As she got closer, she began to recognize some of the voices. One was definitely Danny Tyler's voice.

A shiver of anxiety crept up her spine. She was just considering the wisdom of altering her course when she realized she'd been spotted.

"Well, well, *well*..." The familiar, sneering voice grated on her. "Who do we have here?"

There stood her nemesis, muscled arms crossed over a barrel-sized chest. Berdine could almost swear Danny had grown another six inches since the beginning of their sophomore year. She strongly suspected that even though they were in the same grade, he was at least one, maybe two years older! Danny didn't have the best academic history. Judging by the little fan club that stood gathered around him smirking, Berdine knew he managed to attract the kids who were as insecure as he was. He led by intimidation, which was the reason they all now turned to Danny to find out what their next move was. It disgusted Berdine that the other kids didn't have enough wisdom to see Danny for the bully he was.

"I'm just passing through, Danny," Berdine said wearily.

She started to move by the little group of rebels, but Danny sidestepped to block her path. The group of girls giggled nervously, and the boys aped Danny's challenging stance.

"No, I think *I'll* decide if you're passing through today." A wolfish grin covered the freckle-splashed face of the boy. He turned to his comrades for approval. He was not disappointed. "You and I got a score to settle, don't we?"

The other youths grinned mockingly and moved in closer till they formed a half circle around Berdine. At this point, all she felt was annoyance.

"I don't know what you're talking about, Danny. *I* was the one with the black eye for two weeks." Berdine stared up at the sneering boy.

"You got in the middle of a fight that wasn't your business. *And* a lucky upper cut. I don't like being cold-cocked by a little girl."

At that, the girls giggled. It was the sound of their high-pitched laughter that seemed to push the wrong button in Danny. What might have started as mere bravado suddenly got a little more serious. As the teasing laughter echoed in the background, Danny's insecurities grew. In that instant, Berdine realized that the only way he could now save face in front of his followers was to make her pay. He had too big of an audience and ego to back down now. He leaned in closer, crowding Berdine's space.

"Did Mikey reward you later with a big smooch? Did you two come here to your little love nest for some make-out time?" He gestured toward the tree house, and the group laughed crudely. "Yeah, I bet that's what you did. And now Mikey's run away and left little Berdine all alone without a boyfriend to look after her. I say she needs a *new* boyfriend. But you know what I hear? I hear that Berdine is too good for anyone here in Mount Holly."

"Just get out of my face, Danny. Don't even say his name. You're not good enough to speak it. We were *friends*...That's it. But I'm sure you don't know anything about that!"

Berdine felt the adrenaline starting to pump through her veins. It masked any sense of fear that might have warned her to flee. She stood, quivering in anger, with hands fisted tightly on her hips. Her face was flushed, and her hair curled wildly around her pixyish face. If her own ire hadn't risen to such a dangerous level, she might have noticed the change in Danny's eyes. When he spoke, his voice was ominous and hushed.

"Someone needs to teach you a lesson. And I think that someone is me." His hand struck out like a snake and grabbed a handful of the honey curls. He yanked her head back and abruptly, cruelly, ground his mouth onto hers. Several of the girls gasped, and the boys just stood there slack-jawed while Berdine struggled to push Danny away. The more she fought him, the tighter he gripped her. One of the boys coughed uncomfortably, sensing the situation was getting out of hand.

"Hey, Danny, c'mon. Let's go. Thought you just wanted to give her a hard time."

Danny didn't even acknowledge that he heard. Berdine twisted and turned, flailing her fists helplessly before he wrapped his arms around hers, pinning them to her sides. Panic began to billow up inside her as she realized how much stronger Danny was. Instinct took over, and she stomped as hard as she could on the top of his foot. Danny yelped and let go of Berdine for a second. His rage exploded, and he reached out with his great paw and grabbed the front of her shirt. "Why, you little ... !" Danny yelled. He flung her to the ground, tearing the front of her shirt and landing heavily on top of her. Berdine gasped as the air left her chest under the crushing weight. Sucking oxygen desperately, she fought like a wildcat as Danny struggled to pin down her arms and legs. The other kids began to look frightened and started to hurry out of the grove of trees.

Suddenly, the heavy weight on top of her was yanked instantly away. She opened her eyes cautiously and was shocked to see the wiry figure of Mr. Caraway whirl Danny around. In a flash of movement, he had Danny back on the ground facedown. Mr. Caraway's knee pressed into the middle of his back. He had Danny's wrist stretched painfully behind his back in a vise grip.

"Now you listen to me, boy. Don't you ever put your hands on this girl again. Better yet, don't you even look her way. You do, and I'll find out about it. I got my eye on you, and I'm gonna be watchin'... You hear me, boy?" Mr. Caraway's voice was low and harsh.

"I hear ya," Danny muttered angrily.

But Berdine caught the venomous expression on Danny's face, and she couldn't help but fear that this was only the beginning. She had scooted back away from the two, her back to a tree and her arms wrapped around her knees. She had pulled her shirt together as best she could and she rested her forehead against her folded arms.

Mr. Caraway, small as he appeared in comparison to Danny, yanked the stocky boy back up by the collar of his shirt. Mr. Caraway gave him a light shove forward and said, "Then go on. Don't forget what I said."

The boy stumbled forward, his face beet red. His mounted color was more the result of humiliation than exertion. He rolled his shoulders cockily and started forward. Stopping suddenly, he turned his head and speared Berdine with a malicious smile.

"This ain't over ..." Danny looked like a fighter unwilling to return to his corner. He swaggered off slowly, not bothering to look back.

About the time Mr. Caraway turned back to Berdine, the shaking started. Her slight shoulders, hunched over her knees began to quiver uncontrollably. Her teeth began to chatter, and a small sound of distress escaped from the back of her throat. Mr. Caraway came to kneel beside her. Removing his gray sweatshirt, he murmured soothing words as he pulled it over her head.

"He's a bully, Berdine. You stay away from him now, you hear? He's nothing but trouble. You see him, you go the other way, okay? You're all right now, girl. You got ten times the courage and guts that kid has. But he's bigger'n you, and he'll take any advantage he can get. You want me to walk you home?" He patted her head awkwardly, and when Berdine looked up and saw that gentle, crooked smile on his face, it made her heart sting. He looked so much like his son in that moment that Berdine wanted to cry.

"N-no, sir. I'm-I'm okay. How did you ... Why were you out here?" Berdine lifted a pale face to question the man. Mr. Caraway ducked his head slightly and rubbed the back of his neck. He looked a bit sheepish, but finally he spoke.

"Well, I've been coming out here to patch up this old tree house, and yesterday I brought a couple of boards to see about rigging a sturdier ladder. Came back today with the rest of my tools." He barely met Berdine's eyes, but when he did, she could almost swear she saw a gleam of moisture in the corners.

Berdine tilted her head to one side, studying the older man as understanding dawned on her. "You miss him ..."

A closed look came over Mr. Caraway's face even as he stood reaching out a hand to help Berdine off the ground. His voice was once again distant and a little gruff.

"Michael's in a good place right now. He'll have a better chance this way. My sister and the major will take good care of him. He'll be a man when he graduates."

He couldn't hide the tiny note of pride creeping into his voice. He looked off into the distance, his eyes not really focusing on anything in particular. It was as if he were seeing some future vision, and it pleased him.

Suddenly, he shook himself from his thoughts and turned back to look at the young, hopeful girl in the oversized sweatshirt standing in front of him. His expression softened ever so slightly, and he lowered his voice so that she could barely make out his words.

"He won't forget about you, girl. Don't you worry."

Berdine merely bowed her head, not wishing the man to see the doubt in her eyes. "I better get on home. Thanks for helping me, Mr. Caraway. I'd appreciate it if you'd not mention any of this to my parents. It would only worry them."

She waited for his response, and though it felt like a long time coming, Mr. Caraway slowly nodded his head. She could tell that he wrestled with his conscience, but she was satisfied he'd keep her secret.

XII

Fortune seemed to favor Berdine in the coming days as she was able to sweep the incident under the rug. It made her feel a little guilty that it had gotten so easy to make excuses for things. But with the eve of her sister's wedding now upon them, there had been little time for anyone to notice Berdine or a ruined shirt. Berdine even found herself getting caught up in the celebratory atmosphere around the house. It was almost a relief to forget her recent hardships in the wake of joyful anticipation. She and Kathryn had steered clear of each other since their last uncomfortable conversation, so it was quite a surprise to Berdine when her older sister approached her before going to bed that night.

"Hey, Berdine... this is my last night in this house. Want to spend the night in my room for old times' sake?" The smile on Kathryn's face was reflective and almost hopeful. It was that last emotion that prevented Berdine from turning her down, even though it was her first inclination.

"Sure, I guess. Let me grab my pillow."

"Great... I've got Oreos and Diet Pepsi!" Kathryn giggled like a little girl. "But it's *your* responsibility to hold me to only two. I've got to have a flat stomach when I put on my wedding gown tomorrow!"

Berdine rolled her eyes at the absurdity of that statement. The only place Kathryn *didn't* have curves was her flat-as-a-board stomach!

Surprisingly, it turned out to be a serendipitous time, with plenty of laughter, a couple of tears, and just the right amount of chocolate. It was late when the girls had finished brushing their teeth, washing their faces and settling in for the night. They lay facing each other, in opposite twin beds, with their pillows tucked under their heads. The house had grown quiet, and both sisters were beginning to feel the pull of sleep. It was in one of those glazed moments between wakefulness and sleep that the invisible walls between the girls came down.

"You nervous about tomorrow, Kat?" Berdine asked sleepily.

"Of course not! I've been planning this for years. Rodney is the man I've been dreaming of. Married life is going to be wonderful..." Kathryn's confident tone trailed off, and she finished in a small voice. "Well... maybe, just a little..."

"It'll be great. He looks at you with his heart in his eyes... I wish..." Berdine sighed wistfully and yawned.

For a moment Kathryn didn't reply. Berdine's breathing deepened, and Kathryn knew sleep would soon claim her as well. Hovering just above consciousness, Kathryn murmured, "I only did it to protect you, Berdie... It's for your own good..." Her voice trailed off to a whisper as she too drifted off to sleep. Berdine never even heard the beginnings of the quiet confession.

The next day passed at a frenetic pace, beginning with Kathryn wailing from behind a locked bathroom door barely past dawn. Berdine and her mother both stood outside the door banging frantically.

"What's the matter, Kathryn? Have you hurt yourself? Are you all right?" Mama was panicked, especially after realizing Kathryn wasn't opening the door.

"Open up, Kathryn! You've already woken up the whole house; you might as well let us in!" Berdine couldn't summon the note of compassion she heard in her mother's voice. The only thing she felt was irritation.

"*I'm hideous!*" Kathryn sobbed from inside the little bathroom. Berdine rolled her eyes, marking this down to another of her sister's personal dramas.

"What is it, honey? Let me in, and I'll help you. We'll fix whatever it is!" Her mother was starting to sound a little hysterical herself. Suddenly, the door flung open, and Kathryn stuck her head out, jabbing a shaking finger at her own cheek.

"Can you fix *this?*" she shrieked.

Both females leaned forward, squinting in the direction of Kathryn's finger. Incredulous that neither was reacting with significant enough emotion, Kathryn also leaned closer, nearly bumping heads with the other two.

"It's a *pimple,* for heaven's sake! Are you both *blind?*" Kathryn stood frozen in suspended drama, her finger still pinpointing the evidence of her misery. For a moment, no one said a thing. Suddenly, Berdine's eyes widened as she raised her palm to cover her mouth. She used every fiber of her being to stifle the laugher threatening to erupt, but it was to no avail. Struggling to regain her composure, Berdine realized that the offended amazement on her sister's face had quickly changed to murderous rage.

"You little *troll!*" Kathryn growled. "It's *your* fault! You sat there and watched me eat *four* Oreos last night!"

Kathryn was brandishing her hairbrush, and Berdine knew this was her exit cue. Turning swiftly, she took off in a flash down the hall. Between gasps of mirth, she yelled back over her shoulder, "But at least your stomach is still flat!"

In spite of the rocky start, the day turned out to be everything Berdine knew her sister had dreamed of. Kathryn was a beautiful bride. The shrieking banshee from the early morning hours had transformed into a graceful, poised young woman, greeting her guests at her wedding reception. By the time it was time to toss the bridal bouquet, Berdine's feet were starting to ache. All she could think about was getting out of her bridesmaid's dress and heels (something as foreign to her as her swept-up hairdo) and back into comfortable shorts and a T-shirt. She grumbled to a few other single girls standing close by.

"I'm telling you right now; *no wedding for me.* I mean it. What a lot of fuss!"

The other girls looked alarmed at the determined tone of Berdine's voice. To them, her words approached sacrilege! One of her friends peered intently at Berdine's frowning face. In a perplexed voice, she asked, "What do you mean *'no wedding'?* You don't want to get *married?*" The last word ended on a gasp.

Berdine rolled her eyes, explaining simply, "I didn't say I didn't want to get married. I just don't want all this wedding fluff."

She paused, and a slow smile crossed her face. She continued in a quiet voice. "I'm picturing the beach, at sundown... seagulls and crashing waves as our music. We'll write our own vows, and we'll be barefoot." She trailed off, seeing the vision perfectly in her mind's eye. When she realized no one had spoken, she looked back into the faces of her friends surrounding her. All of them shared a mixture of expressions, ranging from blank confusion to horror. Berdine sighed, thinking to herself this was just another example of how different she was from her peers. Fortunately, she was growing accustomed to the feeling.

There was a sudden stirring of activity to her right, and the wedding coordinator was trying to corral all the single girls into a huddle. The photographer was barking commands, competing with instructions called out by both the coordinator and Kathryn. All the other adults stood crowded in closely, indulgent smiles on their faces. In the cacophony of the moment, Kathryn turned and stared meaningfully at Berdine. The group of girls pressing into her, hoping to catch the bouquet, caught the pointed look and moved slightly away. Berdine just stared back blankly, wishing they'd get this over with.

"Ready?" Kathryn looked over her shoulder, her eyes gleaming with laughter. "One, two, three!" It was a perfectly aimed toss. It could not have been more on target, heading in Berdine's direction. In a belated moment of understanding, Berdine lifted a hand. The bouquet bounced off her fingers and onto the floor at her feet. Everyone groaned in disappointment.

"Gee, Berdine. That's bad luck, y'know." One of the young men standing off to the side teased.

Some of the guys standing near him, quipped, "Depends on whose perspective you're talking about! At least some guy's still in the game!"

They all laughed uproariously at their own joke. Berdine just smiled and shook her head. She had already forgotten the fallen bouquet as she wandered away, looking for a glass of water.

That night, after the good-byes, the well wishes, and the farewell waves to the happy couple, Berdine lay in her bed thinking. *Did Michael like the ocean? They had never really talked about that…* She drifted off to sleep with the image of Michael and her walking hand in hand through the foamy water lapping at their ankles.

XIII

"Berdine!" her mother called up the stairs. "You have to be at the school in twenty minutes! I told you last night to get everything laid out and ready so you wouldn't be rushed! I can't believe you'd be late to your own graduation ceremony! Kathryn and Rodney are going to meet us there because they'll need to head back to Charleston right after lunch. *Berdine?* Are you listening to me?"

Berdine stuck her turbaned head out the bathroom door. "Mama! I'm not gonna be late! When have I ever been late to anything?"

She couldn't help teasing her mother since her tardiness had always been a bone of contention. It struck her suddenly that she might not have many more opportunities to tease her parents since she was leaving right after graduation for the College of Charleston to start summer studies. She felt a little guilty jumping right into the next stage of her life, when Mama and Pop both dropped continuous hints about "How quiet it's going to be around here with both your sister and you gone!" Still, it was not enough guilt to keep Berdine from grasping at the first opportunity to put her high school career behind her. The last two years had crawled by at a snail's pace. She remembered the agony of the last month of her sophomore year trying to avoid Danny Tyler and his cronies. Fortunately for her, it turned out to be fairly easy since he spent more of the year suspended than in school.

The summers were the bright spots in those remaining two years. Berdine had found an ad in the *Mount Holly Herald* for a summer job in Charleston. Something resonated within her as she read the description and necessary qualifications. It wasn't the requirement of administrative skills that caught her attention, although she had a knack for organization. It was the description of the rustic camp, geared solely toward kids with challenges. With a sense of purpose, she answered the ad. It was not a matter of arrogance or overconfidence. Berdine just knew she was the right fit. She was hired as the general assistant to the director at the Outward Bound Wilderness camp for at-risk and delinquent children. Since she was under the age of twenty-one, she was not yet qualified to be a counselor. She was still able to observe enough of the camp's philosophy in action while doing office work to feel a growing sense of calling.

It was during these summers Berdine discovered a beneficiary for her champion's heart still buried just a few layers under a protective shell. At the beginning of each two-week session, she found herself studying the belligerent, angry faces of the troubled children as they descended the steps of the bus. They always stood apart—as if there were an invisible force field surrounding them, shielding them from having to interact with each other. At the end of the sessions, however, she witnessed an incredible transformation in the same group of kids boarding the buses for home. It was a defining moment in Berdine's plan for her future. Over and over she watched disjointed bands of rebels evolve into a supportive, cohesive group of kids. The counselors swore by the core values played out through the challenge and adventure built into each session. The whitewater kayaking and outdoor survival training was designed to teach kids teamwork, tenacity, acceptance of responsibility and most importantly, a sense of their personal value to the group. But in Berdine's estimation, the greatest catalyst for change was the offer of unconditional friendship from counselor to camper. Berdine learned that these kids were masters at detecting insincerity. When they came to realize that the counselors were there because they genuinely liked their jobs, loved the kids, and believed in each child's potential, walls came crashing down. Nothing Berdine had ever experienced in her life could rival the sense of triumph she felt when it finally happened.

And so she watched and learned and planned. Knowing she'd only have an abbreviated term with Outward Bound this final summer, she was ready to soak up every experience afforded her before college classes started. Her bags were already packed: one set aside for camp and the rest for school.

Berdine was looking forward to starting college and being on her own. The summers at camp had taught her independence. It was something her family, especially Kathryn, had never understood. Her older sister had simply moved directly from one protected environment to another. It was probably why she tried on several occasions to convince Berdine to stay with her and Dr. Caulfield when classes for the second half of the summer session began.

"We have such a giant house," she had said. "There's no reason for you to move into the dorms before the fall. It'll be so lonely! Hardly any students stay in the dorms over the summer sessions." She cajoled to no avail.

If Berdine were to be perfectly honest, it was always in the very back of her mind, that maybe, *just maybe,* she'd run into Michael sometime. Oh, not that she would ever seek him out. Absolutely not! His lack of communication made it very clear to her that their childhood friendship was a distant thing of the past. No, it was mainly just mild curiosity that perpetuated her continued interest in him. She defended her interest as being the same kind of casual inquisitiveness she might feel if she were to attend her ten-year high school reunion. That's all it was, she stubbornly maintained. She never allowed herself to look more deeply at the little white lies she told herself. It was important for her to keep the shell around her heart intact.

"*Mama!*" Berdine leaned over the stair rail, yelling. "Can you see if my black pumps are down there?"

She waited for an answer, all the while grumbling to herself how stupid it was to wear nylons and heels under a great, billowing robe. It's not as if anyone even looked at your feet. In *her* opinion, a graduate ought to have the privilege of choosing whatever they wanted to wear under that unflattering, voluminous gown. If it were up to Berdine, she'd be in her pajamas and slippers. She wouldn't even have to bother with her hair. It was tucked up under that hideous square pancake cap anyway!

She was sitting at the top of the stairs having a good pout when her father came up, holding the offending shoes in his hand.

"Looking for these, Irony girl?" He chuckled and bent down to kiss the top of her head. "If I know my Berdine, she's about half a second away from chucking the whole idea of shoes altogether... am I right?"

Berdine had to laugh. "See? That's exactly my problem, Pop. I've become way too predictable. I'll have to change that before I come home from college to visit. It's time for 'little Berdine' to become a grown-up college student!"

Pop winced, chuckling softly as he lowered himself to the steps a couple down from Berdine. "Aaahhh... that gave me a little pain right here, honey."

He pointed at the place over his heart. Berdine leaned down and the kissed the top of her father's head. She wrapped her arms around him and rested her cheek on the place she'd kissed.

"Oh Pop, even when I grow up, you'll still be my hero!"

Her father smiled, a knowing look on his face. "It won't be long, Berdine, till a young man comes along and fills those shoes. That's how it should be, you know. Your mama and I want the very best for you. We're so pleased that Kathryn found a man who loves and takes care of her. We want the same for you."

Berdine just leaned her cheek against her father's head and murmured lightly, "Well, funny thing is, Pop, a young man *did* come along... but it turns out your shoes were too big to fill, so I guess you'll have to wear those shoes awhile longer."

Silence reigned uncomfortably for a moment. For a weighted moment, Berdine hoped her father would respond to her quiet words. But her hopes were dashed in the next second.

"Well, Berdie, my girl." Pop jumped up a little too enthusiastically, holding out a hand to pull her to her feet. "It appears we now have less than ten minutes to get you to the school! We better get a move on, or we'll never hear the end of it from your mama."

Berdine smiled sadly, letting her father pull her up. She allowed the words welling up in her heart to die away. Instead, she brightened her expression and said, "Pop, just tell Mama to quit worrying... Our last name is Williams, isn't it? You know how long it takes to get to the *W*s?"

Pop laughed in response. "Well, you *do* have a point. Still, I'll meet you downstairs in six and a half minutes. Don't fail me!"

XIV

As Berdine later looked back over the day, she had to admit that the whole event was really nothing more to her than a depot station on the way to the main destination. She found herself looking around at the graduates and their families laughing and taking pictures, appearing almost reluctant to leave the school grounds. It made Berdine feel disconnected. She was *eager* to move on. There were no feelings of nostalgia as they walked out of the cafeteria, crossing the courtyard to their cars. It was not that she wasn't grateful she had a supportive family who wanted to share this time with her—she truly was. But there was a perverse side of her simply wanting to shout, "*No big deal!*" Once again, however, Berdine suppressed the temptation to spout her true feelings and went along dutifully to her celebration lunch down at Nell's Café in town square.

Nell's Café was almost an historical landmark in Mount Holly, South Carolina. It had been around under different ownership for as long as Berdine could remember. The latest owner, Nell Baker, was a young woman in her early twenties—not many years older that Berdine. She was a no-nonsense, tough as steel, young woman. She worked hard to help her mother support her five younger brothers and sisters. Her daddy had taken off sometime around Nell's early high school years, and they had not heard from him since.

Nell had dreamed of going to college after graduation, but money was so tight. Even with earning enough academic scholarships to pay her tuition, the stark reality was that her family needed her salary to keep food on the table. When her mother was well, she did what she could to help her daughter clean houses, take in laundry, sew for people—but it was never a steady enough income to keep them comfortable. It could have been so easy for Nell to become hardened and bitter, having to sacrifice her dream of going away to college. Most people didn't know that beneath that tough exterior, Nell was intuitive and kind, with enough dreams to last two lifetimes. But dreams had no place in the stark reality she found herself in. She had learned early in her life that if you wanted something, you had to make it happen. Nell knew how to make the best of her circumstances. It was a waste of good energy to mope around, whining that life wasn't fair. Of course, it wasn't fair! The point that really mattered was that life was *short.*

Running a café might not have been in her original plans, but when the window of chance flew open, Nell jumped through it, using every talent and resource the good Lord had given her. It had been one of those timely and unexpected opportunities, and it simply fell into her lap.

Nell had gotten up early on a Monday morning, hurrying to help her mother fix breakfast for the other kids. As soon as she got them out the front door and on their way to school, she'd be able to leave for the bank. She wanted to be there as soon as the doors opened, before it got busy. Her file of papers was already placed neatly on the old, scratched table by the front door, along with her purse and sweater.

Unfortunately, it was another one of those mornings when her mother's depression was debilitating. It worried Nell that her mother's bouts with depression were coming a little more frequently these days. Her worsening condition had seemed to coincide directly with the day Nell graduated from high school. It was as though her mother held things together just long enough for Nell to finish her school obligations, so she could then take over the reins. Nell didn't resent it. It wasted too much of her energy to harbor resentment. She simply recognized that her mother was fragile. Some days were good ... and some days, like today, required a little more of Nell's patience. She had finally shooed her mother back to her bedroom with a promise that she'd come talk to her a moment before leaving the house.

"Teddy! Stop kicking Anne!" Nell tapped her little brother on the head as she set his bowl of cereal in front of him. She held up a hand to silence his protestations of innocence, knowing they would escalate in volume if anyone doubted his claim. "No, don't even say it. I saw your foot swinging under the table."

The kitchen table was a hum of activity. She unconsciously counted heads and bowls of cereal, all the while keeping watch like a sentry for the possibility of minor uprisings. Nell's eyes narrowed in on the solitary bowl of cereal at the end of the table, presently without an owner. Immediately, she mentally went down the roll call. *Becky!* Nell sighed wearily. Not the best morning for dealing with her recalcitrant, sometimes too-big-for-her-britches, fourteen-year-old sister. Of all her younger siblings, Becky was the one who most resisted Nell's firm, competent running of the family. Nell suspected that it was more than that. Their mother's emotional instability caused a great deal of insecurity for the young teen. Becky was also at an age when she wanted desperately to assert her independence yet didn't quite have the confidence to pull it off. Fortunately, Nell's skin was thick enough when Becky turned all of her resentment and anger on her older sister, yet remained thin enough to empathize with the scared little girl underneath.

Nell pushed back from the table, glancing around once more. "Howard. Howard? Stop reading a second and listen to me. Please help the rest of the kids finish up their cereal. Margaret, you can clear the dishes away when everyone's done. Yes, *I know* that's Becky's job, but as you can see, she's nowhere to be found. Now hurry up, you guys! You need to be heading to school in less than fifteen minutes!"

Nell left the kitchen, glancing once at her watch. It would be a miracle if she got away from here in time to be at the bank when it opened. She rounded the corner, headed for Becky's room. The overpowering scent of perfume stopped her in her tracks. She knocked loudly on the bathroom door. She could hear Becky inside, humming a tune as if she hadn't a care in the world. The knock did not gain any response whatsoever. Nell leaned against the door.

"Becky? Could you come out here, please? You're not going to have any time left now for breakfast. It's already eight thirty!"

She counted to ten slowly, waiting for Becky to answer. The humming had stopped, and Nell could hear the drawer opening and a sweep of cosmetic compacts clattering into the drawer.

"Becky?"

"I *hear* you, Nell! Stop bugging me! I'll be out in a second. I don't even want breakfast anyway," Becky snapped.

"Fine. I'll wait right here for you." Nell folded her arms and leaned back against the wall outside the bathroom door. She could hear Becky huff in disgust. A second later, the door flung open. Nell's eyes widened slightly when she took in the dark, heavy makeup on the younger girl who was now staring back at her in defiance. For a moment, Nell said nothing. She just studied her sister's face.

Becky became self-conscious, retorting defensively, "*What?* I already asked Mom if I could wear her makeup. She said it was fine!"

Nell knew she needed to tread lightly. "I think it's a little dark for you, Becky. Why don't you lighten it just a bit?"

Becky crossed her arms over her chest, and her tone was bitter. "You're always telling me what to do! You don't even *wear* makeup, so how would you know what does and doesn't look good? Quit trying to be my mother!"

Nell could see how fragile Becky's self-esteem was, and she hated putting any more dents in it, but Nell was nothing, if not truthful.

"I'm sorry you don't like hearing my opinion, Becky, but you're going to. You don't need to wear that much makeup to school. It looks trashy, and you're not that kind of girl. If you don't like hearing it from me, go ask Mom what she thinks."

"*Just forget it!*" Becky whirled around and slammed the bathroom door in Nell's face.

Shaking her head with regret, Nell pushed away from the wall and headed back to the kitchen to herd the kids toward their book satchels and sack lunches.

Ten minutes later, Nell had eight-year-old Margaret and six-year-old Anne standing by the door, ready to go. She had Teddy in the bathroom, washing a chunk of oatmeal out of his hair. She saw a flash of white pass by the open door, and she noted that Becky had, indeed, scrubbed her face clean. In a small measure of rebellion, however, the younger girl sported an oxford shirt that she had tied tightly around her middle so that at least two inches of skin showed above the waistband of her jeans. She had turned the cuffs up at the bottom so that as much leg as possible showed above her bobby socks, and her hair was pulled up high in a ponytail with a big white bow in the back. Nell kept her attention on Teddy, who wiggled and squirmed, trying to avoid the washcloth.

"*Be still,* Teddy! This will just take a second. You don't want to go to your class with a big glob of goop in your hair, do you?" She held the little boy's chin steady in her hand, while she wiped the last of it away.

With almost a tone of weary resignation, Teddy answered solemnly, "It's kindergarten, Nell. We're *supposed* to have globs of goop in our hair."

Nell couldn't help but laugh, kissing him on top of his head and swatting him as he hopped out of the bathroom. She hustled all of them through the front door. As Becky passed by, Nell tugged firmly on the knot at her midsection, coaxing the shirt down a couple of inches. Becky made an irritated sound of protest and moved quickly away. Finally, Nell stood in the doorway, waving good-bye to her siblings. Suddenly, she realized Howard was not with them. Throwing up her hands in frustration, Nell turned back into the house. The solemn boy sat motionless, perched on the edge of the couch, reading his book. *In all of that commotion, he probably never even looked up,* Nell thought. She shook her head. At least Howard was no trouble! Thank God for small blessings!

After finally getting the last one off to school, Nell hurried back to her mother's darkened room. It wouldn't surprise her if her mother had taken a sleeping pill and gone back to sleep. On her bad days, it was the only thing her mother wanted to do. She peered into the shadowed room. Her mother was lying on her side, eyes wide open. Nell moved into the room, coming to stand by the bed. "Mama, I'm headed to the bank now. Do you need anything while I'm out?"

Her mother shook her head, tears welling up in her eyes. "We're gonna lose the house, aren't we, Nellie?"

Nell went down to her knees and took her mother's hand in her own. "We'll be fine, Mama. I just need to talk to Mr. McClain and explain the situation. He's worked with us before when we've been in a tight spot. Don't worry. The Lord always looks out for us, doesn't He, Mama?"

"You're a good girl, Nell. You work so hard. I don't know what we'd do without you. As soon as I feel better, I'm going to see if I can find a few more houses for us to clean." Her mother smiled sleepily.

"That's good, Mama. Why don't you go back to sleep? I'll look in on you when I get home." Nell stood, giving her mother's hand a light squeeze. She turned and left the room, closing the door gently behind her.

By the time she stood outside the bank doors in town square, Nell felt as though she had been on the fast track for half a day. She'd hardly had time to comb her own hair and make herself presentable. She glanced at her reflection in the big, plate glass windows. Her neat, brown bob shined and hugged a firm little chin. She was taller than average and athletically slender. Her crisp, white blouse was tucked neatly into the straight, camel-colored skirt, skimming just below her knees. Frowning, she noted that her low-heeled, brown pumps could have used a quick dab of polish to disguise the scuff-marks. She studied her complexion with a critical eye, and for just a second, wondered if makeup actually *could* transform her plain features. Chiding herself for the narcissistic thought, she tossed her head, sending her shiny hair swinging. She straightened her shoulders, standing taller, and marched into the bank. A receptionist at a tall oak desk greeted her, her voice echoing across the lobby.

"Good morning. May I help you?"

"I'd like to see Mr. McClain, if he's not too busy." Nell spoke politely, garnering her confidence.

The receptionist asked, "Do you have an appointment?"

"No, ma'am; that's why I came early."

"If you'll just have a seat, I'll see if Mr. McClain is available. May I give him your name?"

"Yes, thank you. It's Nell Baker."

Nell turned and walked to the brown leather couches in the center of the bank lobby. She sat perched on the edge, her back straight. A moment later, the receptionist returned, her heels clicking out a staccato beat on the marble floors.

"Please come with me, Miss Baker."

The receptionist was not familiar to her, so Nell mirrored the formality, maintaining proper decorum although she had known John McClain since she was a little girl. He was an elder at the Mount Holly Community Church where Nell had committed to a life of faith in the Lord. He had taught Nell's fifth grade Sunday school class years ago. Even at nearly sixty years of age, Mr. McClain was still teaching in the children's department, and he was a great favorite.

She rounded the corner and saw Mr. McClain—tall, silver haired, and distinguished, leaning over slightly to better hear the low, gravelly voice of an even older gentleman. She recognized the older man as the owner of the café in town square. He was round and ruddy cheeked, and he had the great booming laugh one expected of an Irishman. At the moment, the older man was shaking the hand of Mr. McClain, and Nell happened to catch his parting words.

"Now, John, I appreciate your advice about what to do about the café. I'm hoping to have a buyer by the end of the month. My daughter and son-in-law have a nice little garage apartment up there in Greenville, and I've a hankerin' to be closer to the grandkids. If you know of anyone interested in taking over the place, I'd sure appreciate hearin' about it." The older man winked and pumped Mr. McClain's hand once more.

"You know I will, Patrick. That little café is in a prime location, and a lot of folks in town would sincerely regret having to change their lunch routine if it shut down."

The men finished their good-byes as Nell's mind worked quickly on the beginnings of a plan.

Nell had always been the type to analyze and deliberate over every idea she had. She liked to map out the logical steps and consider all possible outcomes of a project. But, for the first time in her life, she felt a strong prompting to take a risk on something that did not seem the least bit logical! She knew this plan was undeveloped, irrational, and … *absolutely perfect.*

"Um, Mr. O'Rourke, could I have just a word with you?" She had reached out and touched his sleeve as the round little man had turned to leave. He looked startled for a moment until he recognized Nell. A big smile spread across his cheeks, and he greeted her warmly.

"Why, you certainly may, Miss Nell! Didn't know you were waitin' on me."

"Actually, I was coming to see Mr. McClain, and I'll do that right after I speak with you—if that's all right with you, Mr. McClain." She looked at the banker, who nodded pleasantly, a friendly twinkle in his eyes.

He spoke in a stage whisper to the older man. "I've seen that gleam in this girl's eye before, Patrick. You best be sharp!"

The round, little Irishman nodded, grinning at his old friend. He turned back to Nell, offering his arm to Nell in a courtly gesture. "How may I help you, my dear?" he asked as he led her to the soft leather couches from which she'd just come.

Nell never doubted herself when it came to her goals and aspirations. She believed she had a fair assessment of her abilities and was confident in her solid work ethic. Sometimes, though, her self-assurance put off her peers, which was why Nell didn't have an abundance of friends in her age group. Most of them, at her age, were either finishing up college or getting married and having babies. Right now, neither of those scenarios fit into Nell's immediate future.

She smiled warmly at the sweet, old gentleman and considered briefly how she wanted to propose her idea. Not having had the time to think it completely through, she took a deep breath and plunged in.

"I'd like to buy your café, Mr. O'Rourke. I believe I can keep it running in a manner you're accustomed to seeing. It's in such excellent condition; I don't believe many changes or improvements are needed." Nell spoke calmly, with a maturity belying her years.

Mr. O'Rourke was silent, surprised at Nell's determined words and curious to hear the rest of her proposal. "Go on."

"I wouldn't be able to buy it outright, but I believe if you would be willing to work out kind of a lease-to-own plan, I could have the place fully paid for within two years. During that time, I would pay interest until the café is completely in my name. It's a small enough place that I can run it without a lot of extra help, so I wouldn't need to pay employees. But if I were in a bind, I believe my family could help out."

Nell sat very still, allowing Mr. O'Rourke to digest her words. She knew that if he was willing to accept her proposition, it would be because he was a generous man with a big heart and an even bigger wallet.

"That's quite an ambitious plan for a young lady such as yourself. Now, what would protect me should you not be able to pay off the café in two years?" Mr. O'Rourke thoughtfully tapped on his cheek with a finger. He was kind, but he was also shrewd.

Nell breathed in deeply. She rarely made impractical or impulsive decisions. Even when she was a child, she thought through her plans carefully and methodically. So when she felt the rush of adrenaline, coupled with the unpleasant sensation of desperation, she knew she was about to take that final leap of faith.

"I can put up our house as collateral." *Did that just come out of my mouth?* As insane as the words probably sounded to the old man in front of her, Nell realized she had no desire to retrieve them. In fact, as they rung in the air between them, she felt a sense of peace settle over her. She waited anxiously for his response.

"Well now, Miss Nell, that's a big risk. I know you got a houseful of brothers and sisters, not to mention your mama—who *does* actually *own* the house!" The old man smiled gently, yet Nell did not get the feeling he was shutting down on her proposal.

Nell leaned forward, passion flowing in her eyes, her voice nearly quivering with conviction. "My family *needs* this, Mr. O'Rourke. We need a place we can be proud of—something that will bring in a regular salary. I know with all my heart I can make it a success. I just need you to believe in me."

Mr. O'Rourke sat silently for a moment, studying the earnest expression on the young woman's face. It made him remember a time long ago when he had found his way to Mount Holly, bringing his young family with him. He had desperately wanted to get them out of New York, away from the fast-paced city life and bitter winters. All he needed back then was for someone to give him a chance. He identified with the eager confidence he could hear in Nell's voice. He sighed loudly, knowing he was won over.

"Ahhh, Nell. Hearing you brings back memories. Let's go talk to Mr. McClain and see what we can work out." He grinned at the joyous light in Nell's eyes, and his heart squeezed when she leaned over and kissed him on the cheek.

XV

And so, Nell's Café came to town, in a manner of speaking. In less than a year, she had more than halfway met her goal in paying off the place. She was even turning a small profit and was able to tuck back a little here and there into her savings.

Looking back on that day, she knew that the Lord had whispered into the hearts of two men. Not only had Mr. O'Rourke agreed to a financially risky proposal, but Mr. McClain had given her time to catch up on her house mortgage so that she would not be starting out in the red.

The café had turned out to be a blessing in so many ways. Her mother was able to help out, and her "bad" days were not near as frequent. Her brothers and sisters had weekly responsibilities that gave them a sense of ownership and a humming, energetic place to come to after school to do their homework. Nell gradually made a few changes here and there. An inviting, green and white striped awning out front framed the big picture glass windows. A few quaint tables with bright, cheery umbrellas and matching chairs were arranged casually along the sidewalk in front. Large terra cotta pots with masses of wildflowers spilling over the sides were tucked in and among the tables. Inside, she had added lots of greenery, a fresh coat of light, butterscotch paint, and white, linen tablecloths. By day, little crystal vases held fresh flowers on each table. In the evenings, they were replaced by aromatic votive candles. Antique floor lamps tastefully arranged in among the tables created a soft glow at dusk. Not a day went by that Nell didn't hear comments like "Love what you've done to the place, Nell!" or "What an inviting atmosphere you've created here!"

It was no surprise that Nell's Café was the location the Williamses' family had chosen for a special celebration lunch following Berdine's graduation ceremony. Berdine's mother had consulted with Nell just last week about the menu. Nell had put together a tray of tasty chicken salad croissants and another of ham and cheese tarts. Fresh fruit compote in tiny crystal bowls accompanied each place setting. Vegetables, cut julienne-style, artfully adorned yet another gleaming silver tray. Raspberry iced tea in tall glasses with wedges of orange glistened on the table. The desserts simply defied description! Nell had already made a name for herself for her strong coffee and her incomparable desserts. She enjoyed researching magazines and recipe books for the most tantalizing confections she could find. Her personal talent was in the tiny bit of altering she did to the recipes.

By the time Berdine had gotten away from the graduation ceremony, her parents and sister and brother-in-law were already at the café. Nell had entered the spirit of celebration and had brought in bundles of balloons and streamers to decorate—all in school colors of forest green and white. Nell's mother and siblings were enthusiastically joining in the festive mood. When Berdine entered, her cap askew and robe unzipped to reveal a sleeveless knit shirt and pedal pushers, everyone stood and cheered. She swept off the ridiculous cap and bowed with flourish, tossing it in the direction of Nell's younger brothers and sisters. They leapt for it and took turns parading around with it on their heads. Berdine's mother wore an expression of weary resignation when she finally got a good look at how Berdine was dressed under her robe. She had indeed worn nylons and black pumps. From the knee down, she was every bit the elegant, poised graduate.

But over the pantyhose, she had worn slim, white pedal pushers with a bright red knit shirt tucked in at the waist.

"Berdine! What *were* you thinking? This was a solemn, formal occasion! What if your robe had flown open? What would people think?" Her mother lamented.

Kathryn rolled her eyes, teasing her mother, "Right, Mother, *that* happens all the time! I think it was a great idea, Berdine!"

Berdine just laughed, bending down to kiss her mother on the cheek. "Sorry, Mama, just had to make my last statement about the dress code. Everyone go ahead and start. I'm just going to slip back here into the restroom and get rid of these hose and shoes!" She pulled a pair of red sandals from her handbag and slipped out of sight.

On her way back, Nell reached around the counter and tugged Berdine in for a quick hug.

"That's the girl we all know and love! Congrats to you, Berdie! If you get a chance to hang around a few minutes after everyone clears out, I'd love to sit down and have a chat with you. It seems like it's been forever since we had any girl talk."

Nell beamed at her younger friend. They were about four years apart, so they had missed being schoolmates, but over the last two years, their friendship had grown rapidly. There wasn't much about each other that they hadn't discussed. There was something in each of them that met a significant need in the other. Nell knew, without a doubt, that Berdine could see inside to the real Nell. Not many people got beneath her exterior of a hard-working, self-reliant, young woman who managed her home, her family, and her business with efficient, organized precision. Yet Berdine saw the softer side of Nell—the dreamer and scholar. She even saw the deeply hidden core of fear that sometimes bubbled inside her friend.

For Berdine, Nell was the *true* sister of her heart. She had the ability to sit very still and listen, without judgment, as Berdine poured out her soul. Occasionally, Nell would ask a thought-provoking question or speak words of comfort. During the last couple of years, when no one else had time for a teenage girl's distress over her first love, Nell not only listened with compassionate interest, she validated those painful emotions. She never tried to reason away her hurt, or pour out platitudes. She listened with understanding and respect. Berdine was going to miss their weekly talks when she left for the camp and then, college.

The graduation celebration was in full swing when Berdine returned to the table. Other patrons seated at some of the peripheral tables couldn't help but join in and feel a part.

It was midafternoon before Rodney and Kathryn came over to say good-bye.

"Well, you did it, Berdine. Now you can run away to college and go wild!" Kathryn loved to get a reaction out of her parents, and she wasn't disappointed.

"Don't you *dare* tell her that!" Mama scolded. "Berdine has serious plans for the next four years, don't you, dear?"

Berdine couldn't help but play along with her sister. Mama could be so adoringly gullible.

"I sure do, Mama. Now that curfew is a thing of the past, I'm going to catch up on all the movies I missed, spend my money at fancy restaurants, and fall in love with dozens and dozens of marines right there close on Parris Island!"

"Berdine! You stay away from that marine recruit base—I mean it!" Her mother looked at her with worried consternation. Kathryn and Berdine exchanged mischievous grins.

"Don't worry, Mama. I'll be able to watch her every move since we live in Charleston, you know. If she goes over to Parris Island, I'll be right there behind her!" Kathryn quipped, tongue-in-cheek. Rodney peered over her shoulder and cleared his throat, jokingly offended.

"What was that, Mrs. Caulfield? You're going *with* Berdine to check out the marines?"

Rodney didn't have a jealous bone in his body, but he pretended to as he towered over Kathryn, a teasing frown on his face. Kathryn laughed delightedly, enjoying his playful proprietary reaction. She placed a hand on his chest and giggled flirtatiously.

"Now, Rodney, why would I care about a few overly muscled *boys* when I have my handsome, distinguished husband by my side?" She batted her eyelashes dramatically.

Berdine pantomimed a gagging motion.

"Cut it out, you two. We all just ate lunch. It's not like you haven't been married three years already!"

Berdine walked them out, thanking them for coming. Her mother and father weren't too far behind them. Berdine told them to go on ahead so she could stay and chat with Nell. Most of the customers had gone, and there was the usual lull between the lunch and dinner crowds. Nell had made them both a cup of coffee and motioned Berdine over to a table in the corner. This was usually the only time of day Nell could catch a breather.

"Nell, this was so great. I know you went to a lot of extra effort. Thank you."

Berdine pulled out a chair to sit. She looked around the café, once again seeing it afresh. In the nine months Nell had taken over the ownership, the place had been transformed. It always amazed her that the girl sitting across from her—not even much older than Berdine—had taken on a project of this magnitude and had made it work. What kind of inner fortitude and drive did one have to possess to do what Nell had done? Berdine shook her head, amazed. She hoped that she too would be able to work toward her personal goals with the same amount of focus and passion.

"Oh, Berdine … it was nothing. You're just easy to please! A few chicken salad sandwiches, and you're happy!" Nell smiled.

"Well … " Berdine began, "if you had *really* wanted to make me happy, you would have made *fried* chicken. That's what I *really* wanted!"

Both girls laughed. It was a big joke between them that Berdine, tiny as she was, enjoyed a diet of calorie-laden, deep-fried, gravy-covered food. Nell was forever trying to persuade Berdine to eat healthier.

Nell suddenly leaned forward on her elbows, fixing Berdine with that familiar, forthright stare.

"So! What's next on the schedule?"

Berdine laughed, wondering why she still hadn't gotten used to the way Nell cut through the small talk to get straight to the matters at hand.

"Well, remember I told you I was going to try to get in at least two sessions at Outward Bound before the second summer school session? So I leave here in four days. I can't wait to get back to the camp. I wish you could experience it, Nell. All of these delinquent kids trudge off that bus the first day, looking like they'd just as soon spit on you as look at you!" Berdine paused, looking off in the distance.

Nell looked askance and muttered out of the side of her mouth, "What's so incredible about that? I live with that pretty much every day!" Berdine returned her attention to Nell and laughed heartily in response.

"Now... I *know* you're not referring to your sweet brothers and sisters... those paragons of virtue!"

Nell rolled her eyes, dramatically dropping her forehead to rest on her folded arms. When she lifted her head again to look at Berdine, she had a mischievous grin on her face.

"Okay, let me rephrase that. The 'bookends' are mainly the problem! Everyone else is fairly low maintenance. Mom has gotten more involved though, and that's good."

Berdine knew what a relief it was to Nell that her mother's depression had gotten steadily better. It had always amazed Berdine how Nell had somehow ended up in the role as the stable caretaker of her large family.

"Okay... I'll bite. What do you mean by 'the bookends'?"

"Well, that would be Teddy on one end and Becky on the other. Those two will probably send me to glory long before Mom goes!" Nell shook her head in dismay. "Teddy is a bundle of energy way beyond my ability to match, and Becky is... well, Becky is Becky."

Berdine knew exactly what Nell was talking about. She had sympathized with Nell over the last few months when Becky had pushed her limits. She knew that Nell worried constantly about her younger sister.

"You have your hands full, as usual. I guess the others are okay?" Berdine asked.

"Thank heavens, yes. Howard is so quiet I hardly know he's around. Sometimes I worry about him too because I never know what he's thinking. I couldn't tell you if he was happy or sad. Things must bother him just like the rest of us, but he never lets on! At least he's no trouble. Anne and Margaret really enjoy coming to the café and having little jobs to do. Margaret gravitates toward the cooking, and Anne likes to arrange the flowers in the vases. Mother has been a big help with dishes and washing the linens and things like that. I really don't have anything to complain about!" Nell ended with a smile on her face.

"Nell, you never *do* complain. You're one of the hardest-working people I know and, still, probably the most contented!"

Nell saw her opening and leaned closer. "You know why that is, don't you, Berdine?"

Berdine saw that familiar light in Nell's eyes that she'd seen many times in the last couple of years they'd been friends. Her defenses rose automatically, and an invisible barrier fell between them.

"Yes, Nell, you've told me a million times. It's because you go to church and all that. It's just not for me right now. Maybe later on!" Berdine grinned, hoping to soften the rejection in her tone once again. She hated to disappoint her friend, but religion had never been a big part of her family's lives.

Nell shook her head sadly. It was so hard to communicate how utterly vital her relationship with the Lord was. Without Him, she'd never have had the strength for all of her responsibilities. She paused, choosing her words carefully.

"I don't want to nag you about it all the time, Berdine, but you're about to head off to college. Who knows what challenges await you? If you don't have faith, where will you turn when life tramples you?"

Berdine sighed, covering the hand of her friend with her own. "I'm not planning on getting 'trampled.'" She paused for a beat, and her smile brightened. "And if that *does* happen, I'll just run home to the strongest friend I know!"

Nell's smile was sad as she reached out and squeezed the younger girl's hand.

"Berdine, you know I'll always be here for you if you ever need me, but even I'm not strong enough on my own for some things." The two girls shared an almost surreal moment as a chill raced down Berdine's spine.

Suddenly, the mood was broken when Teddy came tearing around the corner in a panicked dash. Nell reached out an arm to stop him.

"Slow down there, buster. You're going to break something."

"Nell! You gotta come *now!* The toilet in the boy's bathroom is overflowing! It's a *flood!*" Teddy's eyes were as wide as saucers. He looked more awed than he did worried. Both girls jumped up at the same time, heading for the bathroom.

"*Why* exactly did it overflow?" Nell asked suspiciously.

Teddy looked down at the floor, a guilty expression on his face. About that time, Nell pushed open the door, and water rushed out, covering their shoes. As water flowed by, so did several varying sizes of toy ships. Nell raised her eyebrows in disbelief and then turned to the squirming boy beside her. "Teddy, what did you do?"

He squinted his eyebrows together in a look of concentration, as if he were trying to remember the sequence of events. His expression was so serious, Berdine almost laughed.

"Let's see, the ships were sailing out on the high sea. But a storm came up and then a giant whirlpool trapped the commander's ship and pulled it to the ocean floor and maybe all the way to China!" He looked up at Nell, amazement on his face. It amused Berdine that she could not see one tiny bit of regret in the boy's features.

Nell just shook her head and sighed, "Teddy . . . what am I going to do with you? Go to the utility closet and bring back a couple of mops. We're gonna play a fun little game of cleanup, now."

Nell met Berdine's mirthful eyes, and she frowned, shaking a finger at her. "Don't you dare laugh, or I'm giving you a mop too. You better go on. I'm going to be dealing with this little problem for a while. I'll catch up with you later."

Berdine hugged her friend, amused sympathy on her face. "Another boring day in the life of Nell Baker."

"Don't I just wish!" Nell took a mop in one hand and Teddy in the other and disappeared into the bathroom.

XVI

The next few days passed in a blur for Berdine. She spent the time washing clothes, packing up her room, sorting through memorabilia, and consoling her mother. Every time her mother passed by Berdine's room, she had a nostalgic, wistful look on her face.

"Mama … *really!* I'm going to be less than an hour away! I could come home for dinner if I wanted to," Berdine said.

"But that's just it … you won't want to! Once you get that taste of freedom, we probably won't see you till Christmas. You were always the one we had to hunt down on those late summer evenings …" Her mother sighed mournfully.

Berdine rolled her eyes and grinned teasingly at her mother. "Well, why don't you bring out that wretched bell you used to ring? I'll probably hear it all the way in Charleston!"

She was pleased she could coax a laugh out of her mother. She didn't like thinking of Mama and Pop all by themselves in this big, rambling house. Kathryn was always dutiful about calling their parents and coming home on the many weekends Rodney was away at medical conferences. In fact, she heard Kathryn coaxing their parents to move closer to her and Rodney because, after all, "He is a doctor, and you two are not getting any younger, you know!" Pop said he'd think about it if Kathryn would quit rushing them into the grave.

Berdine finished boxing up most of the things she wouldn't be taking. Pop groaned when he realized he was to be the keeper of yet another daughter's "treasures" in his already crowded garage.

"But, Pop, these are my *memories!* We can't just toss them!"

"Well, can't you just take your 'memories' *with* you, then?" Pop teased, knowing he'd get the expected reaction from his youngest.

"Kathryn didn't take all of *her* boxes! In fact, she still has stuff in her desk and closet!"

"That's true. So ... since you're packing things up, why don't you go ahead and pack up *her* stuff too?" Pop laughed when a stuffed animal came flying at his head. Berdine could still hear him laughing on his way down the stairs. She was going to miss her father's wry sense of humor.

The morning she was to leave, her car was packed to near bursting. Mama tried one last time to offer to bring some of her stuff in their car, mainly so they could see her settled in Charleston, but Berdine remained firm.

"There's no sense in that, Mama. I have everything I need all packed up in my car. I'm going to swing by the dorms, drop off my college stuff there, and then head on over to Outward Bound. I have a tight schedule since I have to be checked in at the camp before noon. How about if I just call you and Pop this evening when I'm in my cabin?"

It wasn't what her mother had hoped for, but she knew she had to let go. "Well ... all right, Berdie. I'm not going to say good-bye though; that just makes it sound permanent. So just drive safely, and we'll talk to you tonight."

Her mother dabbed at her eyes with her tissue, and Berdine calculated she had less than thirty seconds before the dam broke. She grabbed her mother in a quick hug and kissed her on the cheek, whirled around to her father and did the same thing. She hopped in her car and started the engine, cheerily blew them both a kiss, and headed away from 311 Apple Grove Lane.

At last! She breathed deeply, thrilled to feel the sun shining on her shoulders through her open window and the wind tossing the strands that escaped her braid. She honked her horn as she passed Nell's Café and then headed out Highway 52. It was as if the cares of the last four or five years melted off her shoulders in the warm Southern sunshine. *Chapter two in the life of Berdine Williams!* she thought, amused at her analogy. *Surely, this is where the story starts to get interesting…*

XVII

It was late morning by the time she drove through the camp's main gates. A few of the counselors whom she'd gotten to know very well over the last two summers came out to greet her and help her haul her stuff in. One of the guys tossed her heavy duffel bag over his shoulder, bumping his hip into Berdine's side and knocking her off balance.

"How's it goin', Berd-brain? When you ever gonna get old enough to pull your weight and become one us?" He grinned playfully and dodged when Berdine turned to shove him.

"You know, Blair, if I weren't around to keep you guys organized, you'd probably never find your way back from your little wilderness expeditions. Hey . . . that gives me a good idea. I could just mix up all the different trail maps I give you and see if your navigation skills are really as good as you keep telling me." Berdine smirked. The other counselors walking with them laughed.

Blair used his free arm to grab Berdine and pull her into a headlock. He rubbed his chin across the top of her head in lieu of knuckles.

"I heard you were only with us for two sessions this summer—that true?"

Berdine had become like a favorite younger sister with the counselors who were all in their midtwenties. They appreciated Berdine's maturity but also enjoyed her adventurous heart. She had earned their respect when they learned that she gave as good as she got. She was never stingy in her words of admiration for their skills and talents. Essentially, they were her family away from home each summer she had worked here.

"Oh, it's true, Blair. I've got a degree to earn and a career to train for. I can't be spending all my time with you yahoos!" She snickered, looking sideways at one of her favorite counselors. Blair put a hand over his heart, pretending to stumble.

"I can't believe you said that. Ungrateful, little brat. Here you've had the best on-the-job training, observing the most masterful professionals in the field, and all you can do is call us 'yahoos.' I don't know, guys ... that really hurts. I'm thinking a little water baptism is needed to save this child's soul! Who's with me?"

Blair had already sloughed off the duffel bag where he stood. He grabbed her wrist and pulled her arm around his shoulders. One of the other guys mirrored the action with her other arm. Two of the girls in front grabbed Berdine's legs, and they hoisted her in the air. Wiggling and squealing, Berdine voiced her protest; but she was laughing so hard, her words only sounded like jibberish. They carried her across the dirt road, through the cluster of cabins and down the hill to the river. With great flourish, they swung her three times over the water's edge before launching her, fully clothed, into the shockingly cold water. She came up sputtering and laughing, vowing vengeance upon their heads without even the slightest measure of credible sincerity. It was classic precamp hazing, and Berdine loved every minute of it. When the campers arrived, however, all of the counselors' attention and energy would be focused on them.

As much as Berdine loved being part of the lighthearted camaraderie, she already hungered for the sight of those lost, angry faces that would appear in the windows of the buses. She had experienced it and now eagerly looked forward to the miracle of transformation that inevitably took place at the end of the sessions. Nothing in Berdine's past had ever matched the awe and wonder of that moment.

After Berdine had managed to get dried off, cleaned up, and settled in to her tiny cabin, it was nearly lunchtime. There was an administrative meeting scheduled in the mess hall immediately following the meal. Berdine hurried over to the offices to find out what paperwork was necessary to have on hand and anything else the camp director needed her to prepare.

Ben Davis and his wife, Carol, had been in charge of this branch of Outward Bound for nearly twenty years. They had fallen in love with the philosophy of the camp when, in desperation, they had sent their own adolescent son through two consecutive sessions. They could identify firsthand with that feeling of utter helplessness so many other young parents feel when they watch their happy, engaging youngster change into an angry and sullen preteen. Nothing had seemed to work. Many hours were spent in both the school counselor's office as well as their pediatrician's office. It was explained to them that some children unknowingly resist the rocky transition into adolescence. The hormones, the struggle for identity, the self-esteem issues all can become overwhelming in a very short span of time. The longer amount of time the child spends suspended in transition, the more powerless and angry he can become.

It appeared that the Davises' son was trapped in his own inner war zone. It was actually by word of mouth from some friends that they discovered the Outward Bound program. Ben had driven from Greenville down to Charleston to talk with the people in charge. It was the first time in eleven months that he felt a glimmer of hope. By the time he'd returned to his wife and son, he was a firm advocate of the program.

Later, Ben and Carol said that if they could survive the trauma of forcing their son onto that bus, defiance and anger churning on his face, then they could survive anything. But the change they saw in their son the day they picked him up from the bus station four weeks later was, in their minds, nothing short of miraculous. Here was a boy who had been through the fire and come out refined.

Five years later, when Ben heard about the camp needing an administrative director, he and Carol were first in line to apply. Because the position was largely managerial in nature, Ben was perfect for the job. There was a team of onsite child psychologists as well as a whole staff of young counselors, most of them in post-graduate studies in the same field. Neither of the Davises had ever had a great deal of experience in working with at-risk children—other than their own personal one, but they had gained an incredible amount of on-the-job training over the last twenty years just by observing their team work.

"Hi, Mr. Davis! I'm back and reporting for duty." Berdine grinned and saluted the sandy-haired man, sitting at his desk, peering over the top of his bifocals. He shuffled the papers in his hands and smiled at the girl standing in front of him.

"I heard we had a little welcoming party greet you this afternoon."

Ben Davis could tease right along with the best of them, which was probably one of the many reasons Berdine kept coming back to this camp each summer.

"I'm sure you've thought of an appropriate way to show your appreciation." His gray eyes twinkled playfully as he worked to arrange his features into a serious expression.

Berdine grinned at the director. "I'm working on that. Of course, I'm open to any creative suggestions."

Mr. Davis winked then invited Berdine to sit. "All right, business first… Carol has been working on packets for the counselors. We've got everything sorted by session. I'm glad you were able to be here for the beginning of the summer because we've added a few new expeditions, and you're welcome to choose one of the groups to go with. Besides, I'm told that every time you've volunteered to go along and observe, you end up working just as hard as the lead counselor!"

Berdine shrugged casually and smiled. "It's work, but I like being included. Being able to see the inner workings of this camp has pointed me in the direction of the field I've chosen to study."

Mr. Davis nodded thoughtfully. "Based on what some of the kids say about you, Berdine, I think you'd have found your way to this field even without Outward Bound. You have a natural ability to establish rapport quickly. They seem drawn to you. I know you'd rather have more hands-on opportunities with them than the administrative end of all of it, but, of course, we're bound by the age requirement for counselors."

"I know that, Mr. Davis. I'm grateful for the exposure I do get. I don't know what setting I'll end up in, but I do know I want to work with these kids."

They discussed some of the tasks Berdine would be doing in the weeks she was there, and then Mr. Davis helped her load all of the packets and other materials onto the cart.

Berdine's stomach was growling noisily by the time they had walked to the mess hall together. Carol greeted Berdine with a quick hug and helped her distribute all the packets amongst the counselors. Berdine was a good sport dealing with the teasing as she moved among the staff. It was a fun atmosphere, and Berdine was glad to be back with all of them. She finished handing out the last packet then returned to the front of the room. Passing behind Mr. Davis, she turned and pointed her finger slowly at Blair, a menacing look on her face. Blair's eyebrows rose in innocent inquiry. Confident that she had his complete attention, she slowly, dramatically, drew her finger across her throat in a slashing motion. The whole room erupted in laughter. When Mr. Davis turned to look behind him, all he saw on the face of his young assistant was a sweet, docile expression.

As the meeting got underway, the counselors became focused and serious. There was no doubt they understood the gravity of their responsibilities. So much depended on their ability to win the trust of the kids at the beginning of the sessions. No one on staff had a perfect record. Occasionally a child went through the program whom they simply could not reach. Those faces always remained in the forefront of their minds.

Mr. Davis took time briefing the staff, explaining the contents of the packets and asking for questions. As the meeting was drawing to a close, he asked them all to turn to the last flyer in the folder pocket.

"You'll see we've added a new 'expedition' this summer. We've been in contact with the marine base on Parris Island and have been invited to conduct scheduled sessions right there on base. The challenge for this session would involve bunking in a barracks, participating in drills, and observing the marine recruits in some portions of actual boot camp. After a few days of observation, we, along with a drill sergeant, will lead the kids through a shortened, simulated version of marine boot camp. At the end of the session, there will be a ceremony right there on base for the kids—similar to the graduation ceremony after the thirteen weeks of real boot camp. If you would like to take your group through this challenge, I'll need for you to sign up today. There are four different date options, beginning with this first session. Of course, you may still choose the regular expeditions instead of, or in addition to, this new one. I believe that covers everything. Please see me afterwards if you have questions."

The meeting broke up and the young adults enjoyed a casual, leisurely lunch. It would be the last one in such a relaxed atmosphere until the end of the summer sessions. This time was an important part of emotionally gearing up, as well as reestablishing community among the leaders. Berdine sat with Blair and several other counselors, listening quietly as they discussed this new opportunity. Several of them were intrigued—as much for themselves as for the kids.

"You know," one of them began, "it's not uncommon for troubled kids to be attracted to the military as a future career."

Blair laughed lightly. "Now that's a scary thought. What does that say about our armed forces?"

"It's not a bad thing. Kids who get into trouble early in life have the same potential to succeed in the military as those who move smoothly into adulthood trouble-free. It's just that boot camp is the first time they experience real boundaries. Many of the at-risk kids just have not had the rules and structure in their home lives that non-risk kids have. There's an incredible amount of insecurity when a youngster doesn't know where the line is and he's expected to govern himself. There was actually a study done with kindergarten children on a playground. Experts wanted to see how they would behave if all the fences were removed. While the boundaries were in place, the children would lean on the fence, even climb on the fence. But guess what happened when they took the fences down?"

One of the other counselors quipped, "They ran screaming for the hills like escaped convicts?" Everyone laughed.

"No... In fact, not only did they *not* run away, but the psychologists found that they huddled together more closely toward the center of the playground. None of them wanted to play or even move away from the group. I'm not saying all military personnel are drawn to that career because of an innate need for rules and structure, but I am saying there is a common thread among troubled kids to gravitate toward a field that is built on structure, boundaries, and clear objectives."

Several in the group nodded. Blair added, "There are some similarities between what the kids experience here and what draws them later to the military life. Here, they basically experience just a simulation of life. We take them on these adventures where they must trust and depend on the next guy. If they can't do that, everyone loses. Obviously the stakes are much higher in the life of a soldier, but think about how much more crucial it is for those recruits to develop intense and unwavering commitment to their unit.

"How do you think the kids will do with this particular challenge?" Berdine asked.

"I think their observation of the real soldiers is critical. As they watch them train and go through some very intense physical challenges, that image will stick in their minds when it's their turn. They'll be able to identify with the accomplishment a young recruit feels when he's made it through basic training. It sounds good to me. I'm taking one or two groups, if not more, through it," one of the counselors said. Several others nodded agreement.

Berdine felt a twinge of excitement deep inside of her. For a moment, she allowed herself to wonder if Michael had gone through basic training? It made sense that he would choose that path, given the fact that he lived with an uncle who was a marine. Would it be wrong for her to go along on one of these challenges, hoping to catch a glimpse of him? She didn't allow herself to explore that thought for very long. She knew she would end up chastising herself for wrong motives. This was about the kids. *They* were the focus of this camp … not some blast from her past.

She had nearly made the decision firm in her mind to avoid this expedition when Blair leaned across the table and spoke,

"Berdine, you want to go along with my group? I've got a small one this first session, and it might be the least chaotic for our first run. I also saw on my list that Chelsea is back for another round. She really connected with you last summer. How about it?"

Berdine looked back at Blair, struggling to decide. She was grateful that he allowed her time to consider without questioning why she was hesitating. It wasn't a far stretch for her to imagine Blair sitting across a desk someday waiting for a patient to respond to his gentle questioning.

Berdine sighed quietly and then smiled at Blair. "I think I *would* like to join your group. I've heard all kinds of things about boot camp, so it'd be nice to see what it's really like. I'm also curious to see how the kids react to it. You don't think the drill sergeants will get in their faces and hurl insults, do you?"

Blair smiled, shaking his head. "They are aware of our program and our objectives. They'll do enough yelling so that the kids will feel they are getting the true experience, but it won't be demoralizing or designed to break their will. Their focus will be to push them, demand their best efforts, and force them to depend on each other. They will demand respect, but then, we do the same things . . . and if I remember last summer, sometimes at the same decibel level!" Blair laughed as he remembered his "rally the troops" speech after a particularly frustrating and unsuccessful whitewater rafting expedition.

Berdine nodded, beginning to feel the anticipation build. The kids would all be arriving midafternoon, which would give them just enough time to put together the gear they would need for their two weeks as marine recruits on Parris Island.

XVIII

The ride on the bus out to Parris Island the next morning was remarkably quiet with ten kids wearing scowls that said they'd "rather have both legs broken than be at this stupid camp!" She recognized the familiar invisible circle each child drew around himself or herself to keep out any and all intruders. It would have worried Berdine had this been her first experience. By now, though, there was an ironic measure of comfort in recognizing the familiar pattern. She and Blair continued to talk quietly, casually scanning the faces of their charges in the rearview mirror periodically.

Arrival at the base caused a charge in the atmosphere aboard the bus. Ten pairs of eyes stayed glued to the windows. They were greeted at the bus by a staff sergeant in full uniform. The next several hours were busy but conducted with precisionlike order. The wide-eyed kids were checked in and run through typical procedures that a marine recruit might experience upon arriving on base.

The first phase was called "recruit receiving." For a true marine recruit, their first few days on Parris Island were spent receiving their first haircut and their initial gear issue, which included items like uniforms, toiletries, and letter-writing supplies. The young men would also have full medical and dental screening, meet their senior drill instructor, and take an initial strength test to see if they were in shape to begin training. The drill instructor assigned to the Outward Bound group conducted them through a modified version of all those experiences. By the time their ten desperados were receiving preteen-sized "cammies" and going through an abbreviated medical exam, the personal invisible circles were already beginning to collapse. Berdine smiled inwardly as she watched several of the kids beginning to whisper to each other, impressed by their surroundings. All of the military personnel created a sense of awe—not only in their twelve- and thirteen-year-old campers, but also in Berdine. As an observer, she would continue to wear civilian clothing and would not go through all the procedures. Blair, however, participated in every experience the kids had. As he came out with his new military haircut and his gear issue under his arm, Berdine had to laugh at the childlike excitement she read on his face.

The next phase was called "forming." This was the period when recruits were taken to their training companies and introduced to their drill instructor for the first time. It was here that they learned the basics; how to march, how to wear their uniforms, how to secure their weapons, and the like. It was a time of adjustment for the young men before the actual training day. Berdine could sense the anticipation building in their own young group, along with a growing sense of importance. They had not seen any actual recruits in training as yet, but she could tell from the growing buzz that it was the one thing the kids were most eager to see. It had been communicated to the Outward Bound program director that the groups would be allowed to observe some of the exercises in the coming days, but it would be in such a way that the recruits would be unaware of their observation. It was a requirement of true basic training that the recruits were cut off from all civilian life for the full term so there would be no distractions. Thirteen weeks was a relatively short time to turn a company of individualists into one tough, unified collective.

Berdine's first exposure to a true drill sergeant was not too far off the mark from what she had imagined. She sat under a tree far enough away from her little ragtag group so as not to intrude but close enough to see the expressions on the faces of the kids. Of course, she could have been on the other side of the base and still have heard the drill sergeant's voice! And yet what made the difference between her movie-generated image of a drill sergeant and the one assigned to the Outward Bound group was how he communicated with the kids. There was passion in his voice as he barked out what it meant for them to be temporary marines. He talked about the marines' core values: honor, courage, and commitment. He marched up and down the line of the previously belligerent preteens and looked into their faces, engaging their attention while he impressed those values upon them. By the time he was yelling about courage, Berdine found herself drawn in by the instructor's words. It made her grin as the thought occurred to her that values and character could be taught in the most unlikely settings.

"Courage," he shouted, "is *not* the absence of fear! You may have been told that you are a coward if you are afraid! If someone said that to you, they did not *know* the true meaning of courage! I am here to tell you the truth about courage. Hear me well, junior recruits. Courage is not the *absence* of fear. It is the ability to *face* fear and overcome it! Do you think a marine goes into combat without experiencing fear? You show me a marine who says he has no fear, and I'll show you a marine I don't want in my platoon. I want a marine at my back who admits his fear and is willing to do what it takes to face it down!"

Berdine's attention shifted to the young bodies standing at attention. Was it her imagination, or had ten young pairs of shoulders lifted and straightened? A chill ran down her spine, and goose bumps covered her arms. It was that miraculous moment... and it had come so *early* in their expedition. It made Berdine want to bury her head in her arms and weep. She glanced over to catch the awe on Blair's face, and she knew he was caught by the same emotion. Somehow, it never got ordinary. Oh, how grateful she was that it never got ordinary!

By nighttime, Berdine was sequestered away in her own private barracks—an officer's vacant quarters. Earlier, she had been allowed to share in what they called "family time" with Blair and the group before the drill instructor came through shouting commands about lights out and warning them about reveille. The words she heard coming haltingly out of the mouths of some of their fiercest charges caused her heart to ache. Unknowingly, the drill instructor had opened the portal to some of the deepest buried fears in the lives of these youngsters. Confession and sharing poured out. The most amazing thing of all was that not a soul in the room scoffed or pretended superiority. The floor on which they sat had become undeniably level. Berdine left before it was all over because she was no longer able to contain her tears. It was on her way back to her barracks that she wondered how in the world she would ever manage to lead a group when it caused such an overwhelming emotional reaction in her. She didn't doubt that Blair was just as intensely affected as she was. He allowed the kids to see his emotions because part of what they wanted to teach was vulnerability and honesty, but the difference between him and Berdine was that Blair was able to continue leading the sharing time with tears in his eyes and still maintain his role as objective facilitator. It was one thing her mentors had tried to impress upon her. *You must get to the place where you can sympathize without being completely swept away by their pain yourself.* So far, she had not arrived at that place.

She lay in bed that night, listening to the mournful sounds of the bugle signaling lights out, and she pondered her future. Her heartbeat, her very *passion,* was to rescue these lost, angry children. If she could just *love* them enough, *believe* in them enough—perhaps she too could have a part in saving them.

XIX

It was dawn on the last day of their two-week basic training. The orange-streaked sky was beginning to herald the sun's presence with its prelude of colors. Berdine realized she had not even heard reveille at 0500 hours. She sat up, sleep-induced confusion causing her to wonder where she was. The last thing she remembered was a shadowy vision of her and Michael hammering nails into the tree and arguing about whether or not their tree house needed a roof. Berdine rubbed her eyes; the spare furnishings of the room coming slowly into focus. O*kay*... She was not in the tree house with Michael. She was in an officer's quarters on the final day of Outward Bound boot camp on Parris Island... and where were the recruits?

Oh no! she thought. *I'll be late for commencement! Only the most significant event of this session these kids will experience!* She mentally kicked herself for failing to register the piercing sounds of that wretched bugle. Every other morning, she was already up *anticipating* its piercing notes! She mentally added another demerit on her mental record of readiness for a future position as a counselor. In the next fifteen minutes, Berdine was sure she had probably set a record for showering, dressing, making her bed, and dashing out the door. She knew she looked rumpled and thrown together, but it couldn't be helped.

She was hurrying across the campus, taking a shortcut through the training yard. A double line of marine recruits were jogging by to the cadence of their drill instructor's voice. It was a curiously rhythmic beat, almost musical. She stopped to let them pass, listening as the instructor half chanted-half sang to the beat of forty pairs of boots pounding on the pavement. As the last of the line was moving past her, Berdine started forward. She stepped off the curb and took about three steps when she stopped again ... frozen in her tracks. One of the recruits in the line nearest to her, briefly flicked a glance her way, and Berdine's heart stopped. *Michael!* She needed no more than the flicker in his eyes to know it was him. His hair was military-short; his height and build were no longer that of a boy's. His eyes were still stormy, and in that brief millisecond, she saw surprise ... and then an icy hardness. His step faltered for a split second before his eyes whipped back to the shoulders in front of him, and he continued on without missing another beat.

She continued to stand motionless, watching the double line weaving around the curve of the road and disappearing from her view. It seemed an interminable time before Berdine was able to command her legs to move. Even then, she felt shaky and unsteady. As she walked, a kaleidoscope of memories came rushing forward: Michael hoisting her up on his thin, young shoulders to hammer in a board for their tree house ladder; Michael lying on his back beside her, pointing out constellations in an ink-splattered sky; Michael running to catch up with her on their way home from school, casually lifting the books out of her arms to carry them. So many images! It was difficult to mesh those visions of young Michael with the hard-bodied, mature recruit who had just jogged past. Of course, it shouldn't have surprised her that he would be here, after living with an officer of the Marine Corps for two years—eating, drinking, *sleeping* military life. It had been his dream all along to join their proud ranks. Berdine felt a tiny pocket of warmth melting a corner of the shell around her heart.

Then, just as quickly, she remembered the look in his eyes. There was a coldness there. What did that mean? Wasn't *she* the one who should feel betrayed and deserted? And hadn't she tried her hardest to honor his implied wishes to end their friendship? It would have been so easy for her to find out how to contact him, but she held back, knowing it was his move to make. When no word ever came, she did her best to shut the door on their past. Now they were adults. Life goes on. End of story. *Period.*

When she joined up with her group, Berdine determinedly entered into the spirit of things for the sake of Blair and their newly graduated "marines." The expedition had been a resounding success. Later, after they were able to debrief with the director and the rest of the counselors, "Outward Bound Marine Basic Training" was made a permanent addition to their list of expedition options. Berdine and Blair spent a whole afternoon with the staff, answering questions, narrating their experiences and brainstorming ways to make the challenge even more realistic and impacting for their young campers. They had not been back two days before letters came flooding in from grateful parents who remarked on the amazing changes they were seeing in their children. One parent wrote, "I hardly recognize my son as the same boy I put on the bus two weeks ago. He's been talking about courage and commitment—things I've never heard out of his mouth. I know we still have more challenges ahead, but I have hope we'll face them differently now. Thank you, Outward Bound and the Marine Recruiting Depot at Parris Island, for a great two weeks and some lasting life lessons!"

Berdine's term at camp was coming to a close, and the staff good-naturedly teased her about it being time to switch into scholar mode. She was swamped with mailing addresses, camp souvenirs, and plenty of well-meaning advice about college survival. It felt like her time with Outward Bound this summer had rushed by before she'd had a chance to experience it! She'd only had the opportunity to go along on two expeditions since she was needed in the office half the time for administrative duties. She would have a week's break before summer classes at the College of Charleston were slated to begin. She still had not decided if she'd rather just get moved into the dorm and catch her breath there for the week or go home for a brief visit. Maybe she could have the best of both worlds and split up the week between the two.

Berdine was hauling her gear out to her car—weary, but in the best sort of way. Any energy or effort expended at Outward Bound always had such incredible returns on her spirit. She felt restored and ready for the next challenge. She'd just never expected it would come in the form of the one thing she wanted most to avoid.

Blair called out, "Berdine! Hold up a minute! I wanted to catch you before you took off." She turned to see the young man jogging out to meet her as she was preparing to get into her car.

"Hey, Blair . . . what's up?" Berdine was looking into the sun and had to squint as she looked back at him.

"The drill instructor we had for our expedition last month sent me an invitation to family day and graduation at the base. It appears that the group of recruits we had a chance to observe is finishing their basic training tomorrow. On Saturday, they have a time for family and friends to come hang out on base and attend their formal graduation ceremony and parade the next morning. I thought since you and I experienced Outward Bound's first expedition this summer, we could go together. How about it?"

He leaned casually against her open door, grinning with the expression she remembered seeing as he emerged for the first time in fatigues and sporting a military-style crew cut.

"Well, I was . . . um . . . I'm . . . thinking about going home for a visit before classes start . . . but *you* should go . . . definitely." Berdine smiled, trying not to sound like she was hedging. She should have known that excuse would not be enough for Blair.

"You want to visit for ten days? If you go home now, for *that* long, you'll have to do the whole 'cutting-the-ties' thing all over again! Besides, don't you almost feel like you owe the recruits the honor of proving that they survived it?"

Blair was hard to resist when he put it that way, but Berdine's fear of running into Michael again was heightened by what she remembered seeing in his eyes for that brief moment their paths crossed.

"I don't know, Blair . . . I just . . . let me think a minute." Berdine pinched the bridge of her nose, and she knew without looking that Blair's radar was up. He sensed there was more to her hesitation than she let on. She figured she had roughly three seconds left before he started delving, and *that* she wanted to avoid. As she started to shut the door on the invitation, whispered words played through her mind.

"Courage is not the absence of fear! You may have been told that you are a coward if you are afraid! If someone said that to you, they did not know the true meaning of courage! I am here to tell you the truth about courage. Hear me well, junior recruits. Courage is not the absence of fear. It is the ability to face fear and overcome it!"

Berdine sighed out loud, shifting her weight, and spoke in a resigned voice. "Sure, Blair. I'll go. Help me take this bag back into my cabin."

Blair was astute enough to guess that Berdine had a reason for her reluctance, yet he respected her privacy.

"I knew you didn't want to leave this cozy cottage of yours. You know once you leave here and enter the world of academia, your skin will turn pale, and your eyesight will grow dim. An 'evening out' will just be a trip to the library. You'll grow a permanent hump at the base of your neck from all the time you spend with your head hunched over a book. It's not a pretty picture, Berdine." He was trailing along behind her, keeping up a steady stream of nonsense. Berdine stopped suddenly and turned as Blair bumped into her back.

"Blair!" She retorted sharply. "Do us *both* a favor and *shut up!*"

She turned back around and marched forward, trying to maintain a stern visage that was belied only by the mirthful shaking of her shoulders. Blair grinned at her back, pleased with himself.

"I'll pick you up at 0900 hours tomorrow morning. Try not to make us late." He laid her bag at her cabin door and tossed a salute as he trotted off toward the rec field. Berdine watched him leave, shaking her head.

XX

Morning came too soon. Berdine was up before dawn coaching herself on the appropriate mind-set she should have for this coming trip back to Parris Island. No matter how much she tried to bolster her self-confidence, she kept coming back to that cold look in Michael's eyes. By the time Blair knocked on her door, she was sure she was making a terrible mistake. Now she would be adding the humiliation of having him think she was pursuing him to the already painful experience of his previous rejection. There was nothing to be done about it at this point.

Berdine was quickly swept along in Blair's enthusiasm and excitement about the day. He talked about getting to meet some of the recruits and asking them firsthand about the training. He loved to hear people's stories. What drew them to the military, and more specifically, the marines? What did they think about the possibility of actual combat? What was the most challenging thing they experienced in boot camp? Berdine had to smile as she listened to Blair ramble on. She wondered if his fascination didn't reveal a small part of him that wished he were one of them.

As they crossed the bridge onto Parris Island, Berdine felt a strange sense of fate settle into her heart. She felt herself releasing the anxiety and mentally leaning back against the headrest of her seat to await the day and what it held in store. She had a weak, fleeting thought as they pulled onto base and parked their car. *Maybe I won't even see him . . .*

Civilians and troops in uniform were milling about everywhere outside on the grounds. The sun was hot, and although a humid breeze was blowing off the ocean, Berdine was glad she and Blair had come early in the morning. Above the happy din of the crowds, she could hear the raucous cries of the gulls off in the distance. She had a sudden longing to leave this place and walk along the beach. Regretfully, she shook her head, drawing herself back to the excited, happy reunions between families and recruits.

It was a celebratory atmosphere, and Berdine felt privileged to be included. Booths were set up with food and beverages. Music from a band played, and young children ran amongst the adults. Berdine watched as a young man stooped, holding out his arms to what must have been his little sister. She squealed happily and ran as fast as her coltish, young legs would carry her to jump into the young marine's arms. He laughed with abandon and lifted her high in the air, twirling her around. Following behind her were an older couple, beaming expressions on their faces. The man hugged his son, unselfconsciously, and the woman cried as she joined in the embrace. It made Berdine's heart turn over to see the pride on the faces of the recruits' families. She couldn't help wondering if Michael's father was here wearing the same expression.

A poster with pictures on it in the booth in front of her drew her attention. Moving closer, she grinned when she saw that it was a display of the Outward Bound Marine Basic Training Expedition. Her eyes filled as she studied the faces of familiar children whom she had watched cross the stage on these very grounds and receive a medal and words of commendation from their drill instructor and the senior staff sergeant. She'd never forget their pride as they heard the applause from parents and staff attending that day. Berdine knew she'd forever be grateful to the military personnel who managed to take a few minutes out of their schedule to be there for the kids. It was a first for many of the kids to have anyone other than their parents cheering them on with wholehearted approval. Berdine knew it was an experience their little group would remember and treasure for years to come.

"Berdine!" She was startled to hear Blair call her name. "Berdine, come over here a second."

As Berdine turned to join Blair, her breath caught in her throat. She felt the color drain from her skin, and it took everything she had inside of her to continue walking forward, a shaky smile pasted on her face. Standing beside Blair was their drill instructor and Michael Caraway. Blair drew her into the circle with a hand on her elbow. Berdine kept her eyes fixed on the drill instructor.

"You remember First Sergeant Garrison, don't you, Berdine? He was just asking me about the kids and if we've heard from any of them. And this is Lance Corporal Caraway. I sort of butted in on their conversation, actually." Blair smiled apologetically.

"No problem, son," First Sergeant Garrison boomed. "I'm glad to hear how successful the trial expedition for Outward Bound turned out to be here at the base. We're looking forward to seeing some of those kids back here in five or six years!"

The imposing man grinned engagingly as he reached to shake Berdine's hand. He then gestured Michael forward and patted him on the back.

"Lance Corporal Caraway here is awarded Honor Graduate of his company, which earned him his promotion. He received highest scores in nearly all categories."

Berdine slowly raised her eyes to Michael's, and a shiver ran down her spine. His face was closed and impersonal, though she thought she saw a flicker of something else in his eyes.

Before Berdine could speak, Blair jumped in hurriedly. "*Oh man!* Please forgive my lack of manners! This is Berdine Williams. She's been a part of Outward Bound for almost three years now. I can't tell you what a natural she is with the kids who come through the program. She's a born rescuer!"

Blair slapped Berdine lightly on the shoulder, and she grimaced when she saw Michael flinch slightly at that last statement. Instead of responding to that, Michael nodded shortly and spoke in a quiet voice, so much deeper than Berdine remembered, "We've met, actually. We share the same hometown. That's about it, though. We don't really know each other well."

Berdine's eyes widened in disbelief at the sting of the cold, underlying message in his words. She couldn't prevent the short, sarcastic laugh that burst from her. She turned to the drill instructor and Blair, intentionally ignoring the tall, tense marine standing just over her right shoulder. Her words were sharp and filled with pain.

"He's right. We didn't really know each other at all. I only thought we did. Silly me. Would you excuse me please? I need a drink of water. Blair, I'll catch up with you later. Good to see you again, sir." She spoke to the two men and merely nodded in Michael's general direction. She walked hurriedly away with a rushing sound of white noise in her ears. Her heart was pumping so hard it would surely burst from her chest. All she could see in front of her were shades of red. Her only goal was to put as much distance between her and Michael before the brittle pieces of her broke off and scattered to the wind. The people she passed were blurry and out of focus, and she hurried on across the grounds. Suddenly, she felt a cold hand grasp her wrist and swing her around to a full stop.

Michael stood glaring into her face, his own skin ashen. "What was all that about back there?"

Furious and shaking, Berdine yanked her wrist from his grasp. "*You* tell *me!* I never took you for a coward, but I guess I was wrong. You didn't even have the decency to tell me our friendship was over."

Michael couldn't have looked more shocked had Berdine grown another head. He laughed out loud, bitterness ringing in his voice.

"What are you talking about? *You* were the one who turned your back on *me.* I asked… No… *I begged* for your understanding and support, and you couldn't even bother to answer my letters!"

His words hung in the air as they faced off, angry, gulping in shallow breaths of air. For a moment, the silence roared. Berdine lifted a shaking hand to push her blonde curls back from her sweat-beaded forehead. Her tongue darted out between parched lips. She swallowed painfully, her voice a mere whisper, "There were *no letters.*" Her eyes were round and wide with hurt.

"There *were,* Berdine. Four of them. You never answered any of them. *Why?*" The look on Michael's face mirrored her own sadness and regret and confusion. She didn't even realize that he'd reached across the gulf spanning between them and taken her cold hand in his own.

"I never saw any letters, Michael," Berdine said, shock ringing in her voice.

The surreal mood of the moment was broken when Berdine heard her name called out. It was Blair walking over, glancing at his watch. Berdine stared back at Michael, a hopeless expression on her face. "I … I … have to go. I'm going back to Mount Holly this afternoon … " Berdine spoke in a rush, trying to get out her words before Blair reached them.

"Please … come tomorrow, Berdine. Graduation is at ten." Michael spoke just as hurriedly, his tone tense and anxious.

"Oh, Michael … What's the point? I don't see … "

Michael cut her off with an urgent whisper as Blair reached them. "*Just come …* "

"Hey, sorry to interrupt, but I forgot about getting back for a debriefing session I agreed to sit in on. Jenson took another group through 'basic training' last week, and Mr. Davis wants me there. Sorry about that, Berdine."

"No—it's fine Blair. I'm ready to go."

She turned uncomfortably to Michael, stating the obvious, "I have to … to … go."

Blair was already heading for the car, assuming Berdine would follow. Berdine stared for a moment into the depths of those fathomless dark eyes. She started to turn away when Michael merely mouthed to her, "Come … "

He held her gaze a moment more, and then she turned and sprinted off after Blair as if the devil himself were chasing her.

XXI

Berdine pulled onto 311 Apple Grove Lane right in the middle of the afternoon. She could hear the lawn mower rumbling across the backyard. The sight of Pop in his shorts and black crew socks had her laughing before she ever stepped out of the car. She had an album of pictures and a couple of matching camouflage T-shirts tucked under her arm. It surprised Berdine to feel the eager anticipation of coming home. For a moment, she paused and glanced up to the second floor. A slow grin spread across her face as she eyed her bedroom window. She was almost tempted to lay her belongings down and shimmy up the tree for old times' sake.

She opened the front door, calling out, "Mama? I'm home!" She could hear sounds in the kitchen and the smell of something delicious teased her nostrils. "What's for dinner?" She skipped down the hall and into the surprised but eager arms of her mother.

"Oh, my Berdie girl is home! Come in, come in! Let me tell your daddy you're here. We didn't know you were coming! I would have baked some cookies or at least planned a fancier meal!" Her mother twirled in almost frantic happiness, and Berdine felt a twinge of guilt that she'd not communicated more often with her parents over the last five weeks.

"I'm sorry, Mama. And I certainly don't need any fancy meal or anything. Fact is, I'm only here for the night. I've got to get back first thing in the morning. I just wanted to check in on you and Pop; see how things are going."

Her mother's face fell for an instant, but she recovered quickly. "Well, we'll just have to make the most of the time you're here. I stuck a chicken in the oven early this afternoon, so we have plenty for supper. How was camp? What did you do? Have you moved your things over to the dorm?"

Berdine laughed and leaned over to hug her mother briefly. Over the years, Berdine had noticed she initiated affection with her family less and less. If she had been pressed to give a reason, Berdine was not sure she could have. Of the two sisters, Kathryn had just always been the more demonstrative, so no one ever really noticed a lack in Berdine, until Kathryn had gotten married and moved out. Now, feeling how her mother held on a fraction longer made her feel guilty that displays of affection never seemed to come as naturally to her.

"Well, Evelyn, don't just use it all up on yourself! How selfish can a woman be?" Both women turned, laughing at the deep, almost rusty voice. There stood her father, a hedge clipper in one hand, the other wiping his brow with a sweaty rag.

Evelyn spoke in a teasingly haughty tone, "Well, I can guarantee if you want a little of *this,* you better march on up and shower!" Berdine laughed and turned to hug her father.

"Don't you worry about that, Pop! This is the first time in five weeks I've been clean myself!" Berdine quipped, and the three of them laughed.

"Now don't start any stories till I come back down. I want to hear whatever your mama gets to hear!" Her father opened the back door and set the hedge clippers back outside on the porch. He mopped his face another time and winked at his wife and daughter before heading toward the stairs.

"Hey, Pop!" Berdine called as she tossed him a camouflage T-shirt. "This is for you. Put it on after your shower. Let's see how you look as a military man!"

Her father clicked his heels together sharply and snapped out a salute before he trudged up the stairs.

Later, after dinner, Berdine and her parents lingered over coffee and pie long after the sun had gone down. She could hear the soothing chorus of the crickets just outside the back screen door. The oscillating fan hummed softly, bringing an intermittent breeze across their faces. Their voices were low and easy. It was a peaceful summer night. Talk was winding down about Berdine's experiences of the first half of her summer. She had regaled them with stories about her expeditions and the staff counselors. She must have talked about Blair and their junior marine basic training quite a bit because her father raised his eyebrows and exchanged a quick look with Berdine's mother on about the third or fourth mention of his name. Berdine intercepted the look and just smiled, shaking her head.

"*No,* Pop. You can just get that thought right out of your head. Blair is only a good friend. We're more like brother and sister."

"Well that's still a good start, you know. Things can change quickly in that department." Pop winked playfully.

"Actually, I *did* see a familiar face while we were at the family day..." Berdine lowered her eyes, wondering at the wisdom of bringing it up.

"Oh?" Her mother asked. "Who?"

"Michael," she said simply. She raised her eyes to meet the expressions on her parents' faces: disappointed but not surprised.

"Really? How *is* Michael?"

Her mother's tone was polite. Berdine wished she had not even brought it up. She had known they would not be receptive to hearing about him. In their minds, that chapter of her life was already firmly closed.

"Honestly, I didn't get to talk to him much. It was a little strange though. It seems he believes *he* was the one who was deserted and betrayed *by me* after he moved to Parris Island. Isn't that odd? He claims he wrote some letters to me. But, of course, that couldn't be true since I never *got* any letters. I mean, if letters from him came to this house, I would have gotten them, wouldn't I?" She spoke softly, but her tone was tense.

Her mother and father stared back, bewildered expressions on their faces. Berdine could tell their surprise was genuine. She didn't know whether to feel relieved or disappointed.

Pop finally spoke, his voice even, "Berdine, if Michael wrote you letters two years ago and they came here, we would have made sure you got them."

Berdine dropped her gaze, disappointment winning out. "I believe you, Pop. I guess we'll never really know." She covered a yawn with her hand and started to push back from the table. She picked up her cup and plate of half-eaten pie.

"Here, Mama, let me give you a hand with the dishes. Then I'm going to head up to bed. I'll be leaving early in the morning, so you don't need to get up to see me off."

Berdine started toward the kitchen when she heard her mother ask, "You don't need to rush off so *soon* tomorrow, do you, Berdine? It's Sunday, after all."

"I'm sorry, Mama . . . I do. I want to be back in time for Michael's graduation ceremony from basic training." She stared back at her parents, not sure how they would take this bit of news. For a moment, only silence fell between them.

"Berdine, I know you're old enough now to make your own decisions, so I'll just remind you to make wise choices. Summer classes are starting up in a week, and you don't need any distractions right now." Pop looked back steadily, seeing his youngest daughter bristle slightly. He watched her struggle with restraint.

Finally, Berdine replied, "I'll keep that in mind." She turned and continued on to the kitchen, missing the worried look that passed between her mother and father.

The dishes were done quickly, and the three of them stayed on lighter topics. Pop asked how her car was running: Had she put oil in it? Was it still idling funny? Mama filled Berdine in on all the news about Kathryn, urging Berdine to contact her when she got back. Apparently, Kathryn had a lot of time on her hands since Rodney was constantly busy with surgeries in two different hospitals. Mama said that Kathryn was dabbling in painting and taking some other classes, hoping to find a hobby.

"Oh! I just remembered . . . Kathryn asked me about a set of brushes she left here. She said if I came across them to hang on to them for her next time she came home. You might just take a look in her room before you go to bed, Berdine. If you find them, you could save her a trip."

"I never even knew Kathryn was interested in art." Berdine puzzled at that.

"There's probably a lot you two don't know about each other. You didn't have a lot in common when you were younger. I'm hoping you'll become better friends in adulthood," Mama hinted lightly.

Berdine shrugged. "We'll see ..."

By the time they were finished, Pop had wandered away to sit in his old recliner, an open paper in his lap. Berdine had to smile as she passed, kissing the top of his head. She was amused at the picture he made: her aging father, bifocals low on his nose, leaning back in his easy chair with the paper and sporting a camouflage T-shirt. Mama had joined Pop in the den with her crocheting, and both sat together in companionable silence. As Berdine called good night to them on her way up the stairs, she marveled that this was the closest she'd felt to *belonging* in her family in some time.

XXII

It was a little strange to be back in her old room. Mama hadn't done anything to it, although both girls had encouraged her to redecorate and make them into something she could use—a crafts room, a library, an office, or guestroom. Still, both rooms appeared to be waiting for the girls to return from a weekend away. Most of their memorabilia was either packed away or had moved with them, but there were still little remnants of the past here and there. Berdine's bulletin board still had a couple of faded, blue ribbons tacked up, representing her superiority in the 100-yard dash in sixth grade. It made her giggle, wondering if Michael still had his red ribbons, reminding him *he* had come in second place! She fingered a dried rose bud that hung upside down. It was so brittle that several of the petals floated to the floor at her touch. Michael had given that long-stemmed rose to her the day they christened their tree house.

Berdine sat down at her desk, slowly pulling out the drawers one by one. There were a couple of old spirals, leftover from high school; a few pencils and paperclips littered the mostly empty drawers. Her most precious possession—the beat-up cigar box of letters and pictures from the last eight or nine years—was still packed safely away in the bottom of her suitcase at the dorm. Probably three-fourths of the contents were funny little notes and cards from Michael. He was always the better note writer. He knew how to fold them up into creative little... Berdine froze. He *always* wrote her notes. He wrote her notes even when he was all wrapped up with Jennie Martin and she didn't *want* them! He wrote her notes when he was mad at her, when he was bored, when he couldn't wait to tell her something... *always.* Berdine stared at her open desk drawers, and a sickening feeling washed over her. Her heart began to thump painfully in her chest as she rose unsteadily to her feet.

She left her room in a fog, walking slowly down the hall and into Kathryn's room. The twin beds were still in the same arrangement; the headboards against the far wall and spaced evenly under the window so that Kathryn could see the door when she slept on her back. She always had a fear of having her back to the door. Berdine stopped in the doorway, studying the matching quilts adorning the two beds. The closet door was on the back wall, and it stood slightly ajar. To its left, was Kathryn's small, white desk. Empty shelves were still affixed to the wall above it. The room had a forlorn, abandoned feel to it with none of Kathryn's personal items anywhere to be seen although Berdine knew her closet still had some seasonal clothes hanging in there and a couple of storage boxes containing sweaters had been rolled under her beds.

But it was the little desk that captured her attention now. Berdine moved slowly, mechanically, to sit in the chair facing the empty surface of the desk. There was a very fine layer of dust settled on top. Berdine drew her finger slowly across, leaving a mark. Her breathing was shallow, and her mind was blank. Her chest felt like there was a weight pressing in on her. In an unhurried motion, she reached for the first drawer and inched it open. It slid easily, and Berdine saw a half-empty bottle of nail polish, a couple of used nail files, and several hair ties. *Apparently, Kathryn had other uses for her desk besides schoolwork,* Berdine thought with grim humor. She eased the drawer closed and reached for the second drawer. Grasping the ornate little handle, she pulled slowly. She could see as it inched open that the contents looked more like a school desk... loose papers, an old Hemingway paperback, some manila file folders. Halfway out, the drawer caught and stopped.

In that moment, Berdine *knew.* Part of her wanted to leave the room, closing the bedroom door behind her. But she was compelled to see it through. She tugged, trying to release the drawer from whatever gripped it, but it would not move. She abandoned it and reached for the third drawer. By now, she was on her knees in front of the little desk. She pulled out the third drawer, feeling a slight resistance before giving way. She pulled it all the way off its rollers and onto the floor beside her. It was full of a variety of things, among which was Kathryn's little case of brushes. Without thinking, Berdine lifted the brushes out and set them on the floor beside her. She didn't bother to look at the other contents. Reaching into the empty space created by the third drawer, she felt blindly behind the jammed drawer. She inhaled sharply when her fingers brushed against three envelopes. Pulling the letters from the back, she was able to release the drawer. She did not look at them as she laid them in her lap. Instead, she finished pulling the second drawer as far as it would go and picked up the fourth letter buried at the back.

Methodically, numbly, she restored the desk to its former condition. She continued to sit on the floor with her back now against the wall, four letters scattered in her lap and a case of paintbrushes beside her. She leaned her head back against the wall, closing her eyes. She would *not* let the rush of feeling come, though it pressed heavily against the wall in her mind. She would *not* give it a foothold... yet.

Wearily, Berdine rose to her feet. She moved zombie-like down the hall, clutching the letters and paintbrushes. When she got to her room, she gingerly set the items on the bedside table and sank to the mattress beside it. She took several deep breaths, feeling as if she could lie down and sleep for a week. How tired she was! She could feel the angry, injured thoughts pounding on the door of her mind, but she would not answer tonight. Instinctively, she knew that if she opened *that* Pandora's box tonight, she'd never be able to close it again.

Berdine lay on her side, fully clothed. She was grateful for the shock that insulated her from thinking. She reached over to click off her lamp and pulled a light blanket up over her body. She lay in the silent darkness, eyes wide open, her mind completely blank. She had expected to fall asleep immediately out of sheer exhaustion, but in fact, the exact opposite happened. It occurred to her at some point during the night that, ironically, it took a surprising amount of energy to keep her thoughts at bay.

XXIII

Berdine wasn't sure if she had slept at all as she watched her childhood room begin to glow in colors of orange and pink. Sleep had played a vicious game of hide and seek with her, never allowing her to grab hold. She rose stiffly and tried to work out a little of the ache in her neck and shoulders. She undressed slowly and wrapped herself in her white robe, taking clean clothes with her down the hall to the bathroom. The hot water from the shower beat down mercilessly across her back, and the almost unpleasant sensation brought some comfort to Berdine. *At least I can still feel.* She tugged the sundress with ties at the shoulders over her head. It was casual and feminine, and it was Berdine's favorite shade of blue. Slipping white sandals on her feet, Berdine then rose to brush out her wet hair. She didn't bother to dry or style it. She finished up in the bathroom and took her things back to her bedroom. She repacked her bag and glanced once around the room. Her eyes lighted on the items stacked neatly on the bedside table. Woodenly, she picked them up and tucked them into her shoulder bag. Turning off the light, she gently closed her door and headed down the stairs.

"Berdine," her mother spoke softly, coming around the corner and meeting her at the bottom of the stairs. "I brought you a cup of coffee for the road. You sure you don't want some breakfast before you go?"

"No, Mama. I couldn't eat a bite, but thanks for the coffee." Berdine's face was pale and drawn. Her mother peered closely into the face of her youngest daughter.

"You okay, Berdie? Did you sleep well?" her mother asked.

"Sure, Mama." But Berdine thought her lips would crack if she tried to smile. Her only thought was to get out of here. "I better go now. Tell Pop bye for me."

"Okay, honey." Berdine's mother pulled the stiff form of her daughter into the warm circle of her arms. "You drive safely, now." She kissed Berdine on the cheek and walked her to the door. The sun was just coming up, and there was dew still on the ground when Berdine stepped from the house onto the front walk. She headed to her car, bags in hand, when her mother called out, "Oh, I forgot to ask you if you had a chance to look for Kathryn's brushes!"

Berdine turned and nodded slowly. Her mother looked slightly confused at the blank expression on Berdine's face. "Well, did you find them?"

"Oh yes, I found them," Berdine spoke softly.

"I'm sure she'll appreciate your bringing them to her, then. Now, don't speed! Call us when you're settled into the dorm." Her mother smiled fondly.

Berdine merely nodded as she got into her car. She pulled away from the driveway, hastening to distance herself from her house, emotionally as well as physically.

It was still early by the time Berdine arrived at the college. An older woman working in the office spotted Berdine as she came in the lobby doors.

"Berdine Williams, correct? I'm Ms. Browning—your dorm mother." She had a friendly smile on her face, and Berdine thought she looked almost grandmotherly. "I knew we were expecting about ten incoming freshman for our summer session. Mostly we have sophomores and juniors staying with us through the summer, but I like to see you young girls getting a head start! You'll be glad you did when it's time to register for fall classes. You'll already know 'the lay of the land,' so to speak!"

Berdine smiled back, shaking the older woman's hand. "I haven't really gotten a chance to look around yet. I saw a few of the buildings during orientation last May, but this is the first time I've been in the dorm."

Ms. Browning looked down at the clipboard on the desk. Running a finger down the column, she stopped at Berdine's name and said, "You're on this first floor down the hall to the right—Room 112. I'm sure you received that information in the mail. Hmm . . ." The woman looked more closely at the chart. "It looks like you have one of the single rooms and bathrooms. Is that what you wanted? No roommate?" She looked a little dismayed, but Berdine nodded her head, smiling reassuringly.

"For now, anyway. Maybe after I get to know some girls, I might change to a double or a suite. But after spending the past two and a half summers working at a camp and having my own cabin, I'm accustomed to managing by myself." Berdine knew it wasn't the norm for freshmen to request single rooms. But she liked having her own space and knew this arrangement would work out fine.

Ms. Browning smiled at the young woman and gestured around the lobby. "Well, you'll certainly have plenty of privacy and space this summer. There may only be forty other students in the whole hall. This is the only women's dorm open this summer because it's the smallest. I'll be in the office every day until four o'clock. If you need anything after that, my room is the third door on the right down the hall on the other side of the lobby. Do you have everything you need for your classes? You still have a whole week to be a lady of leisure, you know!" Ms. Browning chuckled.

"I have my books. I'll probably just wait till after the first day of class to see what supplies I'll need. I'm only taking nine hours for this session."

"That's probably wise. The summer classes go by so quickly. It's a lot of information to absorb in such a short time. But I'm sure you'll manage nicely." The woman beamed encouragingly.

Berdine nodded. "I'm going to unpack a few things in my room, and then I'll be leaving again for Parris Island. I'm going to be attending the Marine Recruit graduation ceremony this morning."

Ms. Browning reacted with a wide smile. A wistful, girlish expression played over her plump face. "Oh, do you have a marine, dear?"

Berdine laughed at the way the older woman had phrased it. She shook her head. "No, I wouldn't say I *'have'* a marine. But I do have an old friend who is graduating, and I want to be there to support him."

"Well, I won't keep you, then. Have a nice time."

Berdine thanked her and pushed through the door separating the hall from the lobby.

XXIV

Soon she was on the road again, heading for Parris Island. She wanted to be there in plenty of time to get a good seat. She wondered if she'd run into any of Michael's family. Her mind drifted easily, still careful, though, to keep pressing thoughts at bay. The letters, along with the paintbrushes were still tucked into her handbag. She mused that it might be a long time before she felt ready to read them.

It promised to be a balmy day. The azure sky was unmarked by clouds, and the ocean waves lapped indolently at the shore. The horizon was dotted with the outline of freighters out in the distance. A sense of calm rested over her. Berdine existed in the moment, because that was really the only safe place to live. In her young life, she had already experienced the heartache of the past and the dread of the future. As she glanced at the paintbrushes in her purse, she shivered slightly. She could hear the cry of the gulls, and her soul was tugged toward the shoreline. Maybe after the ceremony, she could quietly steal away for a long, meditative walk along the beach.

She parked in the designated lot for visitors, amazed at the number of people who were already here. Grabbing her shoulder bag, she headed for the ceremony grounds. A light breeze tossed her hair, and she tucked the errant strands behind her ears. She was glad she'd chosen to wear a sundress because it was already warm this morning. She began merging with other people planning to attend the ceremony. Some were already seated in the bleachers, facing the giant, concrete parade deck. A red, white, and blue banner draped across the base of the stage with the marine insignia proudly displayed in the middle. Many people stood in the grass and talked, lightly fanning themselves with their programs. The activity was a little calmer than the day before at family day, and Berdine noted that not as many younger children were in attendance. The band had assembled off to the left side of the stage and was warming up.

In a few moments, the officers approached in full dress uniform from across the grounds to mount the stage. Berdine shivered at the thrill that ran down her spine. Families moved to take their places in the stands, eagerly anticipating the sight of their sons. The band began to play a soft march, building the anticipation. Berdine quickly took her seat in one of the top rows of the bleachers. Suddenly, topping the hill across the field, came the young recruits in "service bravos"—dark green trousers and tan khaki shirts, marching in perfect formation. As they came into view, the band struck up a rousing rendition of the "Marine's Hymn." A cheer from the crowd went up and brought everyone to their feet. They continued to applaud until they were close enough for the drill instructor's commands to be heard. At that point, the crowd fell silent, listening in awed respect and watching with proud tears on their faces. The marines filed onto the parade deck with exact precision in both their steps and the swing of their arms. Each turned with sharp movements and stood at attention facing forward, his back to the audience. When all the recruits were in place, the commanding officer rose to the podium to speak. The crowd took their seats. Berdine was surprised to find her own cheeks wet. She had not even been aware of crying.

She had found Michael the moment he had marched across the front, and her eyes continued to stay affixed to the back of his dark head. She smiled a little at the contrary cowlick at the base of his hairline that she had never noticed before. It was difficult to pay attention to the speeches that followed. She turned to watch the faces in the crowd and found herself wondering who were sisters and who were sweethearts. As the marine recruits stepped forward to receive their eagle, globe, and anchor cover, Berdine waited eagerly for Michael's turn. She had not seen any of his family yet, but she knew they were here. It was a surprise to feel the prickles skittering across her skin as she heard his name. She watched him step forward proudly to receive his cover. Berdine smiled through her tears, fighting for composure.

The ceremony drew to a close, and the drill instructor barked out, saluting the marine grads, "*Baker Company! Dismissed!*"

The young Marines returned the salute, responding in unison, "*Dismissed? Aye aye! ooh rah!*"

In formation, the company took one step back, did an about-face and began walking toward their families in the stands. Parents rushed forward, looking for their marine, eager to add their congratulations and hugs. Berdine lingered where she was, content to watch the drama play out before her. For a moment, she lost sight of Michael in the crowd. She tried to see around people, hoping to recapture a glimpse of him. A family moved out of her line of vision just in time for her to catch Michael in the unreserved embrace of his father. Their were tears on both of their faces, and Berdine watched with her heart in her throat as Michael's father reached up to cradle the young man's face in both of his hands. She couldn't make out the words, but she could tell by the way he stared into Michael's face, memorizing his features, that it was a poignant, tender moment. Michael's aunt and uncle had stepped back in deference to the father and son, but soon they too were drawn into the embrace. Berdine felt blessed to watch the scene from afar.

She saw Michael craning to look over the shoulders of his family. He appeared to be scanning the crowd for something . . . someone . . . *her?* His eyes roved slowly across the milling groups of people and scanned across to where she stood. Like a missile locking in on its target, his eyes stopped suddenly, capturing her gaze with his. He mouthed something briefly to the people at his side, never taking his eyes from her. He began weaving through the crowd, with deliberate steps toward her. Berdine's heart began to pound. She felt a wave of heat flash through her and tiny beads of moisture build at her hairline. Her legs trembled weakly, and she tried to summon a smile, but all she could manage was an unwavering stare. She took a deep, steadying breath as Michael stopped just inches in front of her. They both stood, simply staring at each other. Berdine was vaguely aware of people milling past them, almost brushing shoulders, but they could as easily have been a million miles away. All she could see was the man in front of her staring down into her eyes with a sense of wonder in his.

"You came."

"Yes."

"I'm glad." His lips curved into a slow smile. They were a breath apart, not touching. Yet the heat swirling between them was as tangible as if he had enfolded her into his arms.

"Michael…" Berdine started to speak, but the words seem to catch in her throat. "I…I…found the letters. I never knew about them. They've never even been opened. I need to show you…" She started to fumble through her purse, fearful that the tears she willed back would fall, and she would never be able to stop. "They're in here. I just put them in here this morning…I wanted to show you…to tell you…" Her agitation increased, and she just couldn't seem to stop babbling. Slowly, Michael reached out a hand to cover hers, stilling the frantic movement.

"It's okay, Berdine…Sssh…It's okay." His voice soothed and slid over her like a caressing touch. "We'll talk about it later. Look—I'd like to get away from the crowds right now, but my family is here, and we're driving to Isle of the Palms for lunch to celebrate. Please come with us. We could slip away afterwards and talk."

Berdine didn't even realize Michael still held her hand, his thumb moving in a slow, circular pattern over her knuckles.

"Oh Michael, I can't intrude. This is a time for you and your family. They want you all to themselves right now. Maybe you could just call me later." Berdine glanced around his broad frame to see three pairs of curious eyes watching their little scene with interest. It warmed her to see a little smile on Mr. Caraway's face.

"Berdine, please don't say no…" His voice was persuasive, and when the corner of his mouth tipped up in that little half smile, Berdine knew she was lost.

"If you're sure I won't be interfering with family time…"

"I promise. Come on over and say hello. I'd love for you to get to know my aunt and uncle better. You'll love them. You already know my dad..."

There was a spring in Michael's step as he turned and tugged her along with his long, tanned fingers encircling her slight wrist. To resist would have been awkward, although Berdine was still hesitant about these sudden changes of event. Could it be that two and a half years of heartache and misunderstanding would suddenly disappear in a single afternoon? It just wasn't that easy for her. Her head was still spinning with thoughts when she found herself standing before Michael's family.

"Berdine, you know Dad already..." Michael began. Berdine nodded shyly to Mr. Caraway, and she thought she detected a curious twinkle in his eyes. He looked as though he had aged some in last two years. Was it a result of the separation from his son? Yet the look in his eyes when they strayed often to the young man bore witness to a restoration of his vitality.

"Major, Aunt Molly, I'd like you to meet Berdine Williams. Berdine, this is my uncle Major Robert Hampton and my aunt Molly—the two people who saved me from shaming the Caraway name!" Michael had a hand at the small of Berdine's back, and it was hard for her to concentrate on anything but the imprint of his flesh burning through the soft cotton of her dress.

"I'm pleased to meet you." Berdine tried to keep the tremble out of her voice. It was a little nerve-wracking standing here in the presence of three people who thought the world of Michael.

"We've heard a lot about you, Berdine. We're glad to finally know you." Molly Hampton was a natural hostess—even out in the middle of a field. "We hope you'll join us for lunch. We have reservations at the Lighthouse Inn on the Isle of the Palms."

Berdine could feel Major Hampton's eyes on her, and she wondered if she was passing muster. It didn't feel like a critical stare, however, merely one of curiosity, with a bit of protectiveness. She wondered what Michael had said about her to these two people over the last couple of years...especially in light of their misunderstanding. She looked between the faces of the three older adults and smiled.

"I...thank you...I'd be honored to join you."

Major Hampton didn't exactly smile, but she couldn't detect

anything disapproving in his demeanor. Maybe that was just part of his being a marine all these years. He held his emotions and thoughts in check and his bearing erect. In any event, Molly more than made up for his stoicism with her natural warmth and ease.

It was decided that Berdine would leave her car on base and ride with Michael. His family would lead the way in the major's car. It had been years since Berdine had been to Isle of the Palms, and she'd never been to the Lighthouse Inn. She asked Michael if her dress was appropriate. Her question was completely innocent, but when Michael turned sideways in the driver's seat to give her a slow, studied perusal, Berdine started to squirm. His eyes darkened, and a thoughtful smile started at the corner of his mouth.

"Oh yeah . . . " he said in a deepened voice.

It was the lascivious wiggle of his eyebrows that caused Berdine to laugh, almost in relief. It somehow reminded her of the way he used to tease her when they were kids. The playful moment seemed to put them back on a comfortable level of friendship. Berdine wasn't ready to handle anything beyond picking up the pieces of a relationship that had been wounded by misunderstanding. She marveled at how quickly Michael seemed able to retrieve that ease with her he'd had in the past. It just wasn't as easy for her. The shell around her heart had grown calloused layers over the last few years. If Michael sensed she was keeping a cautious distance between them, he didn't let on. For that, she was grateful. Besides, there was more to consider than just healing their relationship. She thought about what resuming their friendship would mean to Mama and Pop and . . . *Kathryn.* Berdine was still not ready to probe that open wound!

"We have a lot to talk about. It will be tough for me to sit across from you in the company of my family and keep the conversation general. We need some time alone." Michael began.

"To be honest, Michael, I'm not sure I'm ready for anything more than general conversation. I just saw you yesterday for the first time in nearly three years. We could be completely different people now."

"We'll have to find that out, but I don't think so." Michael shook his head thoughtfully.

Berdine turned to study his profile. Her eyes ran over the chiseled features that were no longer a boy's. There was a faint shadow on his jawline, and she couldn't help remembering the first time she teased him about growing peach fuzz. His eyes were still so dark—hard to tell sometimes if they were navy or black. His lower lip was full, and for a brief insane moment, she had a powerful urge to trace it with her finger. Her scrutiny continued on to the powerfully built shoulders and an upper body that looked like it was carved from a rock. His forearms were veined and muscular and dusted lightly with hair a few shades lighter than his military haircut. One of those arms stretched over the steering wheel, his hand dangling casually over the top. Berdine swallowed deliberately, realizing her throat felt a little dry. Michael continued watching the road ahead of him as he drove.

"See? Still the same old me..." he said lightly, grinning at the blush that rose on Berdine's face in response.

"Hardly..." Berdine muttered, turning back to face forward and wishing she could slow the rapid beat of her heart.

They drove in silence for most of the trip, and Berdine was surprised to find that it was not uncomfortable. She wondered if Michael had as many thoughts whirling through his head as she did. Where would they ever begin to cover all the things that needed to be said?

They were a few minutes from Isle of the Palms when Michael suddenly asked, "Is our tree house still there?"

"Yeah, it is. Did you know that after you left, your dad worked on it?"

"No kidding? I didn't think he even knew about it! Why would he take the time to do that?"

Berdine leveled a look at Michael and smiled gently. "You really don't know?"

Michael turned trying to decipher her expression. When he didn't answer, she continued, "He did it because he missed you... a lot. I think it was a way for him to feel near you. I was there one day when he brought some lumber and his tools to work on our, should I say, *rudimentary* ladder."

Michael didn't respond right away. Berdine could tell he was digesting the information and imagining the scene in his head. He shook his head slowly. "I guess I never really knew just how much my leaving hurt him"—he turned to study her face—"and you."

Now it was Berdine's turn to remain silent. She sat very still, looking at her hands folded in her lap. As much as she wanted to reassure him to the contrary, she could not. So she just said nothing, turning to gaze out the window. Berdine's attention was suddenly captured as they turned onto the ocean-side drive into Isle of the Palms. She gasped at the incredible scene out her car window: sandy dunes with tall reeds waving lazily in the breeze and beyond that, the miles and miles of smooth, foam-kissed beaches as far as she could see. A lone fisherman stood at the end of a long pier stretching out into the rolling waves. His bucket of bait seemed to attract the attention of several greedy seagulls, alternately hovering, then swooping. In the distance, a shrimp boat trolled along, dotted with its usual pelican escorts. The sunlight shimmered on the blue-gray surface at the edge of the horizon, giving Berdine the impression she could see the very edge of the earth. She hadn't realized she'd been holding her breath until she exhaled it in a rush. Michael enjoyed the wonder he saw playing across Berdine's face.

"*I know*," he said simply.

Berdine didn't take her eyes from the scene but spoke in a hushed voice. "I've been to the ocean so many times, yet it's never the same—never ordinary. It still takes my breath away."

Michael laid his hand lightly on hers. Without even thinking, she turned her own hand to link her fingers with his. They rode the rest of the way in companionable silence with the magnificent panorama of the ocean as their backdrop.

XXV

Lunch was a lighthearted affair—with none of the uneasiness Berdine expected to experience. Major Hampton seemed to warm to the conversation and even chuckled a time or two. Though he was more reserved than the rest of them, he left no doubt as to his pride and love for his nephew. The times he was most animated was when he was entertaining them with stories of Michael's boot camp experiences and the feats he accomplished to earn him the tribute of honor graduate in his company. It was heartwarming to see the three adults share so easily in their relationship with Michael. There didn't seem to be any competition or possessiveness among them, and it occurred to her how different this family was from her own. There were no hidden undercurrents! No unspoken words bubbling just below the surface. It wasn't that Berdine's family didn't laugh and tease each other; it was just that unpleasant or unhappy things were not addressed. If you didn't lift the rug up, you didn't have to see the dirt.

She was content to listen to the conversation swirling around her. The men were discussing Michael's next step in his military career, and it was fascinating to watch the invisible tie between the three men occasionally stretch yet still hold fast. Michael talked about staying at the marine recruit base for a couple of years so he could train to be a drill instructor. His uncle nodded in agreement. But Jack Caraway slapped his palm on the table, leaning in with intensity. "I think you should put in your request for orders. There are plenty of bases in this part of the country where you can be stationed and still get your officer's training!"

"He's not ready for that, Jack. The boy is barely past nineteen. He needs to get his feet wet before he moves up in the ranks. He'll be here where Molly and I can still watch over him … not to mention close enough for you to come and visit as often as you want … "

Michael frowned, a note of impatience in his voice. Turning to his uncle, he said, "Sir, you're missing the point. I'm not asking to stay on at the base here because I don't feel *ready* to earn higher rank. And, Dad … " he said, turning to his father, "I'm not even sure that's what I want … to be an officer who sits behind a desk and signs orders. I'm staying here to go through drill instructor training so that I can learn to *lead.* My goal is to lead a platoon of men."

Jack Caraway closed his eyes, summoning his patience. "You only need to learn how to lead a platoon if you're taking them into combat. We're not in a war right now, son. And if that happens, I'd just as soon you sit behind a desk and sign orders!"

Major Hampton looked back into the face of his brother-in-law and spoke quietly, "Jack, he's a marine."

Michael's father looked unsatisfied with that as an answer, and his voice rose. "Well, he can be an *officer* in the marines who signs orders!"

Berdine watched the byplay with interest. Though emotion seemed to rise, she sensed the unwavering stability of the relationships between the three men. Perhaps that was the reason Molly was able to sit peacefully, snatching forkfuls of chocolate cake from her husband's plate. It made her smile to watch Aunt Molly, nodding absently in agreement as she stabbed at bites of the rich dessert.

Michael scooted his chair in as close as he could get to the table. He leaned forward so he could speak clearly above the clatter and din of the restaurant.

"Dad, I don't think you understand. It's my *calling.* I know without a doubt I've been called to lead a group of men, and if that's so, I need to be as well-trained as possible." Berdine saw passion burning in Michael's eyes, and it caused her to lean in closer to the conversation.

Jack Caraway turned to his sister and asked, "What's this 'calling' he's talking about? Has he had some sort of religious experience?" His tone was suspicious, and Molly dabbed politely at her lips before she answered her brother.

"Now, Jack, we told you we'd be taking Michael to church on a regular basis ... " she began.

"It's okay, Aunt Molly. Let me explain it to Dad."

Berdine frowned as she studied the burning expression on Michael's face, and suddenly she knew where she'd seen that look before ... *Nell.* Well, that settled one question she'd had earlier. They were, indeed, different people now.

Berdine found her mind wandering as she stared out the plate glass windows. The dance of the waves mesmerized her, and the delicious seafood meal was starting to work its magic on her. She yawned behind her hand, hearing—but not really listening to—Michael's voice. It was like warm chocolate, smooth and rich. She felt removed from the scene as she watched the expressions of the four people. She could see the earnestness on Michael's face, empathetic support from his uncle and aunt, and a reserved but interested look on the face of Mr. Caraway. But beyond observing their faces, Berdine did not really focus on their words. She would have been content to remain on the periphery of the conversation except Molly, ever mindful of her duties as hostess, finally said to the men, "Boys, where are our manners? Poor Berdine hasn't been able to get a word in edgewise for the last forty-five minutes!"

The men looked startled then regretful. So much so that Berdine hastened to reassure them. "Oh no! Don't give it another thought. I've been content to just sit here and listen. Really!" She smiled convincingly, and Michael reached under the table to clasp her hand in his.

Aunt Molly said, "Well, at least tell us what your plans are for the rest of the summer, dear. We just seemed to have focused so completely on Michael here."

Berdine laughed, and Michael just stared at his aunt, playfully offended. "Well, Aunt Molly, that *is* the point of this lunch, isn't it?"

They all joined in the laughter, but Michael's little aunt merely patted his hand in a conciliatory manner, "Of course, dear, but we mustn't forget our manners."

Michael's aunt was so gentle, without guile and pretense, and it suddenly became clear to Berdine how timely, even fortuitous, it was that Michael found his way here to them. She concluded that he must have discovered a steadying sense of balance in living with them these last several years. Not that it overshadowed his devotion for his own father; she could also clearly see the mutual love and respect between the older and younger Caraways.

"All right…" Michael drawled, pretending disappointment. "We can talk about Berdine."

The focus swung to her, and she cleared her throat, not particularly comfortable with the spotlight. But since the four other adults were looking at her with expectancy, she knew there was nothing to do but launch into her own monologue.

"Let's see, I just finished two summer sessions at Outward Bound Wilderness Camp for at-risk children…which is how I came to meet up with Michael again." She glanced at him and nearly faltered at his warm, almost caressing, smile. Not a good focal point, she reminded herself sternly. "We had a very successful expedition on the marine base, and the kids responded beautifully. I wouldn't doubt if most of them come back to enlist when they finish high school! And now, I'll be taking some classes at the College of Charleston for the second session of summer school. I'd like to get the core classes out of the way as soon as possible so I can start in my major."

Aunt Molly leaned forward, curious interest in her eyes, "What major is that?"

"I'm not completely settled on it specifically, but either social work or child psychology. I really have a passion for these troubled kids." Berdine felt her confidence grow as she talked of her future plans.

Michael broke in. "Berdine can't help but rescue the wayward and the lost."

Berdine turned to study Michael's face, searching for any meanness or animosity at the veiled reference to their last encounter at the infamous fight years ago, but she could find none. His eyes merely held a hint of sad regret, and he smiled, taking her hand. He continued, "I don't know any person on earth more gifted for that task."

It was as if those few tender words suddenly and completely shattered the hard shell around Berdine's heart. It was a blessing beyond any gift she could ever have been given, an affirmation from him of who she was and what she was designed to do. The years of separation between them fell away in an instant. She turned to study the man sitting next to her, and two words sizzled through her mind: *soul mate.* She had no doubt that Michael too felt the moment of connection, because his hand gripped hers more tightly. She sensed a sudden restlessness in him to be away from here.

Whether it was purposeful or just good timing, Major Hampton looked at his watch and said, "Well, folks, I need to get back on base. I'm sorry to be the one to cut things short here…"

Mr. Caraway nodded his head in the direction of his son and winked at his brother-in-law. "I don't think anyone's feelings are gonna be too hurt."

Major Hampton nodded, smiling. "Now, that's a good thing. Michael, son… you got one week's leave. You can stay at our house if you want to get away from the barracks for a while."

"Thank you, sir. I may take you up on that for at least part of the time. I'll probably also spend some time in Mount Holly with Dad."

"That's a good idea. You have a key to our house, so just come and go as you please. I expect you to get plenty of R and R before reporting back to duty. Drill instructor training begins two days after you return."

"Yes, sir!" Michael saluted out of ingrained habit. It made Berdine smile, knowing he wasn't even aware of it anymore.

They all left the restaurant together. In the parking lot, Jack reached for his son and enveloped him in a big hug. "Proud of you, Son. I always saw the raw potential in you if you were just given a chance. I'll always be grateful to your aunt and uncle for giving that to you."

Michael hugged back and said, "Dad, you were the one to start me on the right road in the first place. I just wanted to live up to your faith in me. I may be home in a couple of days, if that's all right with you. Maybe we can do some fishing or something."

"That sounds like a plan. I'll look forward to it. Miss Berdine, it's good to see you again too. I guess you'll know what I mean when I say, 'I told you so.'" Mr. Caraway winked meaningfully at Berdine, delighted to share in a private joke with her.

Berdine blushed, nodding her head. "Yes, sir, I do. That's still just between us, isn't it?"

She knew they were sharing the memory of the day he rescued her from Danny Tyler and then later assured her that Michael would not forget her. She regretted that she had not believed him at the time.

"That's right." He ignored the puzzled look on the face of his son. He turned then to his sister, yawning widely. "Molly, you got space on your couch for me to take a Sunday afternoon nap?"

"Of course, Jack... that's the next order of business for me as well. Robert has to go to the office for a couple of hours, so I say we make good use of the time he's gone and sleep off this heavy lunch!"

Major Hampton bent down to kiss his little wife's plump cheek. "Maybe I'll just wrap things up in an hour and join you in that nap." Molly blushed furiously and hid her smile by digging in her purse. She found the business card she was looking for and handed it to Berdine.

"Here, dear. This has all our numbers on it. I want you to call us or just come by if you ever need anything."

Berdine thanked Molly, not bothering to mention that she had a sister and brother-in-law barely twenty minutes away from the college campus. It no longer seemed relevant to her. She tucked the card into her purse and looked to Michael. He wrapped his warm fingers around the underside of her elbow, and they said their good-byes.

XXVI

They were finally alone. Berdine felt a rumble of anticipation inside of her. She hadn't really taken much time to analyze how things felt different between them. For one thing, it was hard to compare what she felt now with her tomboyish perspective from the ages of ten to fifteen … Suddenly her thoughts were interrupted.

"Where to? We have the rest of the afternoon and evening—that is, if you're not too tired … " Michael was leaning over the steering wheel watching the thoughts skittering through her mind. He could tell she was trying to work out some sort of puzzle. He hoped it had to do with him.

"Oh! No … I'm not tired." Berdine assured him. She thought for a moment and then smiled. "On the drive over to your graduation, and then even here, I've been feeling a strong urge to walk along the beach. Do you think we could do that? Do you still have to be in uniform?"

Michael grinned. "Right back in sync together with our thoughts! I've been wanting to do the same thing … but just been waiting for the right companion. Since I'm on leave, I can wear civilian clothes. I have everything I need right back there in the trunk of my car. As you know, a marine is always prepared!"

Berdine looked skeptical. "Doesn't that motto belong to the *Boy Scouts?*"

"Whatever. I have plenty of clothes back there that I *should* have put up after Aunt Molly washed them for me. *Don't tell on me!* I probably even have a towel and swim trunks."

"Oh, well . . . I don't have a swimsuit with me . . ." Berdine's voice trailed off, catching the raised eyebrows and mischievous grin on Michael's face. She blushed and raised a hand in front of his face. "Don't even go there. I just want to walk along the water's edge. I can do that in my dress."

Michael laughed and started the engine. "I think the beaches here on Isle of the Palms are the most beautiful. Let's hit one of those and see what we discover."

As they drove, Berdine continued her earlier train of thought, trying to define how the two of them had changed and how she felt about this new element, this intangible sense of awareness between them. As far as personal changes, it was clear to her that Michael was no longer the restless, angry boy of yesterday. He appeared to be more at peace with himself. And it was more than just self-confidence or even maturity . . . She couldn't quite pinpoint the source. Maybe it was a matter of finding his purpose. Perhaps she too would feel that sense of peace when she finally accomplished some of her goals. It had eluded her in her high school years. She wondered if she'd feel that way had Michael stayed. But then, intuition told her that dependence on another person to bring fulfillment was dangerous. People were imperfect. People could disappoint. And *some* people could even betray. She shook her head, erasing the fleeting mental image of her sister.

She glanced over at the contented expression on Michael's face as they drove toward the beach. She would be careful of her feelings. She had goals to accomplish, a career to train for. She was not so naive to believe he didn't have his own far-reaching goals. They would enjoy renewing their friendship, and there would be no expectations.

Feeling better now that she had sorted things out in her head, she turned to Michael and asked, "So tell me about basic training.

What was it *really* like? Our Outward Bound expedition probably allowed only a very limited view of the true experience—or at least what I imagine boot camp is like."

Michael rubbed the side of his face, thinking how best to describe the last thirteen weeks. It was difficult, because it was one of the biggest experiences of his life—and the second most character changing. He thought back now to those first few days: receiving his gear issue, meeting his training company, scrambling to learn the dos and don'ts, all the while hoping not to arouse the ire of his drill instructor. After a while, he learned that there was not really *anything* he could do to avoid the earsplitting, face-to-face dressing-down that came from his instructor on a regular basis. At least he wasn't the only one in his company to receive such "personalized attention"! In hindsight, he could see that in the beginning, he'd still carried a tiny bit of attitude. And though he didn't think it showed, he believed now that every drill instructor is taught to "seek out and destroy" anything in a recruit that tried to hold on to his individuality. Michael "dropped and gave fifty" so many times in the first two weeks that the palms of his hands blistered and became calloused from so much contact with the asphalt. There were times that it took greater strength to restrain himself from taking a swing at his drill instructor than it took to complete a six-mile march, in full gear, at 0300 hours.

He could still remember the agony he felt after completing one such march. He was mere seconds from finally being able to drop exhausted into the sack when his drill instructor rallied them all back outside for a three-mile jog in their skivvies. Two recruits in their company hadn't had their boots properly aligned at the foot of their bunk according to regulations. It was the turning point for Michael's company. They each had to individually come to the same conclusion if they were to survive: they had to watch each other's back. When a recruit fell in the knee-deep mud under the weight of his pack, one shouldered his load and another lifted him to his feet, avoiding a slowdown in the line. When, fifteen seconds before inspection, a recruit realized both pairs of his boots were not mud-free, another slid his own extra pair into place just as the drill instructor came storming in. And there were countless other times. At weapons drill, one recruit could not get his weapon fired and reloaded in the allotted time, though he had desperately tried time and again. The drill instructor stood over him, clipboard in hand, ready to fail the marine. Michael jumped to his feet, requesting permission to train the recruit on his own time. Two days later, not only was it a victory for the young marine to complete the drill successfully, but it was a morale boost for the whole company.

Michael was not even aware that his own character was changing and his natural leadership skills were emerging until the day they were slated to engage in war games. Each participating company was given a bunker to defend. The goal was to seize the flags in the other bunkers, eliminating all other companies—either by simulated death or capture. By the end of the night, Michael's company was the only one remaining, and his comrades were convinced that it was due to Michael's ingenious strategizing. What the officers in charge noted in their records was not necessarily the excellent strategy but Michael's natural ability to persuade a whole company of men to follow him. Michael simply marked it down to being a part of a group of men who were rapidly learning to think and work as one. By the end of their thirteenth week, Michael's company was one of the few remaining who'd not lost a single recruit for any reason. They had grown closer than a family, and each would have been honored to guard their brother's back in combat.

Michael smiled now, turning his head briefly to look at Berdine. His tone was light. "I'd say some of what you've seen at the movies is not too far off reality. It's hard to even find the words to describe it other than 'life changing' and 'character developing.' It was the toughest challenge I've ever faced, and now that I'm through it, I think I would still honestly say I don't regret even one single pushup facedown in the mud!"

Berdine gasped, trying to picture the grueling, humiliating experience of being forced to finish the task under those conditions. She felt that familiar protective surge inside of her and scowled. "It's a good thing *I* didn't see that!"

They both laughed at Berdine's unspoken reference to her propensity for rescuing. They talked more about basic training, mainly because Berdine continued to fire away questions. At one point Michael laughed and said, "I'd like to hear about *you,* Berdine. If you keep asking me questions, I'm going to start believing you are strategizing to avoid the topic!"

"I'm just hungry to fill in the gaps of the last two-plus years. I hate incomplete stories! I'm working my way backwards. Next, I want to know what it was like for you when you first came to Parris Island. But I'll be fair. How about we make a deal? You answer all my questions, and then when we get to the beach, I'll answer yours."

"That sounds fair, I suppose. Ahhh ... guess what? We're here." Michael laughed as he pulled the car to a stop in the sand swept parking lot. A wooden pavilion on beams loomed before them, and they watched sun-reddened children rushed to the bathrooms by frantic mothers.

"But I'm not *near* finished with my questions ..." Berdine begged.

"A deal's a deal, young lady."

"Okay. An amended deal: We'll alternate. I'll ask four or five questions, and then you get to ask one."

"One to your four or five? Let's even that out a bit. Four for every four."

Berdine pretended to give his offer heavy consideration. Enjoying the game, she countered, "My four to your three. Final offer."

Michael yanked on a curl and laughingly conceded as he jumped out of the car before she could swipe back at him. It was the same easy rhythm of their childhood that she remembered. And the feeling brought a sense of contentment.

"Do you want to just leave your sandals in the car? I'm going to run up to the men's room and change into shorts." She nodded, trying to fight the hair whipping around her face. Michael laughed, helping her tuck the silky strands behind her ears. Even that casual touch sent a shiver down Berdine's spine. *I am in such big trouble,* she grumbled to herself. She watched him retrieve a pair of shorts and T-shirt from his trunk and then bound up the stairs of the pavilion. She stood motionless, wishing she could tear her eyes from him. She shook her head in self-disgust and began searching in her bag for a hair tie. Quickly, she braided the unruly curls into a thick braid down her back. Even with the bulk of it tamed, the wind still teased curling tendrils out of the braid to dance around her face. She sighed, remembering how she had once wished she could get a crew cut like Michael.

Michael came out of the bathroom at the top of the deck, and Berdine felt her mouth grow dry. He was carrying his T-shirt tossed over one shoulder, and the tanned, hardened muscles of his stomach and chest were no longer just a figment of her imagination.

"Yep," she whispered to herself, turning her eyes quickly away to stare at the ocean. "I'm definitely done for."

By the time, Michael was by her side at the car, she was surprised, then relieved to see that he'd already pulled his T-shirt on. She almost sighed audibly but caught herself just in time.

"Ready to go?" he asked, grinning with the ease of one comfortable in his own skin.

"I am!" she answered.

XXVII

They took off, headed for the outgoing tide's edge. The loose sand was hot to their bare feet, and Berdine was eager to feel the cool, soothing drench of the saltwater. Berdine laughed at the little sand crabs side winding their way to higher ground. As they neared the water, the sand became cool and malleable, sucking at their feet and molding their prints on its surface. Tiny shells offered up by the foam littered the ground and sparkled as the sun glinted down on them. Some tumbled back into the surf as they caught a ride back on the returning tide.

Their first step into the ankle-deep water brought sighs of contentment. For a moment, they both just stood side-by-side staring out at the vast body of water, trying to take in the incredible magnitude of it all. Berdine closed her eyes, enjoying the rhythm of the push and tug of the water lapping over her feet. The constant roar of the waves mingling with the wind and the gulls was a healing, cleansing symphony. The sun beat down on her shoulders, and she lifted her face to receive the warming rays.

Suddenly, she had that uncanny feeling of eyes on her. She turned quickly to catch Michael studying her with a look she didn't even want to define. It was a consuming look, and for a moment, she was afraid. Not of him—never him, but of *herself* and the answering hunger inside her. The moment was intense, and Berdine felt herself tremble, but then it passed quickly as Michael turned his head, shuttering his expression. She watched him swallow deliberately, and suddenly, she realized, he too was wrestling with his own feelings. It gave her a sense of liberation to learn she was not the only one here struggling to swim to the surface in spite of a very strong undercurrent.

She laughed suddenly, shattering the moment. She bent over, swooping up an armful of water and tossing it overhead. It was a shockingly cold sensation, and she loved it.

"Hey!" Michael jokingly complained. "If you want a shower, move on down a bit!"

It just made Berdine laugh even more, and she turned to start down the shoreline, holding the hem of her dress above her knees.

"C'mon!" she called back over her shoulder, her braid whipping around as she turned.

Michael shook his head in mock resignation, but it didn't fool Berdine. She could see the delight in his eyes as clearly as she could feel it in her own heart. They walked beside each other, mostly looking down at their feet, idly searching for treasures. Occasionally, one of them would stoop to pick up a tiny shell and pocket it before continuing on. And as they walked, they talked. They filled in the gaps and the empty places. They each painted a canvas for the other, finally bringing a finished picture into view. Somewhere along their journey, they had linked hands and they walked with the ease of a couple who'd known each other for years. They lost track of time and didn't even care. Finally, it registered that the tide was way out, and it was nearing sundown. Berdine looked up and then spun in a circle, scanning the area.

"Where are we? I don't see anything familiar! Do you have any idea how far we've walked?"

Michael looked up, the same puzzled expression in his eyes. "I have no idea." He laughed shortly. "At least we know that all we have to do is turn around and walk back the way we came."

"But do you know what time it is? I don't have a watch."

"Neither do I, but I'd guess it's close to seven or eight." He shrugged, unconcerned.

She thought for a moment and then realized she had no real reason for concern either. It made her heart feel light and free. "We should probably still head back. It will be dark by the time we get back to the car."

They turned and began walking slowly back in the opposite direction. The Sunday afternoon beachcombers had left, and only a few people dotted the landscape now. It gave Berdine a sense of insulation from the busyness of daily life. Michael once again reached for her hand, and it felt natural now to entwine their fingers together. They talked easily and sometimes they simply walked in companionable silence. Eventually they saw the pavilion in the distance. By the time they neared it, the sun was beginning to sink lower on the horizon. Its orangy pink fingers reached up to the darkening shade above it, pulling the darkness slowly down behind it.

When they were even with the pavilion, Michael stopped and said, "Let's sit here and finish the show." He nodded to the breathtaking painting on the horizon no human hands could ever copy. They sank together into the dry sand, still warm from the afternoon sun. The breeze had picked up ever so slightly, and Berdine shivered once.

"Cold?" Michael asked.

"A little . . ."

"C'mere." Michael held out an arm, and Berdine moved under the shelter of it, leaning in to the warmth of his side. It was a casual embrace, not asking for anything, simply sharing body heat. They watched the sun turn deeper hues of gingery-red. As the fiery ball touched the edge of the horizon, some of the colors spilled off and spread onto the ocean's surface.

Berdine whispered, "Doesn't it seem like it should sizzle when it touches the water?"

Michael smiled at the imagery. "Maybe it does, and we just can't hear it over the ocean's roar."

They sat quietly enjoying nature's offering. Finally, Michael turned his head slightly and quietly asked, "Do you want to talk about the letters?"

Berdine's breath hitched, and it felt as though her heart plummeted to the bottom of her stomach. "I don't know if I can."

Again silence reigned, and Michael was careful not to rush her. Finally, she took a deep breath and began softly, "I haven't even opened them yet. But I will… soon. I'm sorry I didn't trust you or try to get past my own hurt. I could have contacted you on my own initiative, but I just thought you had shut the door on our friendship." Her voice trailed off, and then she murmured, "I won't make that mistake again…"

Michael pulled her closer to his side, encircling her in a comforting hug. "It's *okay,* Berdie. We were both young, and… well, I was spinning out of control on the inside. I made the decision to go to my aunt and uncle's so impulsively, but later, I came to know there were greater forces at work guiding that decision. My dad agreed I should go just as quickly… before I could change my mind." He laughed shortly as he remembered how rapid the transition was made. And then he looked at her. "But the one thing I didn't want to do was to let you think I left because of your involvement in that silly fight. There were so many bigger, deeper issues. So I wrote to you when I got there. When I didn't hear back, I wrote again, and again, and finally I just decided you'd given up on me."

"Oh, Michael… it hurts to hear you say that. I would never have turned my back on you. And yet, there I was thinking the same thing about you. What a mess." Berdine closed her eyes, a pained expression on her face.

Michael knew his next question would probably shake them both to the core, but they needed to get things out in the open so that they could deal with it.

"Berdine… where did you find the letters?"

She pressed her fingers tightly against her eyes. She didn't answer immediately, trying to find the words. When she spoke, her tone had changed. Instantly, her voice was low and cold. "You think you know someone. And then one day you find out that you only *thought* you did. In fact, you never knew them at all. And then you promise yourself that they'll only get one chance to betray you…"

"Berdine? Who?"

"My sister." Her tone became deadened and monotone. "I found them stuffed way back in her desk drawer."

"I'm so sorry."

Berdine moved slightly so she could turn and look Michael full in the face. A chill ran down his spine when he saw the anger and coldness in her eyes. "How could she hate me so much to do that to me? She knew how sad I was."

"Maybe she thought she was protecting you. I know your family worried about us hanging out together so much. I wasn't a good influence on you or anybody back then."

"Don't you dare defend her. I don't care what her motive was. It was wrong. But I do know this one thing: I'll never let her hurt me again." There was steel in Berdine's eyes. She turned to face the ocean, her mouth set in a stubborn line.

"Berdine, don't do this to yourself. Unforgiveness will eat you alive. Confront her, scream at her . . . whatever you need to do, but then you're gonna have to let it go."

Berdine turned back to Michael, and he could see that bitterness already had a foothold. "I'll *never* let it go."

"Berdine—" he started, but she held up her hand, interrupting.

"I'm done with this topic, Michael. She *stole* those letters. She's not going to steal this night from me as well."

Michael bowed his head, his thoughts in turmoil. His heart urged him not to leave things as they were, but wisdom counseled him to let it go for now.

He pulled her back against his side and whispered into her hair, "I'm sorry to have dredged all this up. I can see how much it hurts you. I'll leave it alone for now. We can talk about it another time."

Berdine nodded slowly. She decided it would be easier to let him believe they would discuss it again later than to convince him there was no reason to.

XXVIII

The first stars were beginning to appear in the dusky sky. It finally registered with Berdine that while they were only a ten-minute drive from the college, they were an hour and a half away from Parris Island—where they had left her car. By the time they got to the base and she drove back to the dorm in Charleston, it would be past midnight. She groaned aloud.

"What?" Michael asked.

"My car is still on the base!" Berdine yawned, already thinking about the three-hour round trip.

"Hmm…I forgot about that when we left the restaurant. Let me think a minute…" A second later, he snapped his fingers and said, "How about if I drive you to the college, and then I can bunk with one of my buddies from Charleston. Tomorrow, I'll come pick you up, and we can head back to Parris Island to get your car. We could spend the day there if you'd like."

"It would be nice not to have to get it tonight. Then maybe we can sit out here awhile longer. Are you sure you can find one of your friends to take you in for the night?"

"Sure. Several of the guys in my company are from Charleston, and they headed back there for leave. I just need to make a call when we get back to your dorm."

"No problem."

"Okay then; we're set. Now let's see who can find the most constellations!" He pulled her arm, so she lay back on the sand beside him.

"It's always a competition with you, isn't it? Fireflies, fishing, hundred-yard dash, and now, constellations!" she complained teasingly.

"I can see you're still smarting over the fact that I beat you in all of those."

Berdine could hear the smirk in his voice. She jolted upright, her braid flinging sand into Michael's face. "What did you just say?"

"Well, take it easy. I know it's difficult accepting defeat..." There was laughter in his voice now.

Before Michael was able to see it coming and dodge, her little fist caught him just below his sternum. He groaned dramatically, rolling from side to side.

"Oww! What was that for?"

"You idiot! *I* won the hundred-yard dash. *You* came in second!"

"Now, Berdine... that may be the way *you* remember it, but I was there too, y'know."

Her jaw dropped, and an odd little squeak erupted from the back of her throat. Michael always did seem to know just the right buttons to push, and here he was drawing her into the same trap again!

"*Michael!* I have the blue ribbon to prove it! I left you *in the dust!* I *knew* you never got over that. This just proves it. You're trying to change history to preserve your feeble male ego!"

At that, Michael couldn't restrain his laughter any longer. Berdine still sat over him staring at him in mock disgust. As his laughter continued, Berdine determined it was time for a payback. She leaned over close to his face and taunted him. "And you know what else? I could do it again!"

Before Michael could even respond, Berdine leapt to her feet and shot off toward the pavilion, kicking up sand as she flew. Knowing a challenge when he heard one, Michael followed suit, all the while helplessly trying to subdue his laughter. She was an arm's length away when he reached out and grabbed her braid. He tugged just enough to slow her down and propel himself past her to one of the giant beams supporting the second story pavilion.

Dancing around giddily, his fists pumping the air, he boasted, "I won! I won!"

Berdine was breathing hard, hands on her hips, eyeing him as if he were lower than pond scum. "There is absolutely no honor in winning by cheating."

"Oh? What do you call the giant head start you gave yourself?"

"That was merely superior speed off the block!"

Her quick rejoinder set him off laughing again. He bent over at the waist, his hands on his knees trying to catch his breath. "Okay, okay… I concede. You won."

"*And* I won the hundred-yard dash in the sixth grade." She stood, arms stubbornly folded across her chest.

"*And* you won the hundred-yard dash in the sixth grade." Michael finally stood, wiping his eyes. He took a couple of steps closer to her and held out his hand. "Here, I offer my handshake in congratulations for then and now."

She looked at his proffered hand and then back up at him, frowning suspiciously. His eyes widened. "You wound me! I'm trying to be a good sport here."

A tiny smile started in the corners of Berdine's mouth, and she gave him her hand. As he clasped it, he tugged her gently closer till she stood toe to toe with him and had to tilt her head to look up at him. He stared quietly down into stormy, gray eyes, and she thought he could see the thrumming pulse at her neck. Her breathing became shallow, and her heart pounded wildly. Slowly, ever so slowly, he started to lower his head to hers. Her mind shouted at her, *I'm not ready for this!* And then he paused inches from her lips. Her wretched mind betrayed her, shouting, *No! Don't stop now!*

Those dark indigo eyes peered deeply into hers, and he murmured softly, "I've just had a sudden unpleasant feeling of déjà vu that I've been right here before with you, and I find myself afraid of repeating that scene." He smiled teasingly, holding the same position, his eyes flitting briefly to her lips.

Berdine's own smile deepened in response, and she whispered back, "In that case, the only fair thing to do would be to meet you halfway."

She placed both hands on his shoulders and stretched on her toes, raising her lips to meet his in a whisper-soft kiss. He pulled her in tightly, causing her back to bow slightly and her hands to entwine themselves behind his neck. He deepened the kiss, and all rational thought disappeared from her mind. She could feel the hammering of his heart against her own chest, and she heard herself sigh. Whether it was audible against his mouth, or just in her mind, she didn't know. Finally, he lifted his head, still gazing down at her. He smiled. "I've waited a long, long time for us to get that right."

Berdine giggled softly, surprising herself at the silvery, feminine sound. She didn't reply, instead laying her head against his chest. They stood in the embrace, allowing the beat of their hearts to slow eventually. Michael spoke softly against her hair. "This may be the biggest test of self-discipline I've faced since starting boot camp thirteen weeks ago, but I'm going to step back now and suggest we head on over to the college."

The look on Michael's face was so pained it almost made Berdine laugh. She savored the tingle of pleasure dancing down her spine and nodded quietly in agreement. He led her to the passenger side and helped her in and then walked around to his side and got in. He sat motionless for a moment, both hands gripping the wheel, and all he could say was "Whew!" He shook his head slowly and then reached down to turn the ignition. He then looked over at Berdine and caught her wide grin, shining brightly in the dark interior of the car. He felt as if he had been sucker-punched, and he muttered, "You're enjoying this, aren't you?"

"Oh, yeah ..." The tone of her voice was low and smoky as she laughed lightly.

Michael's own grin deepened, and they pulled away from the parking lot.

XXIX

The ride to the college was brief, and they talked of light, inconsequential things. He asked her about her upcoming classes, and she gave him a brief rundown of her schedule. She scowled as she told him one of the classes was U.S. history. She'd never liked history in high school so she wanted to get it out of the way as quickly as possible. Michael promised her he was probably a genius in U.S. history and he'd lend her the benefit of his excellent tutoring. She rolled her eyes, playfully irritated that she'd probably have to take him up on his pompous offer.

It was nearly ten p.m. when they pulled into the parking lot of Kressler Hall. A few scattered room lights could be seen, checkering the face of the old building. Their laughter echoed across the silent, darkened campus as Michael teased her about the "wild party atmosphere" of college life here. She argued that this atmosphere suited her just fine because she was a serious student with lofty goals. Their bantering continued all the way up the steps and in through the front glass doors of her dorm. There were a few end table lamps lit.

They could hear the muted noise of a television in one corner, where two students lounged on the couch, a bowl of popcorn between them. Berdine saw in her peripheral vision one of the girls nudge the other and tilt her head in Michael's direction. They bent their heads together, laughing and whispering. Berdine slipped her hand through the crook of Michael's arm, sending a subtle message of possession. Michael was looking around the lobby for a phone when Ms. Browning came around the corner from the little office.

"Oh!" she said, startled to see the handsome young man at Berdine's side. Berdine jumped in before Ms. Browning could ask questions. She suspected they might have the potential to be embarrassing.

"Ms. Browning, this is Michael Caraway, the marine I was telling you about and whose graduation I attended today. He was hoping to use the phone here so he could call one of his friends here in Charleston."

Michael smiled warmly at the suddenly fluttering older woman. She stuck out her hand, and he took it in his, shaking it gently. "It's nice to meet you, ma'am."

Berdine opened her eyes wider as she watched Ms. Browning. Why, she was almost simpering! And was that a rosy blush creeping up her neck? Berdine had to suppress the giggle threatening to erupt.

"Oh, young man, the pleasure is *all mine.* I am *honored* to shake the hand of one of the brave young men defending our country against all foes. I never see a soldier on the street that I don't stop and personally thank for his sacrifice in protecting our freedom!"

"Umm, Mrs. Browning, actually Michael has only just finished his basic training." Berdine offered helpfully.

She could tell by the slightly annoyed look on Ms. Browning's face and Michael's quick, "Shush, Berdine!" that their mutual admiration club did not include her! She sighed heavily and just barely resisted tapping her toe in impatience.

"It's loyal citizens like you, Ms. Browning, that make our sacrifice worth it." Michael turned on the charm, and Berdine rolled her eyes at his blatant flirting. Ms. Browning still had hold of his hand when she pointed to the opposite wall.

"Feel free to use that phone over there. And again, it's so nice to meet you. I hope we'll get to see more of you!"

Michael gently extricated his hand, nodding an affirmation. He headed toward the phone, and Berdine started after him. Ms. Browning stopped her with a light touch on her arm. She leaned her head close to Berdine's and smiled conspiratorially. "I *like* your marine!"

Berdine thought briefly about correcting Ms. Browning again, but then decided it probably wouldn't do any good. Instead, she just smiled and patted the older woman's fleshy hand.

Within a few minutes, Michael concluded his call and gave Berdine's a thumbs-up sign. "I'm going to go ahead and get on over to my buddy's house. He's at his parents', and they said they have a spare bedroom. I just don't want them to have to wait up for me."

"Of course. What time should I be ready tomorrow?" Berdine asked.

"Oh six hundred hours," he said with a straight face, and Berdine's eyebrows shot up.

"You've got to be kidding me." She looked at him with skepticism.

"Yes, lazybones ... I'm kidding you. I'll be by around nine thirty or ten. Is that okay?"

"Well, that sounds a little more humanly possible."

Michael shook his head mournfully. "I'm not sure you'd make a good marine."

Berdine laughed, playfully punching him in the shoulder. Michael grabbed her fist and pulled her toward him. "Walk me out?"

They linked arms and headed back out to the porch. They stood talking quietly, and then Michael said he should get going. He started to lean over and kiss her, but he caught the very interested stare from one Ms. Browning leaning over her desk watching the young couple through the glass doors. Michael stopped in midapproach and lifted a hand to wave at the curious little woman, a winning smile on his face. Berdine followed his gaze just in time to see a beaming smile on the face of her dorm mother. They looked at each other and laughed, settling for a brief hug good night.

It was a long time before sleep finally came that night. Too many thoughts turned over and over in Berdine's head, and she found it hard not to replay every moment of their day together. She wondered how they would spend the day together tomorrow and maybe the next one after that and the next and the next. She grinned happily into her pillow, wishing school was not starting just a week away.

It was probably a good thing that Parris Island was over an hour's drive. She could not imagine how she would ever stay focused if the base was just a few miles down the road. They would both be very busy beginning next week, and she'd have to be content to see him on an occasional weekend, she thought sternly to herself. At least, she hoped she wasn't being presumptuous in believing he felt the same way. She sighed, willing sleep to come, and eventually it did, but not before one dark image of her sister's face slipped through her mind.

XXX

The next several days could only have been described as idyllic in Berdine's opinion. Michael and Berdine spent as much time together as they could, both on Parris Island and in Charleston. Berdine had several meals with Michael and his aunt and uncle, and she was relieved to find that she was growing more comfortable in the major's presence. She knew how special this older couple was to Michael, and it was important to her that they approve of her.

Aunt Molly took her shopping one late afternoon when the men pulled out a beat-up chessboard. Molly rolled her eyes and said, "Get your purse, Berdine. We might as well hit the stores. They'll be at that for several hours."

Berdine was delighted for the chance to hear a different perspective on their mutual object of affection. Molly had a storehouse of amusing stories to tell on Michael, and it kept Berdine entertained. They each had several shopping bags on their arms, which they loaded into Molly's car, and then headed into the coffee shop for a cup before returning home. They sat almost knee to knee in comfy chairs. At one point, Berdine slipped off her sandals and tucked her feet up under her. They talked softly, sipping their coffee and enjoying each other's company.

"He was a scared, angry boy when he came to us. I wanted to just suffocate him with love and comfort, but Robert seemed to know better what he needed. He laid out the rules and the consequences for breaking those rules when Michael first got here. It was all I could do to keep from circumventing what I thought was too harsh from Robert. But he was adamant that Michael needed structure and boundaries first. When the boy learned they would hold, Robert said he'd "cut me loose" to do all the mothering to my heart's content."

Molly chuckled. "He seemed fine the first couple of weeks, but then it was like he took a turn for the worse. We learned later, as you know now, that was about the time he was desperate to hear from you but never did. Lord knows, Berdine, we would have helped him if he had just asked or even let on what the problem was. He was such a self-reliant boy then. It just seemed that he closed himself off even more. There was a new edginess about him.

"One of the rules Robert laid down for him was church attendance with us every Sunday. He'd attend the worship service with us, then go to the youth Sunday school. We helped in the babies class, so we usually just met up afterwards. One Sunday, we parted ways for the second hour as we always did. When it was time to go home, we waited for him to meet us at the car, and he never came down. Robert headed up to the room where the teenagers meet and found out Michael had never made it there. It just sent me into a panic. Here we were responsible for my brother's son, and we lost him. He wasn't at home or any of the local hangouts some of the teens typically frequented, and no one seemed to have seen him. I was close to hysteria at that point, so Robert took me home and said he was heading out in the car to see if he could track him down. He called me from a pay phone a couple of hours later to say he had caught up with Michael down at the beach. The boy had somehow gotten hold of a six-pack of beer and some cigarettes, and he was flying high. Robert hauled him home, knowing he wasn't in any condition then to discuss the matter. We put him to bed, heard him in the bathroom a couple of times during the night, and then as soon as it was dawn,

Robert had the boy up, dressed, and out in the yard clearing away brush and digging post holes for a fence!

"I tell you, Berdine, my heart ached for the poor thing. He was pale and sick and sweaty. I had to lock myself in the house! But I could hear Robert talking to him through the open window… bits and pieces all day long… about what it meant to be a man, how to handle those strong emotions, how he believed in Michael and would help him set some goals and work out a plan for the next few years. As much as I could tell, there wasn't a lot of response from the boy, but I know one thing… he was listening… and he never complained, not once. By evening, I had two dirty, hungry men on my hands. They were both a mess, but I saw something different in Michael's eyes. I saw hope. He even stood taller, tired as he was. As he trudged wearily up the stairs for a shower, Robert turned to me, exhausted and filthy. But there was a crooked little smile on his face. He kissed me on the forehead and said, 'I'm turnin' you loose now, Molly.' He couldn't have thrilled my heart more if he'd presented me with a four-carat diamond ring!"

There were tears in Molly's eyes as she finished the story, a hand to her heart. She smiled though her lips trembled. The love Berdine saw in those eyes brought tears to her own.

"You and the major make a good team, Molly. Michael was so lucky to have you both." Berdine wiped her eyes.

The women continued talking a little longer until Molly glanced at her watch. "Oh dear! It's nearly six. We usually eat dinner around five thirty! And it will be too late for you to drive back to the college. You'll just have to stay the night in one of our guest rooms!"

"Oh, but I don't have anything with me…" Berdine began. "Hmmm… if we have time to make one last stop, though, I think I can get what I need. Besides, I already have three new outfits in the car."

"That's the spirit! Let's do that quickly, and then we'll head home and get dinner on the table before the natives get too restless."

Dinner began with a family prayer. There was a brief moment of insecurity for Berdine when she was unsure what to do. The others quickly smoothed over the moment by reaching for each other's hands while the major bowed his head and led the prayer. It struck her as odd that he was so comfortable in addressing "the Almighty" as if he was on close terms with Him. She felt a strange fluttering of her heart and was not sure she liked the sensation. But then Michael squeezed her hand, released it, and the moment passed.

Dinner was an event, Berdine came to decide. It wasn't just about sitting down and eating a meal; it was so much more. There was laughter and warm conversation, teasing and even a bit of the more mundane things, like reviewing their agendas for the coming day. No one hurried to rise from the table when they were finished, and they seemed content to linger over dessert. When Molly did finally rise, gathering a few plates in hand, Michael and Major Hampton also rose, carrying dishes over to the sink. Molly put up the leftovers. Michael took his place at the sink, slipping his hands into the sudsy water and handing the dishes to his uncle to dry. Conversation never even skipped a beat, and Berdine realized this was a very normal routine.

She felt a little left out, so she asked, "How can I help?"

The major turned around and smiled at Berdine, tossing her the towel. "Why don't you scoot in here and take my job. I know where everything goes, so I'll put things away after you dry them."

Berdine almost laughed at herself when she realized how eager she was to be a part of the mundane chore of washing dishes. It seemed only minutes before they were finished and they all retired to the den. Molly had her knitting; the major had a crossword puzzle book. Michael and Berdine sat together on the couch, talking quietly.

"What's a five-letter word for 'a collective'?" Major Hampton asked.

"Group?" Berdine asked.

"Nope, starts with a t."

"Troop?" Michael suggested.

"That's a possibility." He winked at Michael and grinned. "That's thinking like a marine, son." He turned his attention back to the book. "No, that doesn't fit either."

"Tribe," Molly asserted calmly.

"That's it!"

Molly smiled and nodded, not ever looking up from her stitches. The major returned his attention to the puzzle. Michael scooted closer to Berdine on the couch, laying his hand on her knee. She instantly covered it with her own.

"I'm thinking about heading up to Mount Holly tomorrow.

We've only got the weekend now before things get really busy. You want to ride along with me? I can drop you off at your parents and then pick you back up on Sunday."

"That sounds all right. Can we go by way of Charleston? I need to get a few things."

"Sure, no problem."

"I'd like to spend some time with Nell too while we're there. I really miss her."

They continued to talk quietly until Molly yawned broadly and began tucking her knitting back into her bag. "I can hardly keep my eyes open. Sorry to be such a party pooper, but I think I'm off for my bed."

Major Hampton peered over the top of his glasses, a funny little smile playing at his lips. Berdine caught their exchanged glances. She marveled as she tried to reconcile the two images in her mind: the reserved, dignified officer in uniform and the affectionate, teasing husband she'd had the rare privilege of glimpsing. The latter was the image she saw now. Major Hampton laid down his crossword puzzle book and said to Michael and Berdine, "Well, if my bride is off for her bed, I'd be a fool not to join her."

"Oh, Robert!" Molly blushed like a young girl, laughing softly. But Major Hampton wasn't just teasing for the benefit of their young audience. He joined her across the room and bent down to kiss her briefly on the lips.

Taking her hand, he pulled her from the den, glancing over his shoulder to say, "See you kids later. Make sure all the lights are off before you turn in." Berdine and Michael watched them disappear down the hall with laughter echoing in their wake.

"Oh *my*..." Berdine began.

"I know. See what I've lived with? What a standard. You don't see many couples in their thirty-fifth year of marriage acting like newlyweds." Michael smiled.

"Is it really like that all the time?"

"Well, of course not. They fuss like normal people, but I can honestly tell you that the spark between them still burns brightly. I almost feel like an intruder sometimes!" He laughed shortly.

"How do you think they've done it?" Berdine was honestly curious. She knew her own mother and father loved each other and were both affectionate with her and her sister, but when she thought about it, she couldn't really say they were very demonstrative with one another in front of her. But then, she reasoned fairly, maybe some people were just more private in the way they expressed their love for another person.

"They still do the little things. He brings her flowers and tells her she's beautiful. She gives him her full attention when he's telling her about his day, and she still looks at him like he's her hero. But they respect each other's independence as well. They're not joined at the hip, doing the same thing, every minute of the day. They allow each other space to grow and change but still protect their closeness. The way I figure it, those things don't just come naturally unless you make them a priority. I think they just decided long ago to work at keeping their marriage fresh. Of course, the main thing is their dependence on the Lord."

Berdine raised skeptical eyebrows. "How does that help?"

Michael could tell by Berdine's tone that she really wasn't asking for a dissertation from the Bible, so he decided to keep it light. "They've just come to recognize the human tendency toward selfishness. It's our own nature to look out for number one—ourselves. It's only through our faith and dependence on Him that we ever manage to serve and love another person above ourselves."

Berdine frowned, sensing this was going in the same direction so many conversations with Nell had gone. She wanted to back out lightly, hoping to cause as few waves as possible. She shrugged casually and smiled. "I guess different things work for different people."

It was Michael's turn to frown slightly. It was the only point on which they did not see eye to eye. *Not yet,* he thought. He decided now was not the time to pursue the topic. Instead he asked, "What time do you want to get out of here tomorrow?"

"Well, it's an hour and a half back to Charleston and then another fifteen minutes or so to Mount Holly. It'll take a few minutes to make a stop at my dorm ... How about we leave around nine from here? That'll put us in Mount Holly closer to lunch time."

"Sounds good. Would you believe two guys in my basic training company are from Mount Holly? We actually went to school with them."

"Really? Who?" Berdine perked up, her mind automatically reviewing faces she used to see in the halls.

"I'm not sure you knew either one of them very well. One of the guys I hung out with some when I was 'taking my walk on the wild side.' Do you remember Rance Price?"

"You're kidding! I thought for sure he'd be in jail as soon as he cut loose from high school."

Berdine shook her head, remembering the rough loner on his motorcycle, always with a cigarette stuck to his lower lip. It always fascinated Berdine how long the ash could grow before he finally tapped it loose. It made her nervous to see it hanging there precariously, sure to fall any second and burn a hole in his jeans. She remembered he wore his hair longer than code allowed and he was forever in detention because he refused to conform. She tried to picture Rance in a uniform with a military haircut and no cigarette in sight. She shook her head. She just couldn't do it. Even her vivid imagination could not conjure up that vision.

"You'd be surprised, Berdine. He took to it like a beggar at a banquet. I never thought he'd fit. But toward the end of boot camp, I fully expected him to get honor graduate. I think he's been looking all his life for the right identity… and that was it. I'd be proud to have him guarding my back!"

Berdine shook her head, still trying to see it. "It makes a little more sense now, remembering what the counselors at Outward Bound said about the people who choose the military for a career. I'll tell you about it sometime."

Berdine figured she better store that conversation up for a longer space of time. It would be interesting to hear what Michael thought about their theory. Suddenly she remembered he'd mentioned *two* guys from their high school.

"Who was the other guy? Someone I know?" She was curious.

"I doubt it. Remember Danny Tyler? This other guy was one of *his* groupies." Michael shared a look of distaste with Berdine, knowing their feelings were the same. She wondered if his look of disgust was for Danny alone or also included the recruit.

"What's his name?"

"Thomas Sanders." Michael knew he'd see surprise on Berdine's face.

"You're kidding. *Tuck?* That kid who never had one independent thought of his own?" Berdine was shocked. "He didn't even go to the bathroom without checking with Danny first!"

"Yeah, he was kind of a squirt then. What was he like after I moved?"

"You don't think he changed any, do you? He was still a follower. It made me sick to see the power Danny held over him and the others!" Berdine shook her head in disgust.

Michael was a little surprised at the vehemence he heard in Berdine's voice. She suddenly realized Michael was studying her, a question in his eyes. She fumbled to explain the strength of her emotion.

"Well… you know how it always made us mad when Danny got his little posse to do his dirty work. Tuck was one of those kids… just so he could fit in." Then it suddenly struck her how ludicrous to imagine Tuck Sanders wearing the same uniform Michael Caraway wore.

"How in the world did he make it through boot camp?"

Michael was not as harsh in his judgment of Tuck as Berdine was ready to be. After all, he'd sweated and bled beside the kid. It wasn't that the boy was a *bad* kid; he was just one with a lot of fears. He had a father who was impossible to please, according to some of Tuck's late night confidences, and he had an impressive legacy to follow. His grandfather was a marine, his father was a marine, and *by God,* Tuck would be a marine too. So he showed up at receiving, and Michael took one look at his pale face and knew Tuck would never make it without help.

"Remember that story I told you about the guy who couldn't fire and reload in the allotted time? That was Tuck. And the more the drill instructor got in his face, the more his fingers fumbled. But we got him through it. I've never had a greater reward than seeing the smile on his face when he handed his insignia cover to his father." Michael smiled. He turned to Berdine. "I may spend some time with them while we're there if Dad has to work. I don't know where they'll be stationed after leave is up."

Berdine tried to cover the yawn with her hand, but Michael caught it, smiling tenderly. "That shopping will wear a body out, won't it?" he teased.

"Like you'd know anything about that!" Berdine scoffed then tried to twist away when Michael attempted to tickle her. His expression changed in a matter of seconds when his hands circled her waist. He urged her closer to him and bent his head to move his lips gently over hers. The kiss deepened, making Berdine's head spin. She put a hand to his chest, almost in an effort to bring back balance. Michael broke the kiss, his breathing labored. For a moment, they just stared into each other's eyes, both shaken by how quickly their bodies ignited.

Michael was the first to speak, running a hand over his shorn hair. "That's just downright combustible." He was so serious, it actually eased the tension some for Berdine. She laughed shakily in agreement. He peered closer at her as if he were studying a scientific specimen. "You think it will always be like that?"

Berdine shook her head, concentrating on steady inhaling and exhaling. A small frisson of delight ran through her as she registered the word *always*. "I don't know."

Michael eased himself off the couch and stood, holding a hand out to Berdine. "This is probably a good time to say good night. Got everything you need?"

"Yep. Don't wake me before eight o'clock, Lance Corporal Caraway." Berdine was relieved the moment had lightened. Michael's lips curved in that slow, private smile, and he saluted.

He walked her to the guest room door and leaned down to peck her lightly on the lips.

"Sleep well."

"You too."

She watched him from her doorway as he disappeared around the corner of the hallway to his room. She smiled inwardly, thinking it was going to be mighty hard to hold on to her heart!

XXXI

Maybe it was the ease between them when they talked or the way they worked in tandem to load the car after the stop at her dorm. It could have even been the long moments on the road trip to Mount Holly when the only evidence of their connection was their casually entwined fingers on the console between them. Whatever it was, Berdine felt a sudden revelation running through her mind as they drove into town: *we're a couple!* It made her smile as she looked out the window at the buildings in town square. How strange … to come back to a place as familiar as your own reflection in a mirror, and yet, because *you* are different, everything else looked different now too. She stole a quick glance at Michael and wondered what thoughts ran through his mind.

She turned her attention back toward the scenery. Several old men sat outside the Five and Dime on the north end of the square playing checkers on a barrel. They barely glanced up as she and Michael passed, so intent on their game. A few people strolled along the walk looking into stores. Two men in suits marched hurriedly up the steps of the old courthouse, swinging briefcases, their ties fluttering in the breeze. Berdine always wondered how anyone could hurry by, resisting the invitation to pause and linger on the perfectly manicured lawn around the courthouse, dappled by the shade of venerable, old oak trees. A few benches were scattered around the choice shade places and promised respite from the cares of the day. Occasionally, a young mother and her young children could be seen on a blanket under one of those shade trees with a picnic spread out around them. People were always welcome to visit their courthouse and grounds, and sometimes, just as many found their way here as they did to the park on the east side of town.

Michael and Berdine drove slowly by Nell's Café, and Berdine strained to see through the glass windows for a glimpse of her friend. It was nearing the lunch hour, so she imagined Nell had her hands full with orders and customers. The little tables outside were beginning to fill up, and it renewed Berdine's sense of security that all remained right in her friend's world. That was important to Berdine: no matter what else happened outside of Mount Holly, she could always come home and find things unchanged. Could she ever leave this town? Could she live in a big city, passing more strangers than acquaintances every day? *Maybe*... she thought, *for a time... not forever though.* She laughed inwardly when she thought about a time in her life when she and Michael vowed they would leave this boring little town to head for the sophistication of the city. Adventure was *anywhere* beyond Mount Holly, South Carolina, and the sooner they got to it, the better. Now, Berdine wasn't so sure. She never could really envision a future that didn't eventually place her back here in this little town, but she was fine with that.

They turned into her neighborhood, and she was roused from her reverie. She glanced at Michael and wondered if it was only her imagination that his expression tightened ever so slightly. He kept his eyes impassive, his face blank, yet there was something... He felt her eyes on him, and he turned, smiling quickly to reassure her.

"Almost there..."

"Yep... Hey, do you want to come in for a bit, say hello?" Berdine asked lightly.

"Well..." Michael hedged. "I really want to get on over to Dad's and spend time with him before he goes in to work tonight."

"Oh, right! I understand. We timed it pretty well, don't you think? He'll have had time to sleep, and then you two can have the whole afternoon and evening." Berdine smiled brightly, not wanting Michael to feel pressured.

"Yeah, I'm looking forward to it." He paused, thinking. "It's a little strange being back here. It's like everything *looks* the same, but it doesn't feel like it is somehow . . ."

Michael ran a hand over the top of his crew cut. It was an unconscious gesture she'd seen for years, his fingers combing through dark strands of hair. But with his military cut, his hand brushing over the top just made him seem agitated. She laid a hand over his, calming him. His smile was grateful.

"You want to meet at the park later tonight? Maybe around nine or so?" he asked.

"I'd love to. I'll probably be ready to get out of the house for a while." She laughed, knowing that being the focus of her parents' attention was best in small doses.

"Where's a good place to meet?"

"How 'bout the swing set?"

"I'll be there." Michael winked, and Berdine smiled in response.

They pulled into her driveway and got out to retrieve her bag from the trunk. Berdine glanced up at the front window. For a moment, she thought she caught the fluttering of the curtain but wasn't sure. She wondered if her mother had heard them drive up. If she had, why did she not come out to greet them? Berdine shook the thought from her head. It wasn't a good idea to go down that path. Michael offered to carry her bag to the door, but she protested, saying it was such a small thing. They stood for a moment looking into each other's eyes, then Michael seemed to make a decision. He wrapped an arm around her, pulling her in closer. Bending down, he took her lips in his own and kissed her with a passion that stole her breath away. He ended the kiss almost as swiftly as he claimed it, and it left Berdine hungry for more. Her expression was almost disappointed, and it made Michael laugh. He tapped a gentle finger on her nose and said, "Don't look at me like that . . . You'll weaken all my good intentions!"

Berdine sighed, trying to urge herself along toward her front door. She picked up her bag and turned, still speechless from the kiss, and headed up her front walk. She looked back once, her hand on the knob, and caught Michael's slow grin. She groaned audibly, hearing Michael's soft laughter as she let herself in.

Berdine spent a quiet afternoon with her mother. After a time, her mother went to the kitchen to begin baking for her bridge party later in the evening. Berdine stretched out on the couch with a book she'd been wanting to read. Pop was still at the office and due home for dinner in a couple of hours. It was nice to slow down the pace some from past weeks. It didn't take long for her eyelids to grow heavy. She could hear her mother humming softly in the kitchen and the lazy rhythm of the fan circulating the air. She gradually drifted into a light sleep, the book open on her chest. As she started to doze, the thought drifted through her mind, *Mama never asked how I got here…*

She must have slept deeply for a couple of hours because she awakened abruptly to the sound of murmured voices in the kitchen. Yawning and stretching, Berdine struggled to emerge through the fog dulling her brain. She could smell food cooking, and her stomach rumbled in response. Her neck felt a little stiff, and she turned it gingerly side to side as she raised herself up off the couch. Padding down the hall in her socks, she stopped just in time to hear the anxious tone of her mother's voice.

"I *know* her car's not out front… that's what I'm trying to tell you. *He* brought her. They came *together!*"

Berdine peered through the doorway and caught the worried expression on her mother's face before she saw Berdine and instantly cleared it. She recovered quickly.

"Look, honey… Sleeping Beauty is finally awake!" She turned her husband's arm so that they both faced their daughter.

A big grin spread over Pop's face. "It sure feels like it's been a lot longer than a week since we saw you last! I don't know what we'll do when school starts in the fall and we don't get to see you as often!" He gave his daughter a quick hug.

Berdine rolled her eyes but returned the hug with affection. "Well, I'll just finish wearing out my welcome this summer so you'll be glad for the longer breaks later on!"

"That could never happen." Mama smiled at her youngest. "Come help me set the table. Dinner's just about ready. Hope you have an appetite. I've got my chicken and dumplings and homemade biscuits in the oven."

"Oh, Mama . . . you're gonna make me fat."

"That's another thing that will never happen." Her mother laughed, pinching her daughter's slender waist.

Over dinner, Berdine told them about the campus and her dorm. Sadly, she admitted to herself that she was studiously avoiding telling them anything that had to do with Michael. It was ironic that just about everything of significance happening to her over the past week was something to do with him. It would have brought her great pleasure to talk about his graduation, lunch with his family, spending time at their house and on base . . . but she just wasn't sure what their reaction would be. Consequently, conversation about the college wound down fairly quickly. For several moments, no one spoke, and the silence grew. Finally, Berdine's father spoke. "Your car running all right?"

"Sure, Pop. No problems."

"Because we noticed you didn't drive here . . ." His voice trailed off, giving her a chance to fill in the gaps. Berdine studied her parents' expectant faces for a moment then sighed wearily.

"I rode with Michael. He wanted to come home and see his father before his leave is up. We decided to save the gas and ride together." She shrugged nonchalantly.

Her father leveled his eyes on her and asked, "And that's the only reason?"

Something about the way he asked the question got under Berdine's skin. It irritated her that, once again, she had just downplayed their relationship to avoid a confrontation with her parents. She was growing very weary of glossing over the truth, omitting references to Michael and steering clear of her feelings for him.

She put both hands on the table and pushed herself back, standing to her feet. When she spoke, her voice was low and calm, but there was steel underneath.

"No, Pop, that wasn't the only reason. In fact, that was the *least* of the reasons. I wanted to *be* with him. I've spent most of this past week with him and his family. They're good people. And if you'd just take the time to get to know Michael better, you'd learn that he's turning out to be a good man. I've been friends with him for nearly a decade now, and if it's up to me, I plan to be more than that."

Berdine saw her mother's eyes widen at that last statement. Her father too was momentarily taken aback. As the seconds ticked by, Berdine almost believed the subject was closed. She should have known better though. Her father cleared his voice, staring up at his flushed daughter.

"Sit down, Berdine. I think we need to come to some kind of understanding." His expression was grim, and Berdine could not tell which way this conversation was headed. She slowly lowered herself back into her chair, willing to listen but knowing her own mind was made up.

"Your mother and I know that you are past the age for us to dictate who you can and can't see. So we're not going to try. But you are *not* too old to listen to advice from someone who loves you and wants the best for you. We haven't approved of this relationship between you and Michael because we don't want to see you get hurt more than you already have been. Berdine, Michael doesn't put down roots. You know that. You saw that yourself two years ago. Have you asked yourself why he might now be attracted to military life? It's a far cry from a cozy little cottage with the white picket fence and hubby home every night for dinner at six o'clock."

Berdine was shaking her head, unable to believe what she was hearing. Finally, she looked up at her parents. "Is *that* what you think I want? A safe, little, routine married life? Like Kathryn has? You think I want to settle down one street over and make pot roast for dinner and have my hair done every Tuesday at the beauty parlor and iron my husband's shirts on Sunday afternoon so his colleagues will be impressed with his 'little woman' at home?"

"Now, Berdie—" her mother began.

Berdine continued, "That is such a far cry from what I want that it's not even in the same orbit! I have *goals,* Pop. Dreams of my own . . . independent of Michael or any other man. I'm not looking for a husband to define who I am or what I want or to 'put down roots' for the sake of making my life safe and predictable! That would suffocate me within two weeks' time. I don't know where this will lead with Michael, and it's not even my biggest concern right now, but I'm asking you both to respect my ability to make life decisions!"

Berdine felt as if she had just run three miles. She was breathless as she tried to fill her lungs with air. Her father's next words nearly sucked the rest of the oxygen from her body.

"Then you are planning to continue seeing Michael?"

Berdine stared at her parents as if they were speaking a foreign language—or else she was! Had they not just heard everything that she had just said? She debated for a fraction of a second whether or not to once again try to paint the bigger picture for her parents, but instinctively knew it wouldn't help. She just sighed, a heaviness settling around her heart. It hurt that her father was narrowing it to a choice. Michael or them.

"Yes, Pop, I am," Berdine said it quietly, almost sadly. She searched her father's expression and, to her relief, found no anger—only regret. "Please ... just trust me," she begged in a whisper.

Her father reached his big hand across the table and covered her hand with his. "We do ... trust *you.*" The emphasis was so subtle as to almost have been missed. But Berdine got the message, loud and clear. They would not turn their backs on her, but neither would they embrace Michael.

The silence was uncomfortable. Fortunately, Berdine was spared the necessity of thinking of something to fill it. After several beats, her mother stood, saying, "Oh! Look at the time! The girls will be here any minute for bridge, and we haven't even set the card table up! Paul, do you mind taking care of that? I need to pull that cobbler out of the oven."

"Sure, hon ... Now you promised to save me a piece, remember? I'll be upstairs in my office after that. Berdine, are you joining your mother for bridge?" Her father looked at her.

"Uh, no ... No, I think I'll take a walk later ... " Berdine's voice trailed off. So they were back to this now.

"Want some company?"

"No, that's okay, Pop. I need to sort some things out."

Berdine pushed back from the table, intending to spend time in her room before meeting Michael at the park. She still had a couple of hours to go, and it already felt oppressive in her house with all the unspoken, unresolved things between them. If Michael suddenly changed his mind and wanted to go back to Charleston tonight, she would not have hesitated to join him. She was just rounding the bottom of the staircase when the front door flew open and in rushed her sister, arms loaded with suitcases and art supplies.

"Surprise, surprise!" She sang breezily. "Did I miss dinner?"

Berdine stood frozen on the staircase, watching her mother excitedly greet her older sister. Their laughter was easy and free of undertones. It caused a little pain to throb in Berdine's heart.

"What a wonderful surprise! Both my girls here! If it wasn't so close to bridge time, I'd just call and cancel the thing!" Her mother fluttered around, taking things out of Kathryn's arms and setting them aside so she could receive a proper hug and kiss. Kathryn obliged with enthusiasm, craning her neck around at the same time.

"So, the little brat's home too?"

Her laughter trilled loudly and grated on Berdine's nerves. When Kathryn spotted Berdine on the staircase, she made a big show of covering her mouth with her hand. "Oops!" She giggled.

Pop came in with the table about that time and planted a big kiss on his eldest daughter's cheek. "Where's our esteemed Dr. Caulfield?"

Kathryn waved her hand dismissively. "Oh, he's off to another medical conference—this time in Virginia. He asked me to go with him, but I'd just end up alone in the hotel room for three days! Besides, I have my first sculpting lesson on Monday! I don't want to miss it."

"Sculpting?" Pop asked, scratching his head. "I thought you were into painting!"

"Oh, Pop, I'm doing that too! That's on Thursdays." Kathryn scooped her suitcase up and headed for the stairs. "Mama, you got a place for one more in your bridge game?"

"Absolutely! I was hoping Berdine would join us as well, but I don't think we can talk her into it." Her mother looked up at her youngest, a questioning look in her eyes.

"I'm sorry, Mama, I don't think I can focus on a card game right now." Berdine smiled wanly, anxious to escape the inquiring looks.

"What a party pooper! By the way, where's your car?" Kathryn asked, unaware of the tension.

Berdine decided to sidestep the issue, continuing up the stairs. "I got a ride ..."

She didn't pause to listen for reactions, just headed on up to her room. She sat on her bed staring across at the opposite wall, feeling as if the room were closing in on her. How could she have lived here nineteen years and feel like such a stranger now? If she closed her eyes tightly and concentrated, she could almost conjure up the image of her and Kathryn chasing each other down the hall, giggles and squeals echoing. But the vision was old and faded, not so clear to her now. The woman down the hall was someone Berdine no longer knew. Her head began to ache, and she knew it'd be a full-blown migraine if she didn't take aspirin now.

Reaching into her bag, her fingers brushed across the letters, still sealed and beginning to fray at the edges. Her breath caught as she slowly lifted them out to look at the faded, blocky print on the front of the envelopes. Michael always said he'd never gotten the hang of writing in cursive. To this day, he only used it when he signed his name. He had that square, upright, heavy-handed print that almost left an impression in the paper. She brushed her fingertips across her name and address now, closing her eyes and imagining the intensity of the hand that pressed those letters into the page.

In her mind's eye, she could almost see his head bent intently over the paper, pen in hand. She could picture the way his dark, unruly hair shadowed the concentrated look on his face. She envisioned the confusion on his face as he folded the letter, stuffing it into the second, or maybe the third envelope. When he wrote the fourth one, did he resolve to himself it would be his last effort? Was it sealed with frustration and mailed with a sense of hopelessness? Tears gathered in the corners of Berdine's eyes and slowly leaked out. She brushed the side of her face with the back of her hand, trying to shake the images from her mind.

She wanted desperately to open the first letter, but for some reason, could not bring herself to do it. Anger began to burn inside her. All of the tumultuous, angry emotions she'd kept locked up for two weeks began to rumble and stir deep in her soul. Just what had Kathryn's plan been? One letter could have been attributed to impulse. But two, three, *four* letters? As far as Berdine was concerned, after one letter, it was simply nothing other than calculated deception! How in the world could she possibly have rationalized her actions? What twisted sense of altruism did Kathryn believe herself to be motivated by? Was it *Michael* they all hated so much… or was it really *her?* The pain tearing through the deepest part of Berdine was so harsh that she needed the cushion of bitterness and anger to buffer it. It was those emotions that propelled her to her feet and urged her down the hall. She stood silently in Kathryn's doorway, framed in shadows. For a moment, the pain was so intense that Berdine could barely breathe.

Kathryn was humming to herself, her back to the doorway, as she hung a few things in her closet. She never noticed Berdine leaning against the doorframe, trying to breathe evenly. She pulled art supplies from a satchel and laid them on her little desk. As if a sudden thought occurred to her, she paused, standing still, and then sunk to her knees in front of the desk. Kathryn pulled out the top drawer, looked in and then shut it.

As she was pulling out the second, Berdine said, "Looking for these?"

Kathryn jumped, inhaling sharply. She turned to Berdine and laughed a little shakily. She was quick with her sarcasm. "Next time, wouldn't it be fun if you tried to sneak up on me?" She noticed the case of brushes Berdine held in her hand. "Oh! Yes! That's exactly what I was looking for! Where did you find them?"

Berdine smiled coldly, her eyes bright with anger. "Why, right there in your desk drawers…"

Something in the tone of her voice alerted Kathryn, and she peered more closely at her younger sister's face. "What … ?"

Berdine slowly lifted her other hand from behind her back. "Recognize these?"

The color drained from her sister's face as she lifted a shaking hand to her mouth. When her sister didn't speak, Berdine continued in that deadly calm voice. "No? I'd think you would since you've had them for… what… two or three years now?"

Kathryn was shaking her head, trying to form words, but the lethal expression on her sister's face robbed her of coherent thought. "I… I… can explain…"

"No, I don't think you can. In fact, don't bother. It would simply be a waste of your time and certainly of mine."

"Berdine… listen to me. I did it for *your* sake. He was… he was… a *hoodlum,* and you were—"

Berdine snapped up straight, jabbing a finger at Kathryn, her voice dripping ice. "Stop right there. Don't *ever* speak to me about him again. In fact, save us both the time and trouble and just… don't… speak… to me… *ever.*"

She pushed herself away from Kathryn's doorway, tossing the brushes in at Kathryn's feet. The burning adrenaline pumping through her veins gave her the momentum to put one foot in front of the other away from her sister's room and into her own. The rush of energy driven by rage was such a force that Berdine could not slow down. She stood for a fraction of a second while she made some snap decisions. Grabbing her suitcase, she began tossing items back into it, slamming it shut. She whirled and stuffed the letters, now moist from sweaty palms, into her shoulder bag. Grabbing both bags, she snapped off the light switch with her elbow and stormed out of her room. She didn't even bother to look into her sister's room as she brushed past. All she could think of us was to get down the stairs and out of this house where she could breathe.

"Oh! Berdine! Come say hello—" Her mother and her friends looked up from their cards. It didn't take a fraction of a second for her mother to take in the pale, drawn face of her daughter, freezing the words in her throat. She half rose from her chair, reaching out to her daughter. In an instant, her widened eyes took in the bags in Berdine's hands and the tortured expression on her face. The only words she could intelligibly form were, "Paul? Paul! I need you… "

Her husband came in from the kitchen, drying his hands in a dishtowel. He took a second to take in the scene, and he started toward his youngest daughter at the moment she grasped the front doorknob. Kathryn appeared at the top of the stairs, tears streaking down her face.

Berdine turned and held up her hand, saying, "I'm going to Nell's. I'll talk to you tomorrow." Before any of them could respond, she was out the front door, slamming it shut behind her.

The night air outside was heavy and oppressive. Humidity was so high that beads of sweat appeared on her arms and forehead almost instantly. As she walked, trying to fill her lungs with air, her body felt sluggish and weighted down by the heat. The moon and stars were hidden by heavy clouds. It was several minutes before it occurred to Berdine that the air was deathly still and hung heavy with a sense of anticipation. Lightning sizzled and crackled high above her in the billowy, dark clouds hanging ponderously above her head. It seemed hours had passed before reason finally returned to her. The adrenaline still pumped steadily, insulating her from any emotion yet feeding her sense of flight. She slowed momentarily to check her watch, noting it was nearing nine o'clock. Turning east, she switched directions, heading for the park. If she hurried, she might make it before Michael and be able to buy herself a few minutes to calm down. She passed by the tall hedges lining the park gates and was startled by the flash of light and low rumbling of thunder that followed. She felt a few raindrops hit her face. She stared upwards to the tall oak trees starting to sway ominously in a macabre dance to the increasing tempo of the wind. Even as she neared the swing set, she already knew the coming storm would intervene in her meeting with Michael. Lightning flashed now in frequent bursts, accompanied by increasing rumbles of thunder. The treetops were bending and whipping wildly, just as Berdine's hair whipped about her face.

With the first outpouring of rain, Berdine stood beside the swing, exposed and vulnerable to the elements. She made a forlorn picture; standing there, suitcases in hand in the middle of a deserted park, while a storm whipped itself into a fury all around her. She could no longer detect her own tears from the rain stinging her face. Slowly, reason crept from its hiding place and returned to her. She gradually became aware of her cramped, whitened knuckles painfully clutching the handle of her suitcase. Rain dripped from her brow, mixing with the salt of her tears and stinging her eyes.

Nell... she thought. It was the only coherent thought to break through her scrambled mind. Slowly, she compelled her body to move. One sodden foot in front of the other, plodding along, remembering the path her conscious mind could not even summon up. It never even occurred to her as she left the park behind and turned down the darkened street to Nell's house what she would do if Nell were not there.

As fortune would have it, a car turned into the gravel drive, killing its lights and pulling under the carport just as Berdine found herself standing on Nell's front porch.

"Berdine! What *in heaven's name* are you doing?" Nell's shocked voice rang out, piercing through the rumble and crash of the storm.

She called out from under her umbrella then realized her words weren't registering. She hurried across the yard, grabbing the frozen form of her friend and pulled her under the shelter of the umbrella. Nell knew misery when she saw it. She didn't bother with questions. She peeled Berdine's stiff fingers off the suitcase, wrapped her strong arm around the younger girl's waist, and urged her toward the covered carport.

"C'mon, girl. Let's get inside. This storm is just getting started. I'll be countin' our blessings if we only get one or two twisters out of *this* one!"

She herded Berdine's numb body under the carport and in through the utility room door. Sticking her head around the corner, she yelled, "Mama? Becky? Someone bring some towels and a blanket!"

Becky and the two younger girls appeared, wide eyed and half scared from the storm but then even more bewildered at the sight of their bedraggled guest. Nell took charge in her calm manner.

"Becky, take Berdine's suitcases and put them in my room. Put some water to boil for tea. Where's Mama? I'll need one of my nightgowns laid out on the extra bed in my room. *Mama?*"

Becky shook her head. "Mama wasn't… feeling well. She took a pill and said she was going to lie down for a bit." The younger girl looked uncertain then turned to peer curiously at the dulled, blank expression in Berdine's eyes. "What's wrong with her?"

"Hush, Becky. Let me think. Go run some hot water in the tub. I need to make a phone call. Could you help me get the younger kids to bed?"

Nell glanced at Berdine, a worried look on her face. Then slowly it registered that she was barking commands at her younger sister without doing her the courtesy of explaining anything. She took a deep breath and tried to reassure Becky.

"Something's upset Berdine terribly. I need your help, Becky. Please forgive me for these demands without a lot of explanation. If you'll be patient, I'll let you know what's going on when *I* know. If Mama is asleep, I'm going to have to count on you to help me. Do you think you could show Berdine to the bathroom so she can take a hot bath? Take her my nightgown and wait outside the door till she's finished. I'm just going to go in the other room and call her parents."

"*No!*" It was the first word they'd heard from Berdine's blanched lips. They turned to study the pale face that slowly began to color with an angry, red flush.

Nell faced her young friend, hands planted in fists at her hips. She studied the angry countenance, stubbornness starting to register in her expression. But Nell was having none of it. "Berdine Williams, I don't care *what's* happened tonight... we'll deal with it. But we won't leave your parents worrying about you all night. I'm calling them and telling them you're here, and that's final."

Berdine stared back at the fierce expression on her friend's face, and her shoulders slumped in defeat. Nell took in the dejected stance, and pity washed over her. Knowing now was not the time to give in to it, she nodded toward Becky. "Now, go on with my sister and soak a little bit in a warm bath. When you get out, come to my room, and I'll have a nice hot cup of tea for you, and we'll talk."

Berdine glanced helplessly from the firm expression on Nell's face to the uncertain one on Becky's. It was the latter one that caused her to reach deep inside herself and regroup.

"It's fine... *I'm* fine. Thank you, Nell. I'll appreciate a hot bath and, if it's not much trouble, a spare bed for the night." She turned almost formally and walked unaided to the bathroom, pulling the door closed behind her. Nell exchanged a puzzled look with her young sister and then galvanized herself into action.

The phone call was brief, and it caused even more confusion for Nell when she was unable to detect anything from the succinct conversation with Berdine's mother.

"Mrs. Williams? This is Nell. I just wanted to let you know Berdine was safe and is staying over at our house."

"Well, of course. Berdine *told* us that's where she would be."

Nell held the phone away from her, staring at it in confusion. Berdine's mother almost sounded offended! What was going on here? She shook her head and spoke carefully. "Right... *umm*... naturally... I was just thinking, because of the storm and all... you might want to know she's safe..." Nell's voice trailed off. She was careful to keep the note of censure from her tone.

"Oh... yes... Thank you for calling." *Click.*

Huh! Nell slowly replaced the receiver into its cradle. *Well, that was strange...*

By the time the tea had steeped and Nell brought two cups into her room, Berdine was bundled up in Nell's nightgown and robe and leaning back against two plumped-up pillows. Her color was better, and she looked a bit chagrined. Nell handed a cup to Berdine and perched on the side of the spare bed, searching her friend's eyes. She waited patiently as Berdine sipped the hot liquid. Outside lightning flashed, and rain pelted the window with no signs of easing.

"Nell, I'm sorry. This was crazy for me to show up here like this ... I ..." Berdine stumbled, not even sure how to begin.

Nell simply shook her head, interrupting. "Don't apologize, Berdine. You don't even have to talk about it tonight if you don't want to. You know you always have a place here."

"No ... I want to. It was Kathryn. I'll *never* forgive her, Nell. We've never been close, but I had no idea she could ever do something like *this* ..." Berdine lifted anguished eyes to Nell, still trying to sort out her thoughts.

"What happened?" Nell asked.

"She *stole* four letters Michael wrote to me back when he suddenly left Mount Holly almost three years ago. I thought he was angry with me for interfering and wanted nothing to do with me anymore or maybe that he'd just outgrown our friendship. Nell, we'd been *best friends* for five years. I couldn't understand how he could change so abruptly. I never got over that! The last two years of high school were miserable for me. And she *knew!* She knew those letters were the answers to all my questions, and she ... she ... hid them from me! And now she has the nerve to tell me she was trying to *protect* me." Berdine laughed bitterly, anger glittering in her eyes.

"I'm so sorry, Berdine. She's hurt you deeply." Nell leaned over, hugging her friend. She had tears in her own eyes as she breathed a silent prayer for healing.

"They never took me seriously because we were so young. They've *never* accepted Michael," Berdine continued, appearing not to have even heard Nell. "They just keep waiting for him to do something horrible, I guess, so they can feel justified. I just don't get it. How can they all be so close minded?" She shook her head in frustration, taking a slow sip of her tea. She paused for a moment, trying to understand something that had never made any sense to her. Berdine looked back at her friend, her voice quivering, and tears shining in her eyes. "He's a *good* man, Nell. I … I … might be falling in love with him."

"Oh, Berdine … " The picture starting to form in Nell's mind was convoluted and rife with misunderstandings and miscommunications. It was difficult for the older girl to hold her tongue and restrain from jumping in with a solution. She knew Berdine needed an empathetic ear right now more than she needed a three-step plan to fix the whole mess. Berdine had finished her tea and had scooted down farther under the covers. Nell could tell the girl was exhausted. She switched off the lamp and picked up Berdine's cup.

"Why don't you see if you can sleep? Things always look different in the morning. We'll talk more then. Sleep in, if you can. When you wake up, come to the café. I need to be there by eight, but we'll have time to talk there."

Berdine responded with a wan smile. "Thanks for listening, Nell." She closed her eyes as Nell quietly left the room.

XXXII

There was an incessant humming (or was it buzzing?) penetrating slowly through the edges of Berdine's consciousness. Without trying to open eyelids that were swollen and heavy, she lifted a hand and waved it aimlessly around her face. If there were mosquitoes, she hoped the sweeping gesture cleared them away. The annoying sound, however, merely seemed to grow in volume. She pulled the sheet up until it nearly covered her head and waved her hand around again. Suddenly, it was silent, and Berdine breathed a deep sigh of relief. She burrowed deeper into the covers, trying to keep morning at bay. In the next instant, she heard muffled giggling. Squinting her eyes cautiously, she could see Teddy sitting cross-legged at the foot of her bed, using her covered legs as a runway for his toy airplanes. He was completely engrossed in play and seemed oblivious to whether Berdine was asleep or awake. The noise she'd heard was the takeoff and landing sounds Teddy supplied as he ran the airplanes from her ankle up to her hip before going airborne. For a moment, Berdine remained motionless, amused at Teddy's ability to make any surface his playground.

Her voice was scratchy when she finally spoke, "Those planes better not make any crash landings!"

Teddy looked up, grinning shyly, as he continued his flight pattern above Berdine's hip. He stretched, leaning on her leg, so he could turn the airplane and bring it back down for a landing, coming to rest on her ankle. He stopped, cutting his eyes toward Berdine, and they both laughed simultaneously.

"Nice landing, Captain." Berdine teased.

Becky stuck her head around the corner just at that moment and rolled her eyes at her little brother. "Teddy! You were supposed to let Berdine sleep! C'mon out of here."

"It's okay, Becky. I was awake." Berdine winked conspiratorially at her little companion. "What time is it?"

"About ten, I think."

"Wow! That late? I need to get moving. Are you guys heading over to the café this morning?"

Becky shook her head. "Nell said she just needed us for the dinner crowd. Saturdays get pretty busy later in the day."

"Well, if it's okay with you, I'll just hop in the shower and head over there in a bit. Any damage from the storm? I didn't hear a thing after I fell asleep. We could be in the Land of Oz for all I know!"

Teddy giggled at that, covering his mouth. "No silly! We're still in Mount Holly. You can see for yourself!"

Berdine gave him a disappointed look. "Oh, *darn!* I thought you might be one of the Munchkins!" She reached over and tickled the tow-headed little youngster.

"Do you want some breakfast? I can get you something while you shower," Becky asked. She was looking more grown up in recent months. Her need to rebel was slowly fading, and Berdine was glad for Nell's sake.

"No thanks, Becky. I'll grab a bite at the café. Is your mother here?"

"No, she went in with Nell to help get ready for lunch."

"Okay, so I guess you're in charge here. I'll just take a minute, and then I'll be out of your hair." Berdine smiled at the younger girl.

By the time Berdine walked into Nell's Café, her stomach was growling in protest. The smells were heavenly, and it made her mouth water. As her eyes adjusted to the indoor lighting, she saw Nell sitting at the back corner table across from a tall, handsome young man. Berdine felt her heart trip over as she made her way back to them. Nell caught her eye and smiled over the marine's shoulder. He turned just as Berdine came to stand beside him. He grinned, reaching his long arm to snake around her waist and pull her playfully to perch on his knee. Leaning over, he kissed her briefly on the lips.

"Wondered if you'd be up before dinner, lazy-Berd," Michael teased.

Berdine laid her head on his shoulder, sighing contentedly. "So you two have been talking, huh?"

Nell smiled, compassion in her eyes. "Michael called our house last night trying to find you. It seems he left a message at your house and no one ever called him back. He then thought you might have decided to come on to my house when the storm got started. You were dead asleep, so I filled him in and told him you'd be here this morning."

"You filled him in? About *everything?*" Berdine had a funny look on her face, and Nell surmised that it might have more to do about her shaky declaration of love than of the breech in her relationship with her sister.

"Well, about your conversation with your sister last night." Nell subtly reassured her.

Berdine turned to look down at Michael, still holding her captive on his lap. His eyes were sad and regretful. They mirrored the look in Nell's. Their expressions caused a momentary feeling of defensiveness to rise up in her. Her chin lifted, and her eyes darkened with some emotion.

"You don't need to look so sad. I told you we weren't close. This just proves why we never had any kind of relationship. It actually makes it easier now to live our separate lives." The other two could see Berdine bristling and pulling a mantle of pride over her hurt.

"Berdine..." Both Michael and Nell spoke at the same time. Nell conceded, gesturing for Michael to continue.

He said, "Berdine, you can't just cut yourself off from your sister.

You need to talk with her about what happened. Yes, she wronged you. Hurtfully. But if you hold onto this, it will eat you up."

"He's right, Berdine. You need to work through it with her."

Michael could feel her stretching away from him, and he loosened his arm so she could stand. She looked at the two people she cared most for, and disappointment clouded her vision. "I'll handle this the way I need to. I don't want to talk to her or see her right now. I'm not saying I never will; I just want you both to respect my need for some distance between us."

Nell reached up a hand to tug Berdine gently down to sit in the chair between them. Though her eyes were still sad, she nodded her head in acquiescence. "Okay, Berdine, we respect that. We're just warning you not to let bitterness fester. It only hurts *you* in the long run."

Michael reached over, massaging her neck. He knew it was better not to push. "Are you hungry?"

Berdine was grateful for the respite from the tense topic. She nodded enthusiastically. "Anybody know what's good here?"

Nell jumped in, also eager to move on to lighter fare. "*Everything!*" The three of them laughed. Nell held up a finger, saying, "I'll surprise you!" and then disappeared into the back.

Michael had both arms folded on the table, and he leaned forward to claim a quick kiss from Berdine. In the private moment, he studied her thoughtfully, taking in the shadows under her eyes and the stiff way she held her shoulders. A curious expression lit up his eyes, and his lips curved upward in a secret smile. Berdine's eyebrows lifted, questioning. Michael whispered softly, so that she had to lean forward to hear.

"What would you do if you found yourself falling in love with your best friend?"

Berdine's eyes widened, her breath catching. "*What?*"

Michael just smiled, not saying anything. Slowly, her lips curved in delighted response as her heartbeat quickened. A warm delicious thrill swirled through her. She leaned even closer to Michael, folding her arms on the table in a mirrored action. "I would definitely tell them."

"You think? You'd tell them? "

"Definitely." She nodded her head determinedly.

Michael was a breath away from her lips. He whispered, "I love you…"

Berdine's own lips curved under his, smiling at the warm pressure. She murmured against his mouth, "I love you too."

Nell came around the corner and saw the couple. She never broke stride as she did a quick about-face right back into the kitchen. Her light chuckle alerted the two as they caught a flash of her yellow shirt disappearing into the back.

"Geez, Berdine! She's walking away with our food!" Michael slapped his palm on the table, making Berdine jump. She laughed.

"Don't worry, I'll get it back." Berdine hopped up from her chair and practically skipped after Nell, eager to have the opportunity to share her news.

What a roller coaster ride this weekend had been so far! As it was, the couple decided to head back to Charleston early. Berdine rationalized that she wanted at least one day to relax before classes started, but they all knew she really just wanted to avoid any chance of having to deal with her family. Nell convinced her to at least call her parents and let them know of her change of plans. She dreaded the call but knew that the sooner she got it over with, the sooner they could get out of Mount Holly. Michael dropped her off at Nell's to get her things together while he went back to his house to say his good-byes and collect his gear. It gave Berdine some time to rehearse what she wanted to say before actually making the call. It was with a damp palm that she finally lifted the receiver and began to dial.

"Hello?" Her mother's voice was crisp.

"Mama? This is Berdine."

Pause. Silence. Breathing.

"Mother?"

"Yes, Berdine. I'm here."

"I guess you know what's happened between Kathryn and me."

"Yes, she told me, and she's a wreck. She wants to talk to you about it."

"There's nothing to say, Mother."

"Berdine, this is ridiculous. That happened years ago. She was trying to look out for her little sister. The least you can do is hear her out!"

More silence. So much silence, it rung in her ears … or was that the pounding of her blood rushing through her veins?

"So you're taking her side."

"Berdine! Of course I'm not 'taking her side.' This is just childish. You were only a child then … and … and … you're still acting like one now!"

"I need to go now, Mama. We're heading back to Charleston. I'll call you and Pop after classes start."

"Berdine? Is that all you have to say?"

"Yes, Mama. Good-bye now."

Berdine gingerly returned the receiver to its cradle. She sat woodenly, staring at the phone as if hoping it would play back a different conversation in her head. Never had she felt more alone. The people she most expected to understand had just turned their backs on her. What did she *really* want? Did she want Kathryn to grovel and beg for her forgiveness? Did she want her parents to tell her she was justified in her behavior? Was she wanting to punish Kathryn so she would suffer as she herself had suffered? It was just too exhausting to pull out all that emotion and examine it. It was much easier to stuff it back behind the closet door of her mind and slam the door shut. Berdine took a deep breath, desperately working to ignore a small inner voice that continued to whisper, "Let it go."

As Berdine would later look back over the next three years, she would define them as some of the richest times in her life but also some of the most bitter. Her relationship with Michael became her lifeline. They spent every free moment together, and they grew closer, under the watchful, caring eyes of Major Hampton and Aunt Molly. Although Berdine continued to talk to her parents on a regular basis and even listened to unwanted updates on her sister and her husband, she turned more to Michael's family for comfort and advice. She followed their guidance in many areas, grateful for the personal interest they took in her. But the one thing she would not allow intrusion from anyone on was the subject of her estrangement from her sister.

Berdine continued to spend weekends with Nell, always making sure she dutifully stopped by her parents' house for a short visit.

Amazingly, she never ran into her sister during any of those times. It was difficult for her to ever stay more than a few hours, however, because the topic inevitably came up about resolving the conflict with Kathryn. It appeared to Berdine that her sister was no more inclined to take the initiative than Berdine was, and it eased the encroaching feelings of guilt that sometimes seeped through the cracks in Berdine's stoic veneer. She had taken to spending her holidays with Michael and his family and finding a day or two to see her parents. As hard as Michael and Nell tried, separately and collectively, they could not persuade Berdine to change her heart.

Michael had talked to Nell on several occasions, hoping she could shed some light on the best way to approach Berdine. They discovered they shared common ground: they both loved Berdine, and they both loved the Lord. But to Michael's continued disappointment, the one person he most wanted to share his faith with was not receptive.

"It's the only thing we don't see eye to eye on, Nell. I'm not sure how to convince her that it's the one thing she needs," Michael would say, frustrated that no ground had been gained spiritually with Berdine.

"That's not your job, Michael. Your job is to love her to the best of your ability and trust the Holy Spirit to draw her to Himself." Nell would cover his hand, squeezing lightly, trying to encourage the young man.

"I just keep praying ... " Michael would trail off, trying to ward away the disappointment.

"Me too. Don't give up. Keep talking to her when opportunities present themselves."

"It's just that her heart is so hardened because of the deep hurt she still harbors." Michael would rub his hand over the top of his head in frustration.

"I know, Michael. Don't lose faith. *He* can reach her." Nell smiled, hope in her eyes.

"*When?* I want to *marry* her, Nell. But I want it to be at the right time. It just doesn't feel right yet." Michael seemed to wrestle with a conflict deep inside himself.

"What do you mean?

"I can't explain it. Every time I think about asking her, something holds me back." Michael looked bewildered staring back at Nell.

"Are you doubting your feelings for her?"

"No, of course not! That's the one thing I am *most* sure of. It's more a sense that the Lord is telling me it's not *His* timing yet." Michael shook his head in confusion. As disconcerting as it was, Michael was grateful for the small measure of relief knowing that Nell and his family understood and sympathized with the spiritual side of his dilemma.

It was encouraging to him that Berdine willingly visited his church with him and his family from time to time. He noticed, though, that she was always very quiet afterwards and a little withdrawn. Michael tried hard not to push. He just made it clear that if she ever wanted to talk about it, he was a willing and eager listener.

Apart from the spiritual element of their relationship, things couldn't have been better. They laughed a lot, shared the daily ups and downs of their lives together, and talked about their future. It seemed that every day they spent in each other's company, they grew even closer to one another. On rare occasions, Berdine allowed herself the luxury of imagining her and Michael going about their daily routines as husband and wife. Sometimes, when they parted for the evening, Michael would kiss her, holding her body against his, and the longing that surged through her was so powerful it made her ache. Yet an unspoken vow was between them, and Michael had appointed himself keeper of that promise.

Even as their relationship grew, the young couple continued to pursue their individual goals. Michael finished his training to be a drill instructor and, along with that, received a promotion to first sergeant. Berdine loved that he always had plenty of stories about the young recruits in each company he trained. Many of the tales were humorous, but most often, they were intense. The one thing that never changed about Berdine as she listened was that her protective nature was always on alert. Often, in the middle of a story about a dressing down Michael had given a marine, the rescuer in her would surface admonishing him not to "hurt their feelings too much." Michael would laugh, trying to ease her concern. He teased her, saying she'd have to "toughen up" if she was going to be a good military wife!

Berdine juggled an increasingly busy schedule as she studied diligently during the semesters and continued to work at Outward Bound in the summers. Now that she was twenty-two and in her senior year, she had joined the ranks of the other counselors, leading groups on expeditions of her own. She always managed to take at least one group through Outward Bound Marine Boot Camp, where she got the rare privilege of watching Michael in action. He was an incredible leader. It came naturally to him. She watched the recruits scramble to do his bidding, hoping to earn a rare word of praise from First Sergeant Caraway. He was frugal with it, so that when a recruit became the beneficiary of a positive word, it was nearly as great an honor as a promotion.

Berdine's passion for working with troubled kids continued to grow the more she learned and was able to work with them in hands-on situations. Her biggest challenge still remained in setting firm boundaries around her emotions. Time and time again she had heard the litany that it was crucial to maintain a healthy balance in her emotional involvement with the kids and their problems because it could potentially skew her objectivity. Finding that invisible line between caring and becoming too involved was sometimes close to impossible. Mr. Davis, the camp director, continued to give Berdine more and more opportunities with some of the toughest cases so that Berdine could learn to find that balance. If it were up to her, she would have found a way to rescue every child who crossed her path. Sometimes, she gave so much of herself that it nearly made her physically ill. Those were the weekends she most needed the calming, steady influence of Michael. He helped her to see things in a balanced perspective.

When she began her last year of college, her parents finally sold the house in Mount Holly and agreed to move down to Charleston. They told Berdine it would be a relief to be near both girls now, but Berdine had a hard time believing it had much to do with her. Her father's health had begun to decline, and it both saddened and relieved her that her parents would be even closer now to Kathryn and Dr. Caulfield. Her mother continued to give Berdine news about her sister, and Berdine had softened enough to ask questions and show interest. Berdine suspected that her mother did the same thing with Kathryn about her. Sometimes she felt a creeping feeling of regret, but then her mother would push, and Berdine's pride would resist. To her way of thinking, she felt she had made a considerable concession by at least showing an interest in what Kathryn was doing. Yet, deep inside, the nagging feeling that it wasn't enough was always there. Her last conversation with her mother had begun to chip away at the wall of stubborn pride.

"Kathryn went to her gynecologist again yesterday. She and Rodney still have not been able to conceive. She said the doctors don't know what the problem is because both of them check out just fine." Her mother paused and her sigh was heavy. "She's so desperate, Berdine. They've been trying for almost five years now to have a baby. She said she feels sometimes like Rodney is just halfheartedly appeasing her in her desire for a child and that he'd be perfectly happy with just the two of them. He's so busy all the time now." Berdine could read between the lines, and she knew that her mother was also concerned for the strain it was putting on their marriage.

"Why don't they just look into adopting? There are so many kids who have *no one* and they grow up feeling unloved and alone and hopeless. In fact, *those* are the same ones who end up with me at camp in the summer! Rodney and Kathryn could give a kid such a great life."

"Well, of course they could. But they want a child *of their own.* She's really struggling, Berdine. It might do her some good to hear some encouragement from you ..." Her mother's voice trailed off.

"I'm sure they don't need any distractions right now—especially if this is such a tense time for them."

It stung when she heard her mother sigh again heavily. She knew that sound was fraught with disappointment, but things had gone too long and too far to repair the great chasm between the two sisters. She changed the subject. "How's Pop feeling?"

Berdine's mother perked up slightly, "He's doing wonderfully on this new heart medicine. There are not nearly so many side effects as the last one. He'll go in for another heart test in two weeks, and we're hoping he'll have made good improvement."

"That's great, Mama. Is he handling the early retirement okay?" She chuckled, then added, "Are *you* handling his early retirement okay?"

Berdine's mother laughed softly. "Well, other than the few days I wanted to run over him with the lawnmower, it's been good. Rodney introduced him to a few of his retired colleagues, and they try to play golf once a week. It's good for him to get out of the house and get the exercise."

"And what about *you,* Mama? What are *you* doing with your time?" Berdine's voice softened, a note of affection touching her mother across the distance.

"Oh, you know… I still have my bridge night with the girls, and I do some reading and crocheting. I try to walk with your father several times a week." Berdine could hear the smile in her voice. "Oh!" she continued, "I almost forgot! I've been taking some sculpting lessons with Kathryn over the last few weeks. I'm not very good, but, Berdine, I think Kathryn has a true gift. She's created some beautiful pieces! Our teacher wants to hold on to two of her pieces to see if she can find a buyer! Isn't that great?"

"Yes, Mama, that's really great. I'm glad you both are doing that together." Berdine couldn't prevent the wistful note from creeping into her voice. There was a pause and the unspoken words were a tangible, weighty presence. But habit had both her mother and her retreating to safer, more comfortable corners.

"Well…" Berdine smiled sadly into the receiver. "I better get some studying done. The semester is barely underway, and I've got two tests, a research paper, and a speech coming up next week."

There was a moment of silence before her mother said, "We're proud of you, Berdine. You have proven your priorities and have done so well over these last few years."

Berdine felt a sudden glow of warmth at the miniscule reference to a conversation long ago when Berdine had promised her parents that Michael would not be a distraction to her academic goals. But the glow faded as quickly as it came when Berdine realized there would be no expansion of the subject.

"Thanks, Mama. It's not over yet, but I think I'm starting to see the light at the end of the tunnel!" She paused and then said in a quieter voice, "Mama? I'd love for you and Pop to come to the campus sometime. We could have lunch or something."

"We'd like that, honey. Of course, you're welcome to come here when you want to get away from the dorm."

"I'll try, Mama. It might be closer to Thanksgiving, though, before I have much more time than a lunch hour. My nights are packed with studying now."

"On the weekends too?"

Berdine felt herself grow warm, and she was glad her mother and she weren't speaking face to face. She hedged, uncomfortably, "I'm spending a lot of time on Parris Island, Mama..."

There was a prickly pause, and then her mother responded quietly, neutrally. "Oh, right... of course." Berdine could not detect any censure in her mother's tone, which was an improvement, however slight. But neither was there any encouragement for Berdine to explain.

"Well, I better go now. Tell Pop hello for me... and... and I'm glad Kathryn's doing so well with her sculpting." It wasn't a direct request for her mother to deliver a message to her sister, but Berdine justified that at least it was a step. It wasn't as if Kathryn was taking any initiative from her end. It was the best Berdine could concede now. The old sting of hurt and betrayal had faded some, but pride and bitterness had a much deeper grip on Berdine's heart.

The call disconnected, and Berdine lay back on her bed, thinking through the conversation. Her mind drifted to the past weekend, when she spent two days at Major Hampton and Aunt Molly's house. Michael had taken his company out in the field for three days, and she hadn't even seen him. Yet the ease she felt with his aunt and uncle had grown so much over the last few years, she still felt right at home. It was odd how during the times she felt most a part of Michael's family were the times that she also felt the loss of hers. She had fooled herself into believing that his family's love and acceptance would fill the gaps in her own relationship with her parents and sister.

This coming weekend, she had been invited back to Parris Island. It was Michael's twenty-third birthday, and Mr. Caraway would also be coming down to celebrate with his son. Aunt Molly encouraged Berdine to invite Nell, saying the poor thing probably needed a short break from the café! Berdine had teased Nell that she just might find herself a marine too. Nell had rolled her eyes at that, firmly informing Berdine that she had neither the time nor the energy to take on any more responsibilities.

"Is that how you see it?" Berdine had questioned her friend, truly puzzled.

Nell paused, not wanting to get into a lengthy discussion on the subject. "Oh, I don't know, Berdine. It's just not for everyone... My life is humming along, full and busy... and right now, well, I just don't see that in the cards for me."

Berdine was disappointed, as one in love typically would be in the face of such a response. Because she herself was so happy, she wanted the same for her friend.

Nell hastened to reassure her. "Don't look at me like that! I'm not saying I'm *avoiding* it; I'm just saying that looking for a relationship is not on my list of priorities right now."

Berdine tilted her head, peering curiously into the eyes of her friend. Admittedly, the concept of being alone was so foreign to *her;* she just couldn't accept that Nell was being truthful to herself. Still, out of respect for the older girl, Berdine let the subject drop.

On Friday, Berdine finished her last test by noon. Feeling buoyant about her performance, Berdine took off for downtown Charleston, in hopes of finding the perfect birthday gift for Michael. It was late September, and the air was still warm. She had changed into a sleeveless, jersey dress that swung freely about her knees as she walked. Her sandals tapped against the pavement, unhurried and steady. Berdine knew she had plenty of time before Nell was to meet her back at the dorm to drive over to Parris Island together. She felt carefree and almost giddy now that the week was behind her. What a grueling five days it had been! She strolled aimlessly down the walk, peering into store windows, smiling casually at the people who passed by. It was an unwinding time—a few precious moments to relax and pretend that deadlines and grades were part of another reality.

A display in a window she passed suddenly caught her eye, and she stopped, transfixed. It was a sculpture of a churning seascape with the focal point a glittering sand castle. Behind the castle, a moonlit ocean swelled and crashed, almost angrily, stretching to reach the edges of the castle walls. There was a whimsical lifelikeness in the lighting and colors cast upon the waves, hurtling forward and smashing onto the deserted beach. She leaned in closer, her forehead almost resting on the windowpane, and she suddenly found it difficult to breathe. A small carved figure stood in the castle balcony. She could only see the figure from behind as it faced the angry waves. It was the shape of a man. His coat and diagonal scarlet sash draping across his back from his shoulder to the opposite hip reminded her of a fairy-tale prince. He even had the raven hair, long and tossed about by the wind. His arms were stretched out in front of him with his fingers gripping the balcony rail. His head was bowed, and Berdine thought how dejected he looked, though she could not see his face.

Her gaze followed his to where the beach touched the water's edge. It was almost completely obscured by deepening night shadows. The huge painting, providing the backdrop for the scene, was incredibly real. Berdine could not tell where the painting ended and the three-dimensional sculpted beach and castle began. As her eyes roved across the scene, her attention was suddenly captured by another small figure just at the edge of an ebbing, foamy wave. She peered closer. It looked like a girl ... *No!* It was a *mermaid!* She was reaching forth a slender arm, fingers delicately outstretched. Her other hand balanced her body upright in the crystallized sand. Berdine could barely make out the tail, curved back behind her and fading into the ebbing waves. Her hair was long, curling wildly over her shoulders and covering the pale, nearly translucent, skin. Berdine stared so long, squinting in concentration, that her eyes began to sting and then water. How *familiar* the features were on the mermaid's face ... *why, it almost looked like* ... Berdine pulled herself up sharply, shaking her head and laughing quietly in self-mockery. She definitely needed a break! Her nose had been in the books way too long. Any longer, and she'd be convinced that the mermaid was *her!* Feeling a little foolish, she started to push away from the storefront and walk on, but the pull was still strong. She knew in that moment that she wanted Michael to have that figurine.

Turning back determinedly to the front door, she pulled open the heavy glass. A tinkling chime triggered by its opening, announced her arrival. Her senses were first beset by the faint aroma of sandalwood. Music played softly, inviting the customer to slow down and breathe deeply. Blown glass figurines in fragile repose lined the shelves of a cherry wood cabinet. Wind chimes of all sizes hung overhead, stirring gently as she passed. Old books and shells were scattered carelessly about on a smooth piece of driftwood. There were shelves that held pots and jars of sea kelp lotion. Candles burned in little globes here and there. It took a bit of winding around displays before Berdine found the glass countertop. There, perched on her stool, sat an elderly woman completely engrossed in a romance novel and oblivious to her presence. She made such a charming picture in this fanciful setting that Berdine almost hated to disturb her. She smiled and cleared her throat. "Excuse me, ma'am?"

As Berdine anticipated, the woman jumped up, startled, and then began apologizing profusely. "*Oh dear!* I am *so* sorry I didn't even *hear* you come in! I just got caught up in the story." She waved the book at Berdine as she continued. "You know, he had just returned from the war after three long years. And all he wanted was to be reunited with her. But as he steps off the bus, he sees her across the street in a little café window with *another man!* And ... and ... she's *kissing* him!"

The little old woman looked so grieved, Berdine wasn't sure how to respond. Fortunately, the woman suddenly gathered her composure and chuckled. "Good gracious! Just ignore me! Now, please ... tell me how I can help you."

Berdine smiled. "I wanted to know if the little clay figurine in the window display was for sale?"

"Which one, dear?"

"The mermaid."

"Ah ... that one! You're not the first to inquire about her today. We just got the two of them—her and the prince—yesterday." The little woman beamed proudly.

"Oh ..." Berdine sighed disappointedly. "So they're a set?"

"Not necessarily. I asked the artist about that—*she's local, by the way!* She felt that if either were sold separately, the story would not be harmed, merely changed. Here ... let me get the figurine for you."

Berdine leaned against the counter, waiting for the woman to return. In a moment, the storekeeper bustled back, the mermaid cradled gently in her palm. Reverently, she handed it to Berdine. With the figure cupped in her hands, Berdine studied it closely. When she looked up at the woman, she was met with a curious smile. "What is it?" Berdine questioned.

The older woman chuckled lightly, shaking her head. "It's fitting you would want her ... She *looks* like you!"

Berdine caught her breath, her own opinion confirmed. She returned the tiny figure to the storekeeper.

"I'll take her. Could you wrap her for me? It's to be a gift." Berdine felt a tiny shiver down her spine and wondered why she was so affected.

"Of course, dear. It will just take a moment. The mermaid is fifty-five dollars—gift-wrapping is free. Won't you have a seat and a cup of tea while you wait?"

Berdine thanked the woman and poured herself a cup of the lemon-scented tea. She sat in the overstuffed chair, barely resisting the urge to kick off her sandals and curl her feet up under her. Within ten minutes, the woman returned, beaming at Berdine as she presented the silver box, adorned with a shimmery cream ribbon tied in a bow. In the center of the bow was a charming little seashell. Berdine thanked the woman, complimenting her on the wrapping. She said good-bye and headed for the front of the store. Just as she pulled the door open, she heard the storekeeper's voice. "Oh! Dear? I nearly forgot! I'm to give out the artist's card to customers who purchase her pieces! Here you go. Enjoy your day." She pressed a business card into Berdine's free hand and held the door for her. Berdine waved and stepped out into the bright sunlight, slipping the card into her purse. Her heart felt light as she walked away from the little shop. If she had considered it for very long, she would have had to admit that the tiny clay figure of a mermaid was probably a strange gift for the man she loved. Oddly, though, she had never felt more right about something.

Nell and Berdine arrived at the Major's and Aunt Molly's house, assailed by the mouthwatering smells of barbecue grilling in the backyard. Aunt Molly had strewn streamers and balloons along the patio, and the tables sported brightly colored paper tablecloths. She greeted the girls with an excited hug, exclaiming, "I just *love* having parties!" They laughed, quickly immersing themselves in the dinner preparations. The major, Michael, and his father took turns tending the grill and sipping lemonade under the shade of the trees.

It was a festive atmosphere and a beautiful evening. Laughter and easy affection abounded as the evening shadows grew. Aunt Molly brought out the largest chocolate cake Berdine had ever seen, candle flames dancing. They sang happy birthday with enthusiasm, entreating Michael to make a wish before blowing out the candles. A big grin crossed his face as he searched out and met Berdine's eyes. With a slow wink, he took a deep breath and blew out all the candles. Next came the presents, and Michael was like a little boy, exclaiming over the gifts. Berdine felt shy when it was her turn to hand Michael his present. She wasn't sure she liked being under the spotlight, but she handed the little gift-wrapped box to him, smiling quietly. Michael captured her outstretched hand and pulled her to sit closely beside him. Knowing she was feeling conspicuous, he leaned over and kissed her lightly on the cheek. He made jokes about the box being just the right size for a ring and wondered if Berdine was proposing. It lightened the moment just enough for Berdine to laugh comfortably, cuffing him on the shoulder. "That's *your* job, buster!"

Slowly, he lifted the little mermaid from the protective tissue, studying it intently. His eyes widened in surprise, and he breathed, "*It's you!*" The others gathered closely, remarking at the likeness and how coincidental it was. Michael's eyes sparkled as he thanked her for the treasure. Her heart warmed at his sincere expressions of pleasure, and she knew she had chosen well. The little mermaid was passed from hand to hand to the accompaniment of exclamations.

Aunt Molly turned the figurine over, murmuring quietly, "I wonder who did this? It's exquisite!"

"Oh!" Berdine started. "I actually have a card of the artist's! Let me look."

She dug in her purse, found the card, and took it over to a light so she could read it. All eyes turned to her expectantly. In an instant, the color drained from her skin. Her lips moved, but no sound emerged. She closed her eyes tightly, and Michael was at her side in an instant. His voice was worried as he asked, "What? What is it?"

Berdine laughed a little shakily, her hand pushing back the hair from her forehead. "I guess it's not really that much of a coincidence, after all." She held up the card with trembling fingers, smiling weakly. "Kat Williams . . . "

"Kathryn? *Your sister?*" Nell asked, amazed.

Berdine merely nodded, listening to the swell of comments and questions. It was a surreal moment for her and she couldn't quite define what she was feeling. Michael leaned closely and asked in a worried voice, "Are you okay with it? Do you want to return it?"

Berdine shook her head firmly, and when she spoke, her words were sure. "Of course I don't want to return it. I want you to have it. Kathryn did a beautiful job. She's very talented!"

Nell and Michael exchanged looks, hope rising in that glance. He smiled down at Berdine, hugging her tightly. "Good! I wasn't going to give her up that easily, you know." They laughed easily together, and the moment of discomfort faded easily away.

The girls helped Aunt Molly clear the tables, returning with coffee and slices of cake. By now, it was getting dark, and the conversation flowed easily. Major Hampton was sharing military news with Michael and his father, and Berdine turned her attention to the women. They chattered quietly about business at Nell's Café and news from Mount Holly. Berdine spoke softly about her last conversation with her mother, reporting on her father's health and the update her mother had given her on Kathryn. The other two women murmured sympathetically, both knowing how much more deeply affected Berdine was than she let on. So engrossed were they in their own conversation that they failed to notice a rising tension in the air. Had Berdine been facing the men, she would have noticed instantly the change in Michael's body language and the tightened expression on the faces of the three men. It was the abrupt cessation of their low voices that caused Berdine to notice the stillness and turn to glance at them. What she saw made her stop in midsentence and study the faces of the men with curiosity.

Michael caught her questioning look, and he rubbed a hand over his face. Berdine felt her heart drop in the same instant. "What? What's going on?"

Michael breathed deeply, taking her trembling hand in his. He could see on her face that she already anticipated what he would say. When he spoke, he looked directly at her, though his words included everyone.

"This is not the time I would have chosen, but since everyone is here, it's probably the *best* time to do it. I've just received orders for Camp Lejeune, where I'll have a brief time of training before deployment to Korea."

The words hung suspended in the air, and no one responded. Berdine sat stiffly, almost unable to comprehend what Michael was saying. She searched his face as if his expression would somehow deny the truth of his announcement. But the truth stared back bleakly from his eyes. She shook her head, bewildered, looking around at the rest of them. Somehow, it seemed to her that shock had not stung the others as it had her. They were asking questions and discussing the news with Major Hampton, as he explained in a somber tone about the conflict stirring in Korea. Berdine felt as though she'd been sucked into a vacuum as Michael steadily held her gaze. Voices and faces faded as she tried to form the word.

"*When?*" It came out hushed and anguished.

Michael spoke calmly, his voice clear and firm. "I'll be headed to Camp Lejeune in four days. As for my deployment from there to Korea, I just don't know yet."

His eyes were regretful, but underneath, Berdine could see determination. She looked helplessly to his father and Major Hampton, but there was a resoluteness about them as well. Even Aunt Molly wore an expression of understanding support.

"But... but... don't you get more advance notice than that? How can anyone pack up and move in such a short time? Oh, Michael... *Korea!*"

Major Hampton looked at Berdine with compassion in his eyes. He knew what she was feeling. He exchanged a quick look with his wife. She too had felt those same things before. His voice was gentle when he spoke. "I know it's hard, Berdine. Michael has been trained to stand ready, and you haven't had the benefit of hearing that on a daily basis. It's barely long enough for your mind to adjust to it, I know. He'll need your support on this assignment more than he's ever needed anything from you before. Sometimes, that even means *willing* yourself to be strong when you don't know where the strength will come from."

Berdine wasn't even aware how tightly she was clenching Michael's hand. Her eyes were bleak as she listened to the major's words. The whole gamut of emotions ran through her in a flash, yet she felt each one with painful clarity. Shock, then anger, guilt, fear, and sadness, and finally... acceptance.

Aunt Molly spoke softly to the pale, rigid girl. "I know exactly what's going through you, dear. And it won't be the last time you feel all those things. It's okay to be afraid... even angry! I've been right where you are, and it wasn't easy. It was a continuous process."

Berdine nodded slowly. She turned tortured eyes to Michael then glanced around the patio. Their faces were shadowed, but she saw her own feelings mirrored in their eyes. Nell had tears in her eyes, and, oddly, it comforted Berdine. Jack Caraway had his head in his hands, and he looked weary to his soul. It suddenly struck her that she was not alone. However much she struggled with her feelings at this moment, there were five other people wrestling within themselves. She felt irrevocably entwined in the loving network of this family, and it bolstered her courage. She nodded gratefully, turning toward Michael. He smiled warmly at the woman he wanted to spend the rest of his life with. He knew what it was costing her to choose to be courageous.

Speaking to the rest of his family, he said, "Berdine and I will need some time to process all of this. I hope to have time with each of you over the next few days, but she's my first concern right now." His voice was quiet, asking humbly for their understanding, and he was met with words of reassurance.

Talk continued, and it was late when it finally registered with Berdine that Nell was dependent on her for a ride back to Charleston. Guiltily, she apologized for not paying attention to the time. Nell simply shook her head, hugging her friend and reassuring her that Mr. Caraway had already offered to drive her to the dorm to get her car and then follow her back to Mount Holly.

They all walked slowly out to the front, where Mr. Caraway's car was parked. Michael walked ahead alongside his father, apart from the others. The young man had looped his long arm around the curving, thin shoulders of the older man. It painted a poignant scene. Tears burned Berdine's eyes, and she struggled to hold them in. She heard Michael say, "I'll be home in two days, Dad. Will you have some time then?"

Mr. Caraway's voice was rough, but Berdine could hear the tenderness underneath. "You bet,. I'll take the day off." He smiled, giving Michael a quick, firm hug.

Nell took her turn, embracing Michael firmly. She whispered, for his ears only. "You go do your job, Michael. I'll take care of Berdine. You know I'll be praying daily for your protection."

Michael nodded, grateful. But his whispered response was low and urgent. "Pray for *her,* Nell. She needs the Lord now more than ever."

It was the early hours of the morning before the four of them headed for their beds. There was so much to discuss. Berdine had many more questions about Michael's deployment than either man could answer. They either didn't know yet themselves, or they were not allowed to divulge. The major tried to fill them in on the heightening tension between North and South Korea. Earlier in the summer, troops from the north crossed the thirty-eighth parallel into South Korea in an effort to overthrow and reunite the Korean peninsula as one government. The North Koreans captured Seoul on June 28 but did not accomplish their goal of a quick surrender and disintegration of the South Korean Army, despite their being outnumbered and outgunned. At the same time, the U.S. and allied forces had serious supply problems in the region, and the infantry divisions were at 40 percent of their strength. The U.S. Marines were being mobilized to aid South Korea in their resistance of the Communist invasion.

Michael didn't know how long he would remain at Camp Lejeune before his deployment, but the implication was that it would only be long enough for some training and a briefing on the situation. It was more than Berdine could take in, especially as exhausted as they all were. Major Hampton finally stood, pulling Molly up with him.

"We all need sleep. It's been a long night, and it's hard to process all this in an objective frame of mind. My advice would be that we all get some rest and then talk things over in the morning." He sounded, in that moment, like an officer with years of authority under his belt. Then, just as suddenly, his voice changed, and he was simply Uncle Robert. "We love both you kids more than we can say. We're here for you now, and we'll still be here for you when you two have to be apart."

His words made Berdine want to dissolve in a puddle of tears around their feet, but she bit her lip and nodded, accepting a warm hug from Aunt Molly. Michael shook hands with his uncle and kissed his aunt good night. When they had left the room, he turned to Berdine, trying to form the right words. But she put two fingers against his lips then tenderly replaced her fingers with a kiss. He inhaled deeply as his arms wrapped her firmly against him. When the kiss ended, they stood together, Berdine's head resting against the solid wall of his chest.

She spoke very softly. "Let's not say anymore tonight. We'll pretend, just for tonight, that things will go on the same."

Michael leaned back, tipping her chin so she could meet his eyes. His heart filled with an indescribable love for this woman. "Things *will* go on the same. We'll just be apart for a while."

Berdine merely nodded, breathing in deeply the scent of him and committing it to memory.

XXXIII

Saturday was detail day. Michael had errands to run and loose ends to tie up on base. Berdine had a special pass allowing her access to nearly every place Michael needed to go. He had most of his gear already packed in a four-foot tall duffel bag that was nearly as tall as Berdine. In her eagerness to help, she was attempting to drag the heavy bag out to the car. She had gotten about fifteen feet out the barracks door, fighting it the whole way, when Michael noticed her and couldn't decide whether to laugh or berate her for attempting to carry it.

"Hey!" He was grinning broadly. "Are you carrying that thing, or is it the other way around?"

She huffed in frustration. "What in the world do you have in here? A load of cement?"

"Just the usual stuff... boots, cammies, helmets, machine guns, grenades ..."

She dropped the bag instantly and backed up a few steps. It made Michael laugh to see her eyes go wide. "I'm *kidding!* Here, let me take it. You can carry these files."

Berdine sighed in relief as she took the papers from him. He tossed the bag over his shoulder, grinning cockily at her. Berdine rolled her eyes and marched to the car, trying to hide her smile. They loaded his stuff in the trunk and settled into their seats, headed for the next errand.

"Now, *tomorrow,* when we go to Mount Holly—," Michael began, but Berdine held up her hand.

"I'm not going with you."

"What? Why not?" Michael was surprised at the stubborn resolve in her voice.

"Because tomorrow is for you and your dad."

"But—"

"No, Michael. I'll have you to myself the following day and a half. I'm going back to Charleston for the day to see if I can call a couple of my professors to explain why I won't be in class on Monday or Tuesday."

"Will that be a problem for you?"

"That's not even a part of my consideration. I'm only calling as a courtesy, not for permission," Berdine said.

Michael shook his head, smiling. He reached for her hand and held it tightly as he drove. After a pause, he glanced at her, a serious look on his face. "Do you think you could be at my aunt and uncle's house when I get back tomorrow evening?"

"I'll be waiting at the window."

A smile of pleasure lit up his face, and Berdine thought, if it were even possible, that she just fell a little more deeply in love with him.

They parted the next morning, eager to take care of business at hand. Aunt Molly reminded Berdine that she was welcome to come back as early as she could get away. It was a quiet drive back to her dorm. So many thoughts tumbled through her mind. It was quite an effort to keep her worries in check. *How in the world did wives of military men manage to function under the stress of not knowing—daily—whether their husbands were safe or not? That kind of peace had to come from a higher source!*

Berdine shivered, a frown furrowing her brow. *Now where did that last thought come from?* She didn't have time to explore the question before she arrived at her dorm.

She spent the rest of the day talking with her professors and sharing her news with some of her friends in the dorm. Ms. Browning was especially eager to hear the details about Berdine's "young man."

"We'll send a care package! I'll put a box outside the office and send around a notice that anyone can contribute. It will be our way of supporting the troops. You'll have to find out for us where it can be shipped!"

Her enthusiasm was contagious, and it helped to ease some of the reality of his leaving in two days. Berdine hugged the older woman and thanked her, assuring her that Michael would be grateful for the surprise.

It was also comforting to talk about it with the girls she'd come to know on her hall. The dorm was quieter on the weekends, and most of the girls who went home didn't get back until Sunday night. Berdine sat on her bed in the company of three of her closest college friends, trying to process how her life would be different in the coming days. The girls meant well, but they couldn't seem to grasp the depth of fear Berdine struggled to keep from consuming her. To them, the whole idea of "her marine" headed off to war was romantic and heroic. Berdine understood how it looked through their eyes and knew she'd probably feel the same were it happening to another. She tried not to watch the clock, but she just couldn't help it. When the girls wandered out of her room, it was even worse. Each hour brought a new question to her imagination about how it was going for Michael in Mount Holly. *Did Michael and his father talk about the years they'd been apart? Was Michael trying to keep his words positive and reassuring, just as he did lately with her? Did they talk about the future—when Michael would return?*

Finally, she just couldn't stand it any longer. She threw some clothes in an overnight bag and headed for the door. She flipped off the light switch and closed her door behind her. As she hefted her bag to her shoulder, the hallway phone caught her attention. She hesitated. Now, why was the common sight of a dormitory telephone compelling her to pause? She wanted desperately to be on her way to Parris Island!

Be fair, Berdine. They care about you. Regardless of past circumstances, if you are hurting, they would want to know.

She shifted the bag to her other hip, irritated ... impatient ... trying to shut out the voice inside her head. She argued with herself, wanting to continue down the hall.

"Go on!" she told herself. "Why would they even care?"

They love you, Berdine. They've always loved you. Your feelings matter to them ...

"Oh, yeah?" The bitterness rushed in with such force that she almost buckled in surprise. "If my feelings mattered even a fraction to them, they would have respected those feelings years ago."

Even parents get it wrong sometimes, Berdine. You never really let them see your heart. You always built a defensive wall, shutting them out with your anger.

"What was I *supposed* to feel? They judged him from the beginning!"

You were the bridge. You were always the bridge ...

Berdine frowned. Now what was *that* supposed to mean? And why was she standing in the hallway, arguing with herself as if she had a split personality? She looked back at the phone and sighed heavily. Irritated, she stomped over to the phone, lifting the receiver to her ear. She dialed the numbers with unfamiliar forcefulness. Tapping her foot, she listened to the ringing on the other end.

"Hello?"

Berdine straightened, swallowing hard at the unexpected rush of emotion. "Pop?" Her voice quavered, and she cleared her throat. "It's Berdine."

"Well, I surely know the sound of my little girl's voice without her having to tell me!" There was a smile in his voice, and Berdine shut her eyes tightly.

"Pop, I ... I miss you." Berdine wasn't even sure where that came from. It was nowhere on the imaginary script she'd intended to use.

"I miss you too, honey. When are you coming to see me?" Berdine almost laughed at the possessiveness of the question—not even a reference to seeing her mother or sister.

"Soon, Pop. Are you feeling okay? How's the ticker?" Berdine smiled into the phone.

Memories she hadn't thought of in years suddenly washed over her: sitting with her father on the back porch, watching for falling stars; the rhythmic cadence of her father's deep voice as he taught her a poetic method for memorizing her multiplication tables; listening to that same calm, patient voice beside her on the passenger side of her first car as she stalled it for the fourth time. She might have laughed aloud if the lump in her throat hadn't been there.

"Still tickin'! What's new with you?" His tone was cheerful and pleased that she'd taken the time to call. And then he heard the lengthening silence. "Irony-girl, you all right?"

He hadn't called her that in years. A sob escaped her before she could pull it back through the line.

"Berdine?"

"He's going to Korea, Pop. He'll be right in the middle of it. I don't know how long he'll be gone or even what he'll be doing. *I'm scared.*"

Even through her tears, she heard him take a deep breath. She almost braced herself for the disappointment that was sure to come.

"Berdine, I doubt Michael has changed too much from that precocious, ten-year-old boy we knew years ago. My guess is that he probably had to learn how to take care of himself back then so he would be equipped for a greater challenge some day." Her father paused, and Berdine could not have stopped her silent tears streaming down her cheeks if her life had depended on it. "Looks like that day has come. You're gonna have to summon up that lion's heart now, girl, and put that unwavering belief in him into action."

She smiled through her tears. She wanted to laugh. *No,* she wanted to *dance!* His words had cut loose some invisible binding on her heart, and in her mind, she soared.

He understood! Maybe it wasn't his choice for her, but he understood!

They talked for a few more minutes. He asked questions, and Berdine gave him as much information as she herself knew. She told him Michael was leaving on Tuesday morning from Parris Island, and she would be staying with his aunt and uncle until then. He promised to share the news with her mother and sister and asked Berdine to call him again after Michael left. She hung up the phone, amazed at the complete irony of her emotions. In perfect parallel with her fear and sadness was a sense of absolute elation and freedom. She tried to reason it out and realized it was a pointless effort. She shrugged, casting off heavy thoughts. Just as she started down the hall, she heard the words running through her mind…

You see? It's just as I said. Now… about your sister…

Berdine clamped her hands over her ears. "Enough!" she spoke audibly to the darkened room as she closed the door firmly behind her.

XXXIV

Berdine felt a sense of urgency as she drove the familiar route from Charleston to Parris Island. She'd made the trip so often over the last three and a half years, she could almost drive it blindfolded. Time had gotten away from her, and she hoped she could still fulfill her promise to Michael to be waiting for him when he returned from Mount Holly. She drove into the setting sun, and the beauty of it filled her with a longing to walk along the beach. It reminded her of a time several years back when she experienced her first kiss with Michael. But just as the thought began to wax romantic, she was brought up short with an even earlier memory loudly protesting *its* place as "the first kiss"! With perfect clarity, she remembered the embarrassing awkwardness of two adolescents startled by unfamiliar, heated reactions. Berdine laughed softly at the tender memory of an ill-timed, poorly delivered kiss, and ... *still* ... it made her sigh.

She pulled into the Hampton's driveway a little before dinnertime. She was relieved that Michael's car was not there. There would still be time to freshen up before he arrived. Aunt Molly greeted her at the door, and Berdine fell into the easy, familiar routine of getting dinner on the table. As they worked, Berdine shared with the older woman the conversation she'd had with her father. Molly knew how badly Berdine needed her parents' support. Berdine had just reached up to the top shelf to retrieve a gravy bowl for Molly when she felt her waist encircled tightly and a smacking kiss right on the side of her neck.

"Oh! Michael! I nearly dropped your aunt's dish!" She turned in his arms, the gravy bowl still in one hand, and wrapped her arms around his neck.

"Serves you right! You were supposed to be waiting eagerly at the front window." She rolled her eyes, reaching up to kiss him lightly on the lips.

"Hmmm. Waiting at the window—or—getting your dinner on the table? What a difficult choice for you!"

"Yeah ... it's hard being me." Michael shook his head in mock seriousness.

A moment later, Major Hampton came in. He was in full uniform, and Michael immediately straightened and saluted. The major returned the salute and leaned down to kiss his wife. Berdine was curious. "You were working today? On Sunday?"

The major nodded, a grim look on his face. "Things are heating up a bit here. It looks like I may be spending a few weeks at Camp Lejeune as well, training some of the officers there."

Berdine looked startled. "You won't be going over to Korea as well, will you?"

"Not this time." He almost appeared disappointed.

"Will Molly go with you to North Carolina?"

"Oh no, dear," Molly answered herself. "I'll stay here and hold down the fort. I'm used to him being gone occasionally for different things."

The evening was relaxed and their conversation light and easy. Berdine was aware, however, of an invisible clock in her head, now ticking down the minutes of her time left with Michael. She wondered if he felt it too. Molly asked what they had planned for their day tomorrow.

"I hadn't actually had a chance to ask Berdine about it." He turned to her. "Would you like to spend the day at the Isle of the

Palms? Maybe a picnic on the beach, swim a bit, take in the last of this September warmth? We could have dinner at the Lighthouse Inn later on … ”

Berdine smiled, nodding her head. It would be the perfect setting. She made a silent promise to herself to enjoy the moments, not looking ahead. She somehow knew Michael would need her to say good-bye with a smile on her face.

Molly insisted she would pack their picnic basket, despite Berdine's protests that they'd take care of it. "No, let me do this. I want you to have a special treat from me."

Michael laughed, bending down to whisper loudly in Berdine's ear. "The general usually gets what the general wants."

"Amen!" The major mumbled behind his napkin, and Molly punched him lightly on the shoulder.

When Michael kissed Berdine at her bedroom door that night, she held on to him fiercely. "I wish we didn't have to be apart. I wish we could just walk into this room together!" Her whispers were impassioned and fervent.

Michael groaned. He lowered his forehead to rest on top of her hair. For a moment, he didn't speak. Berdine felt a twinge of guilt, but she still wasn't sorry she'd told the truth.

"You know I feel the same, Berdine. And it's even more difficult, knowing I'll be away from you for who knows how long … ” Michael's expression was pained. "But … ”

Berdine interrupted him. "I know, I know … ” She stood on tiptoe and kissed him lightly. "I'll see you in the morning, Michael. Tomorrow will be special."

He grimaced, feeling he'd handled the situation badly, but she merely smiled as she slipped through the door and closed it behind her. He stood leaning against the wall outside her room, a multitude of emotions running through him. He finally started down the hall, smiling wryly to himself. His frustrated whispers echoed in the air. "Now tell me again … exactly *why* we have to do this *Your* way?"

XXXV

Michael wasn't sure what awakened him so suddenly. He could tell by the still-darkened shade it was not even daybreak. He started to lay back and pull the covers over his head, but somehow he was compelled to sit up and reach for his Bible. He switched on the bedside lamp and checked the time. Five o'clock. The house was silent. Slowly, he rose up from the bed, stretching the stiffness out of his shoulders. He pulled on a pair of shorts, grabbed a T-shirt and his Bible, and padded down the hall quietly. He paused beside Berdine's door and, hearing nothing, continued into the kitchen. A night light glowed beside the coffee pot. He plugged in the cord, knowing Aunt Molly had it ready to percolate. He leaned against the counter, waiting for the rich aroma to fill the room. When gurgling bubbles began to slow, Michael poured his coffee and took it outside to the back porch. It was a cool morning. He knew it wouldn't be too long till fall arrived. They'd had a long summer, and the afternoons were still warm. He always looked forward to the first cool front. *Of course*... he thought, belatedly.... *I'll probably miss it this year. Not many cool fronts blowing through South Korea!*

He stretched his long legs out in front of him, leaning back in the cushioned chair. He sipped his coffee and stared out at the backyard. His eyes came to rest on the back fence, and he was filled with nostalgia. In his mind's eye, he saw a dirty, sweaty boy, thrusting his shovel into the dirt and turning it into a pile beside the hole. Beside him stood a man, talking calmly to him, pouring out his approval like a balm over the boy's wounded spirit. The vision faded, and Michael smiled, breathing a prayer of thanks for the love and firm guidance he'd found in this home. He knew it would help carry him through—*whatever* he was to face in the coming days. He set his cup on the table beside him and slowly ran his hand over the worn leather cover of his Bible. The major had given it to him the same week he'd arrived.

"This is your manual for life, son. Learn it well." Though the words were echoes from the past, they were still planted firmly in his mind.

Michael knew his aunt and uncle were aware that he'd barely touched it that year, but neither of them said a word. They just continued to quietly model a lifestyle and relationship with the Lord that he eventually came to want for himself. And it *did* become his manual. He learned it as well as he learned the marines' Code of Conduct, and he tried to live by both.

Shades of pink began to crest on the horizon, a prelude to the beginning of the day. The colors of morning never failed to amaze him. He closed his eyes, recording the images in his mind, storing them up for dark days ahead.

Michael…

A whisper floated through his mind. Michael sat up and looked around toward the back door. He frowned, sure that he'd heard his name clearly spoken. He sat in expectant silence… waiting.

Michael…

"I'm here."

I have a promise for you.

"A promise?"

Your steps I *have established. And I delight in your way! When you fall… you will not be hurled headlong, because I AM the One who holds your hand.*

Michael sat stunned. He was fairly certain it was a scripture out of the Psalms. Had the Lord really whispered into his thoughts? His first inclination was to believe his mind was playing tricks on him. He rubbed a hand over his face, breathing deeply. He began to turn the pages slowly through the Psalms, running his finger down the words. He stopped, his finger poised on the thirty-seventh Psalm. There it was. Why did those words burn in his mind? What could it mean? Michael shook his head in confusion.

"Okay, Lord. I don't really know what this means for me. But I'll hang on to it."

In that moment, a sense of peace flowed through him, and his heart was encouraged. He didn't know what the next few weeks held in store for him, but he knew he wouldn't walk through them alone.

He heard the door creak open behind him, and he turned to see a sleep-tousled Berdine ease through the door. She had a cup in her hand. He smiled at her baggy, flannel pajama bottoms and over-sized T-shirt. Her curls were gently tangled, and two perfect ringlets flopped over one eye. He chuckled at the cuddly picture she made.

Berdine raised her eyebrows at him. "What's funny?"

"Not funny… *delightful!*" His smile was tender, and it made her want to climb up on his lap and bury her head under his chin. She sighed to herself, hoping she'd never get over the fluttery feeling in her stomach. She sat in the chair next to him, tucking her feet up under her. She noticed his open Bible on the table but said nothing. They sat companionably, drinking their coffee and talking quietly about their plans for the day. Michael told her he wanted to have everything ready before they headed out to the Isle of the Palms so they wouldn't have to leave early.

"What time do you leave tomorrow?" She tried to keep her tone light and upbeat.

"We have to be on the bus at nine in the morning. It will take us to the airport, and then we'll fly out to Camp Lejeune."

"And they won't tell you when you leave for Korea?" It was still hard for Berdine to understand the lack of information given to the men.

"There won't be much notice; I know *that.*" Michael smiled. He could see the little frown between her brows, and he wanted to smooth it away with his finger. Instead, he settled for a change of topic.

"Will it be all right with you if we leave here this morning around ten? I have a couple of phone calls I need to make, and there are some forms to sign on base. Then we can make our escape to the beach."

"That's fine. I brought my books, so I can get started on a paper I need to write. You go ahead. I'll be ready to go when you get back." Berdine shoved the persistent curls back from her face and yawned. She set her cup down and stretched her arms over her head.

"All right then, I'll be as quick as I can." He planted a quick kiss on her head and stood up with his Bible and cup. She followed him with her eyes until he was inside, and then she turned back to watch the sunrise.

Nine o'clock tomorrow morning! How can we hold on to this day and make it last a lifetime?

She'd make one phone call before they started their day. She wasn't sure if it would mean anything to her family, but she'd promised her father she'd keep him posted about the details of Michael's departure.

XXXVI

When they hoisted the picnic basket that Aunt Molly had prepared for them, they realized it wasn't just a light wicker basket designed to carry food. It was *romance in a basket!* They both snuck a peak after she had seen them off and closed the door. Berdine drew in a surprised breath. A green linen tablecloth with matching napkins lined the side. There were two crystal champagne glasses tucked between the napkins. A small bottle of champagne, fruit, crackers, and a wedge of cheese were artfully arranged inside the basket. Aunt Molly had even tucked in a container packed with ice to keep the smoked salmon and chocolate-dipped strawberries cold.

Berdine laughed delightedly. "This is amazing! Wonder how all this will taste seasoned with sand?"

It could not have been a more perfect day. After eating, they lay back on the linen cloth, sleepy and lulled by the rhythmic ocean waves. They dozed with the sun on their faces and a gentle breeze whistling through the tall reeds on the dunes.

In the late afternoon, they changed into their swimsuits and frolicked like children in the ocean. When they were exhausted, they sat in the wet sand, discussing the design and construction of a sand castle. Without commenting, both of them experienced a hint of nostalgia.

"I may be the muscles of this project, Berdie… but you're *the brains."*

"What muscles?" Childish laughter was followed quickly by splashes of cold, pure creek water…

Shaking her head in remembered amusement, Berdine tried to describe the beautifully sculpted castle scene she'd seen in Charleston where she had purchased the mermaid figurine. Michael grunted in frustration when he couldn't get the balcony of their sand castle to stay aloft. Berdine just laughed, giving up and stretching out on her side. She watched Michael's face as he worked, memorizing even the finest details. The day was passing so quickly, and it felt like time was slipping through their fingers as easily as the sand.

They cleaned up at the pavilion and changed into clothes for dinner at the Lighthouse Inn. Berdine found it harder and harder to maintain a lighthearted demeanor. Even Michael noticed that she had grown quiet through dinner. He reached across the table for her hand and smiled at her across the candlelight.

"It's okay for us to be sad—it's honest. Besides, it takes too much energy to pretend otherwise!"

Berdine nodded. She felt relieved to get it out in the open. "How will I know if you're safe? Will I hear from you after you go over? Will they tell you *then* how long it will be?" Her eyes were bleak as she looked at him.

"I'll try to write you every chance I get. I don't think anyone higher up even knows how long we'll be there. Long enough to do our jobs, I guess."

Berdine looked down at the table, and Michael could tell she found no comfort in his answers. He tried again, "Berdine, listen to me. We both just have to finish out one day at a time. You'll be here, going to class every day, doing what you have to do… and then, you'll go to bed at night and do it all over again the next day. It's the only way to get through this time of being apart. One foot in front of the other…"

Berdine tried to smile, summoning the resources to accept what she didn't like. Maybe the hardest part was the first step.

They finished their dinner and found that the timing was perfect for a sunset walk on the beach.

"It's so beautiful here, Michael. It's a special place to me now. I'll come here while you're gone and when I'm missing you so terribly." Berdine looped her hand through the crook of his arm as they walked slowly along the water's edge.

Michael smiled down at her and said, "And when I'm missing you, I'll picture you here, like this."

He stopped and turned to face her, brushing the gold tendrils from her face. He stared deeply into misty gray eyes, wishing he could store every detail of this woman away in his mind. The beginnings of a smile lifted the corners of his mouth.

"I've noticed something about our relationship, Berdine." Michael shook his head in teasing consternation. "We seem to have a lot of timing issues."

Berdine smiled in response. "I've noticed that…"

Michael paused, running a finger from her temple to her chin, tilting her face to his. "I love you, you know."

"Yes. I know."

Michael sighed, bending down to kiss her lightly. Oh, how he would miss her touch, the softness of her skin, the way her eyes turned smoky when he held her. Michael had never dreamed his childhood pal would become the passionate woman he loved. It made him laugh out loud. He wrapped his arms tightly around her waist and lifted her, spinning her once.

"Michael! She laughed shortly, "Stop! If you drop me in this water, that will be two black marks against you."

Still holding her so that her toes dangled, he chuckled. "Are you still holding a grudge from that little accidental spill into the creek when we were ten? If I remember correctly, I was the one with the wounded ego!"

He slowly let her body slide down his until her feet met the sand. She grasped his upper arms and squeezed lightly. "And who could have guessed those scrawny, little arms would fill out so nicely…" She giggled mischievously. Michael laughed aloud. He took her hand as they began to walk again.

Suddenly he stopped. He looked down at the sand as a receding wave tugged at his feet. Tumbling after the retreating foam was a perfect little sand dollar.

"Oh, Michael . . . Look!" Berdine saw it nearly the same time. Michael stooped down and gently picked up the fragile disc, cupping it in the palm of his hand.

"It's special to find one unbroken and with such clear markings!" He held it up so Berdine could see it. "There's a legend about this little sea urchin. It goes that Jesus left the sand dollar here to tell His story. See the five holes here? Those represent the five wounds of Christ when he died on the cross. This marking here in the middle is the Easter lily, and at the lily's heart, is the star of Bethlehem on this side. Turn it over and a Christmas poinsettia is etched on this side, both reminders of His birth. According to the legend, if you break the center of the sand dollar, five white doves will be released to spread God's peace. There really are five, tiny white bones inside that look like doves."

"I wish I could see them . . . but don't break it. It's beautiful—whole and perfect like that."

Michael handed it to her. "Here, you keep it, Berdine. I know it's just a story, but maybe in the coming days it will remind you of God's peace when you're anxious. It'll remind you of today and . . . us." She smiled sadly, taking the perfect shell from him and slipping it gently into the pocket of her dress.

The evening ended too soon for both of them. Berdine knew sleep would be elusive, not only for her, but for all of them at the Hamptons' house. They had returned home, tired but happy from their day. They spent time talking with Michael's aunt and uncle and planning for Michael's departure in the morning.

"We'll tell Michael good-bye here, when he leaves the house tomorrow," Aunt Molly said. "You go with him to see him off at the bus."

"Are you sure you don't want to go too?" Berdine didn't want to steal time away from his family.

"It's fine. Something tells me it's *your* face he'll want to see last before he boards that bus." Molly smiled, her heart generous enough to share the only son she would ever have.

The major talked with Michael about Camp Lejeune. He himself would not be too far behind the younger man. Hopefully, they would have a little time together there before Michael was deployed. The thought comforted Berdine.

Though she wanted so badly to stay up late with Michael, she couldn't hide the yawns coming more frequently or the insistent downward tug of her eyelids.

"C'mon, sleepyhead. I wore you out today, and if I don't want you sleeping through my send-off tomorrow, we better call it a night."

Berdine made a sound of protest, but she knew her body would not be denied. A good night's sleep would fortify her emotions for tomorrow, and she wanted to be at her best. She said good night and headed for her room. She'd had a feeling Michael might stay up a little later talking with his aunt and uncle, and she was glad they had some time alone with him. She lay awake in her bed, comforted by the muffled timbre of his voice. She'd heard him say he wanted to call and talk with his dad once more before he left, and she wondered if he'd do that tonight. As attentive and sensitive as he'd been to her in the past few days, there was a part of him that seemed restless. She had talked to Molly about it, wondering if she should be concerned. Molly had hastened to explain the little she understood about a marine on the eve of an assignment.

"They're so well-trained to do their jobs, Berdine, that when the call comes—it's the waiting that makes them antsy. Now that Michael has his orders, his training is kicking in, and he's eager and ready to carry them out. It doesn't mean he's not regretful about leaving you behind or that he won't miss you, but his focus and energy are turning, and rightfully so. The success of his mission largely depends on his ability to make that transition completely."

It made more sense to Berdine now as she had watched it happen on the way home from Isle of the Palms. He'd seemed slightly distracted and a little more tense. It was subtle but enough for her to notice the change.

As she lay quietly in her bed, waiting for mind and body to ease into sleep, she thought about their future. If they married someday, could she grow accustomed to the life of a military wife? Could she kiss her husband good-bye, time and again, juggling a toddler in one arm and a baby in the stroller? Could she take care of all of the responsibilities of managing their home, patiently accepting the upheaval his leaving would surely bring? Those weren't easy questions to answer, and Berdine was not so naïve as to take them lightly. As her mind grew foggy with sleep, she welcomed the heaviness in her limbs. It occurred to her in that brief moment before slipping below consciousness that she really had no choice anyway. Her love for Michael had already answered those questions.

XXXVII

She was the one this morning to lie awake long before it was light. She had slept deeply and restfully, so she wasn't sure why she felt suddenly alert. The house was still quiet, although she imagined it would be difficult for Michael to remain asleep much longer. Surely the adrenaline was starting to build in him as he anticipated this day. She debated trying to find her way back to oblivion because it was so much easier than wrestling with her thoughts. She finally kicked her legs over the side of the bed in frustration, tossing the covers out of her way. She felt her way down the darkened hall to the bathroom, where she splashed her face with cold water and brushed her teeth. She pulled the feisty curls back into a high ponytail and then made her way into the kitchen. She realized she'd forgotten to check the time, and for all she knew, it could very well be two o'clock in the morning! It made her chuckle softly. She started a pot of coffee and then squinted up at the clock above the refrigerator. Well, it *looked* like five thirty. That wouldn't be so bad. She would have a few quiet moments to prepare herself emotionally for the day ahead.

As she waited for the coffee to perk, she looked out the back window. It was still dark, though she could see the outlines of the trees. She let her mind drift as she leaned against the kitchen sink before reaching into the cabinet for a mug and filled it to the rim. She took her first sip and felt the warmth slowly spread through the foggy places in her mind. She wandered slowly back into the living room and sank into the deep cushions of the couch. She assumed her favorite position, with her feet tucked under her. For a moment, she closed her eyes, enjoying the stillness. She took another sip, and her eyes rested on Michael's worn Bible, lying open on the coffee table in front of her. She stared at it, aware of a subtle yet insistent urging inside.

Pick it up.

Berdine frowned. *Now where did that thought come from?* Michael didn't talk a lot about his faith, and it occurred to her that it was probably because she'd never been open to hearing about it, but she knew it was an integral part of Michael's life. How could she continue to ignore something that important to him? Why did she always steer away from those conversations, first with Nell and later with Michael? She realized she'd never taken the time to answer that question. Was it pride? Perhaps she felt she managed life fairly well on her own and didn't really need that "crutch." Yet life was about to get very uncertain. Was she really as strong and resilient as she thought? Or maybe it was simply apathy? Faith in something higher—or "*the Lord*," as Michael named it—was never something she'd given much energy to understanding. But didn't she care enough about Michael to explore why he'd committed his life to it? Suddenly, the answer pierced her very being, as clearly and sharply as if it had been a physical arrow.

The answer is fear. What will it cost you, Berdine? What if it costs everything?

Honest introspection at last. The admission brought relief, much to her surprise. To name it didn't necessarily increase it. She thought about the two people in her life who had embraced a life of faith. And it *did* cost. Or at least, it surely didn't guarantee a life of ease. There was Nell, strong and steadfast, making a life for her mother and siblings and running the café. But that was not Nell's *dream.* She had wanted to go to college. Berdine had asked her about it one time. Did Nell no longer yearn for that opportunity? But the older girl laughed. "Of course I still want to go to school. But that's not going to happen right now. And whether it ever does or doesn't, I'll still serve the Lord." She'd meant it. Somehow, achieving her dream had nothing to do with her commitment to her God. Berdine thought of Michael's childhood and how difficult it was. Now he was about to engage in a conflict halfway around the world, removed from a life they were starting to build with each other. It didn't make sense to her. Wouldn't the God they served want to protect and reward those who were committed to Him?

Even as she struggled with questions she seemed to have no answers for, there was a growing awareness of a deep emptiness inside of her. She'd never really noticed it before, but in the quiet early hours of the morning, she felt it and named it. *Discontent* gnawed at her heart. Maybe what Michael and Nell had was the answer to the restlessness in her soul. Peace. Would *He* give her peace?

Slowly, she leaned over and set her cup down. She scooped up the gently scarred, leather-covered book and switched on the lowest setting of the lamp beside her, looking down at the open pages. There were some verses highlighted in yellow with Michael's familiar scrawl in the margins. Her eyes were drawn to the verses.

> 12 For there is no difference between Jew and Gentile—the same Lord is Lord of all and richly blesses all who call on him,
>
> 13 for, "Everyone who calls on the name of the Lord will be saved."
>
> 14 How, then, can they call on the one they have not believed in? And how can they believe in the one of whom they have not heard? And how can they hear without someone preaching to them?

She read the words twice, and her heartbeat began to quicken. Turning the Bible slightly sideways, she could barely make out Michael's writing. His words read, *Please, Lord, help Berdine believe . . .*

Tears filled her eyes. She could hear the urgency in those five simple words written by Michael's hand. She sat for a moment, breathing deeply and willing herself to think calmly. Could she *believe?* It was a decision she needed to make for herself, not because he wanted her to. Could it be that simple, though? She looked back down at the words.

"Everyone who calls on the name of the Lord will be saved."

That's it? No ritual? No exacting of payment? Instinct told her there was no reason to learn any further what a commitment to God required if she couldn't take this first step to believe. So it came down to that. Could she *believe?* Not knowing the next step? Not knowing how her life would change?

And then she knew. *I want what Nell and Michael have. They don't have all the answers to what the future holds, but they have peace.* She laid the Bible back down on the coffee table and leaned her head back against the sofa. She took a deep breath, opening her eyes to see the colors of dawn flooding through the windows. The remnants of an old, hardened shell around her heart fell away as she began with halting words.

"I'm not sure if these are the right words, but *I believe,* Lord . . . and I need You."

Berdine could only describe it later as a quiet assurance blooming in her heart. She had almost expected something a little more dramatic, but would not have traded the calm feeling of joy taking root in her heart for anything more sensational. She continued to sip her coffee, watching the sun peak through the kitchen curtains. *How ironic,* she mused. *On the one day I expected to feel the most turmoil, my heart is calm.* It made her smile.

The bathroom door down the hall opened and closed, followed closely by the sounds of a shower running. Michael must be up. A feeling of excitement fluttered in her stomach, and she realized how eager she was to share the news with him. She jumped off the couch and poured herself another half a cup. She swiped a fresh peach out of the bowl on the kitchen table and took a bite. Berdine wanted to move—*needed* to move! Energy surged through her. She opened the back porch door and stepped outside. The air was cool. Dew sparkled on the grass like tiny diamonds reflecting light from the sun. She set her coffee on the table and rolled up the legs of her pajama bottoms. She stepped off into the glistening carpet of green. The damp grass tickled her bare feet as she tiptoed lightly to the honeysuckle bushes draping the back fence. She breathed in the sweetest fragrance. Her attention was captured by a tiny, fluttering ruby-throated hummingbird. It hovered bravely, just beyond her reach. Its wings were a blur, but the rest of its colors and features were starkly clear. *Oh, God! How beautiful,* and her thoughts, she realized, were addressed to Someone very real.

The tiny bird darted from bloom to bloom. Berdine was enchanted. She followed it down the fence line, tiptoeing carefully across the carpet of grass. She was so absorbed in her quest, she jumped at the sound of Michael's voice directly behind her.

"How lucky can I get? My very own garden nymph!"

She whirled, surprised he was merely a touch away. He laughed and swooped her up in his arms, carrying her back across the lawn. "And now that I've captured her, she'll be mine forever!"

Berdine giggled, wrapping her arms around his neck and burrowing her face against his skin. She breathed in the familiar smell of his cologne and decided honeysuckle couldn't even compete! He carried her into the house, causing a commotion with her squealing over his laughter. The major looked up from his paper, shaking his head. Aunt Molly beamed with pleasure at their playful antics. Berdine was breathless with laughter when Michael finally set her down. Her eyes shone brightly, and her heart felt close to bursting. How could she feel this way on the morning of Michael's departure? Even as she asked herself, she already knew the answer. The empty places were gone. The gaps had been filled. She was whole.

"Breakfast, anyone? It'll have to be quick if we're going to get Michael to the bus on time. What time do you want to be there, dear?" Aunt Molly smiled tenderly at her "borrowed" son.

"I need to be there about eight fifteen, so I'm thinking Berdine and I need to leave a little before eight." He turned to the laughing girl and swatted her playfully on the behind. "So that means if you're planning to shower, you have about thirty minutes."

"Who needs thirty minutes? It'll take me fifteen, tops. I'll be out before you finish your breakfast."

She darted off down the hall before Michael could even respond. He just shook his head, grinning to himself as he pulled out a chair at the table.

Michael's good-byes to his aunt were tender and loving. He enveloped her in his long arms, kissing her soundly on the cheek. She remained composed until his last whispered words, "You're the only mama I've ever known and the best I could have prayed for. Now, don't you forget to send that special candy you make. I'll be the most popular marine at Camp Lejeune!" Tears leaked from his aunt's eyes, even as she laughed at his teasing.

"You take care, Michael. I'll be sending the major up there in a couple of weeks to make sure you're behaving!" Through unshed tears, she tried to summon a frown.

Michael's answering chuckle was tinged with sadness. He turned and shook the major's hand. It wasn't enough. He leaned over and wrapped his uncle in a bear hug. His uncle thumped him on his back. "And if he *doesn't* behave, I'm sure the base up there could do with some new fencing. I've got an experienced post-hole-digger, right here!"

Michael dumped his gear into the trunk of his car and opened the passenger side door for Berdine. She rolled down her window and called out to Aunt Molly, "I'll be back in a bit to pick up my things."

"Well, there's certainly no reason for you to feel like you need to rush off. Robert will be at work, and it'll just be me here. Maybe it'll be a good time for us to 'debrief.'" With the mirrored unshed tears between the two of them, they both knew "debrief" was code for "weep unabashedly."

Berdine nodded, knowing instinctively she would need Molly's support. The couple drove off with the major and his wife waving.

They arrived on base with a little more than forty-five minutes to spare. Michael pulled into a parking space and got his gear out of the trunk. He handed Berdine his keys, and they headed over to "arrivals and departures." Buses had just pulled up, and several dozen men poured out the open doors. A few looked wide-eyed and scared. It amused Michael to see how different the recruits always looked after completing thirteen weeks of marine boot camp. Several more buses drove up as Michael and Berdine entered the lobby where they would await his orders to board. The place was already teeming with activity. Officers waited with their families. Gear was spread out across the large waiting area. TVs in several sections of the room provided the background noise. Berdine began to feel a slight rise in the tension throughout the place. She wondered if the waiting to say good-bye wasn't twice as difficult as the good-bye itself. She and Michael found an empty couch and sat together, holding hands and talking quietly.

Soon, a voice came over the PA announcing ten minutes to boarding. Berdine's heart suddenly plummeted. Her face must have shown her feelings, because Michael leaned over to cup her face.

"I love you," he whispered.

"I love you too, Michael. More than I know how to put into words."

"I'll call when I get to North Carolina. If I find out anything, I'll let you know." He stood slowly, drawing Berdine to her feet.

Berdine stood on her toes, her hands lifting to clasp around his neck. He smiled down at her in that slow, easy way, and Berdine felt the familiar fluttering deep inside her. In one fluid motion he lowered his head and captured her lips in his in a long, lingering kiss. One hand circled her waist, pulling her tightly against him, and the other trailed gentle fingers up and down her spine. She could feel tears on her cheeks and wondered which of them they belonged to. When their kiss ended, they stood staring at each other silently.

Finally she spoke. "There was something I wanted to tell you."

"What is it?"

"*I believe,* Michael . . . I . . . I told God I couldn't do it anymore on my own. I'm giving Him control."

"*What?* When? *Berdine!* That's the most incredible news I've heard in a long time! You need to tell the Major and Aunt Molly. Maybe you can go to church with them. And Nell . . . she's been praying for you for a while now, Berdine. Wow . . . *this makes me so happy.*"

Her news filled him with an amazing sense of joy, and at the same time, he looked disappointed. "Aw, Berdine . . . that thing about *timing* . . . I just wish I could be here these first few weeks to watch you grow. It will be the most incredible change in your life . . . and I hate missing it! You'll have to write me . . . let me know what you're learning."

Berdine smiled happily through her tears. She was so glad she was able to share this moment with Michael.

"Five minutes to departure! Marines, please store your gear in the carrying compartments of the bus and load up."

She was crying openly now, and Michael's expression was bleak. He leaned down, whispering urgently to her. "I want you to be my wife, Berdine. I had planned to ask you before I got these orders, and then I wasn't sure if I should wait till I got back. I just don't think I can wait until then to ask you! I have to know now. Will you marry me when I get back?"

His arms were wrapped tightly around her, his chin curved around her neck. If she had seen his face in that moment, she would have seen the hungry desperation. The longing in him was almost painful.

"*Oh, Michael! I will.* There's nothing I want more than to be Mrs. Michael Caraway. Please come home soon. I love you so much."

They smiled at each other through tear-filled eyes. Finally, he shouldered his gear and gave her one last kiss before turning to walk toward the bus. Suddenly, he stopped, turning back with the most quizzical look on his face.

"I think this means… *we're engaged!*" He looked comically surprised.

Berdine laughed through her tears as she watched him walk away to board the bus.

XXXVIII

"And that was it. That was the last time I saw him. Two months later we learned his platoon had been attacked on a special mission." Berdine sniffed, dabbing at her wet cheeks with the crumpled tissue. She looked across the table at her lifelong friend, grateful for the answering tears on Nell's cheeks. The two of them had been coming to the Lighthouse Inn on this date in September for almost thirty-five years.

"It always makes me cry, Berdie. What a special love you two had." Nell smiled, the piercing brightness of her eyes, undimmed by the years.

Berdine nodded, gazing out of the restaurant window at the unchanging view of the ocean. The irony of the scene struck her instantly. Even though life had whipped her about as freely as it stirred the dunes of sand, this tremendous ocean ... *their* ocean ... maintained its steady rhythm throughout all of time. At least the pain of losing Michael no longer constricted her soul. Thankfully, it only visited her in its fullness on this anniversary each year. *How blessed*

I am, she thought, turning her gaze to the beloved friend across the table from her. She reached out a hand to touch Nell's fingers, now swollen with arthritis. Berdine's touch was gentle, ever sensitive to the pain that was Nell's constant companion.

"Nell, how can I thank you? All these years you've come to this place with me to hear me tell this story. And you always cry as if it were the first time you ever heard it." Berdine spoke softly, love brimming in her voice.

Nell smiled back at her dear friend, wincing as she tried to curl her fingers around Berdine's palm. "Each time you tell it, it takes me back. On the patio, that night, when he first told us he had to go, I watched your face as he said the words, and it took my breath away. I wondered how you would ever survive being apart from him. You weren't a believer then. It may have been the only time I threw a tantrum before the Lord. I doubted Him for the first time in my life. If this was His method for drawing you to Himself, I would have been happy to point out why it wasn't going to work!"

Berdine smiled, comforted that her friend still had a backbone of steel and a will of iron. She chuckled lightly, trying to picture a young Nell, hands on hips, lecturing *the Almighty* on His strategy!

Berdine was thoughtful a moment, reminiscing how soon after that time she had committed her life to the Lord. She chuckled softly, "I remember how surprised you were when I shared the news that I was a believer—not even two days later!"

Nell looked chagrined. "Oh, I remember it well! Sometimes I think the Lord branded it in my mind so I would forever remember that I should have trusted in His timing. What better, more *meaningful,* gift could you have sent Michael off with than to let him know you shared his faith?"

Berdine nodded, continuing, "Things moved so quickly after that! Remember sweet Aunt Molly and Uncle Robert—the major? They snatched me up so fast and carted me off to church on a weekly basis! I took a class so I could learn the basics. Soaked it up like a sponge. After I got to know folks, I started finding ways to get more involved. It's amazing how busy a person could stay just volunteering in a church. As soon as people knew I had worked with preteens at Outward Bound, they had me helping the sixth grade Sunday school teacher before I could barely tell you where Genesis was in the Bible! Those kiddos sure knew how to spot a rookie!" Berdine chuckled, remembering her early experiences in church life.

Nell nodded. "Oh, but they *loved you,* Berdine. There were no pretenses about you. Kids have always been drawn to you—especially the troubled ones. You've experienced such pain and loss in your life. It's given you an insight into those hurting souls like no one I've ever known. You have used your own suffering to reach so many! Remember how many teens you helped as a counselor at the high school?

Nell caught the change in Berdine's expression and knew instantly what she was thinking. A flash of fresh sorrow crossed her friend's face, and Nell reached out to touch Berdine's hand.

"How is Mac doing?" Nell's voice trembled with the shared pain.

Both women were instantly transported back as years began to blur…

Berdine had met McAllister Richmond when he had first come to Mount Holly as a troubled, young boy. Even then, as she was trying to sort through her pain of losing Michael, her heart still reached out to the anguished little boy. Young Mac had experienced an incredible trauma in the death of both his parents in a tragic airplane crash. They had something in common: significant, paralyzing loss. Most of the folks in Mount Holly only saw the young boy's anger and lashing out and were quick to judge him hopeless—but not Berdine. When she looked into those stormy dark eyes, she saw a young Michael. She befriended the boy and gained his trust. It was an odd friendship but one that grew and solidified through his high school years where she saw him nearly on a weekly basis in her office at the school. Sometimes, he just stopped in for a chat. He had such an endearing way about him. Over time, the sullen, withdrawn little boy disappeared, replaced by a gentle, engaging young man with hope and dreams for a future.

The first time he shyly presented one of his sculptures to her, Berdine gasped in amazement. It was a beautiful figurine of an angel. Every detail was exquisite. Its wings were gossamer, and the expression on her upraised face was one of ethereal joy. She lifted slender arms to the heavens, long, curling tendrils of hair trailing down her back.

Berdine remembered cradling the sculpture gently in her hands, surrounded by the bittersweet memories of *another* figurine from long years past. Tears had clouded her eyes as she thought of the mermaid she'd bought for Michael for his twenty-third birthday, just days before he left. The tears escaped the corners of her eyes and ran down her cheek. Young Mac watched in dismay, fearing he had caused his friend pain. He stood hurriedly, stammering a confused apology.

"Miss Berdine … I … I'm so sorry."

Berdine suddenly became aware of the growing fear on Mac's face. She hastened to reassure the boy.

"Oh, Mac, don't worry. This is the most beautiful angel I've ever seen. It reminded me of something I gave to a friend I lost years ago. You know how things can trigger those unexpected ambushes of pain. Grief never truly goes away. Something can bring a memory in an instant, and the sudden pain simply takes your breath away." Berdine reached across the desk and patted Mac's hand. "You know what I'm talking about, don't you?"

Mac was nodding his head with a solemn expression belying his young years. She saw an answering pain in his eyes. "Yes, I do know. That's why I made this angel for you. I knew when I first saw her face, she was for you. It's called 'Hope.'"

Berdine smiled broadly through her tears, nodding in satisfied agreement. She breathed a silent prayer of thanks for the Lord's unique provision in her life through this young friend. It almost brought a smile to her face when the sudden thought crossed her mind. *Now who exactly is the rescuer here?*

Sometimes, Mac came into her office carrying the burdens and pressures of his teenage years. He was somewhat of a square peg trying to fit into a round hole. His peers didn't quite understand his dreamy ideas and distracted, creative brilliance that characterized him. Consequently, Mac was somewhat of a loner. From what Berdine could observe, kids liked him from a distance, but he had no real close relationships. He just operated on a different plane. The girls might have liked to pursue him, but he was petrified of ever having to hold a conversation with one of them. He kept his distance and found his fulfillment in his sculpting. Berdine continued to encourage him and observe him closely for signs that the lack of a social life might have a negative impact on his self-esteem. But she never saw it. Mac continued to keep his cheerful sense of humor and charm, growing in self-confidence and purpose.

They discussed his plans for his future, and Berdine was amazed at how focused and specific he was. He had scholarships to several renowned art institutes around the country. They were simply there for his choosing. He discussed all of his options with Berdine, finally settling on the institute in New York. She would be sad to see him leave; she was as proud as any mother might have been. But she also knew what an incredible gift he had. He had a responsibility to get the best training afforded him. She knew it might be years before young Mac ever found his way back to their sleepy little town of Mount Holly. After all, he had an exciting career looming in his future.

But if Berdine had learned one thing over the years, it was that *nothing*—not things, nor good fortune, nor even people—was hers to hold too tightly to in this life. It was only in the blind ignorance of her childhood that she ever believed *if she were just "good enough" or "quiet enough" to slip through under the wire, maybe she could just tiptoe through this life without heartache and trauma and loss.* It was life itself that opened her eyes to the truth she'd often read, yet never fully understood, in the pages of her well-used, worn Bible. *Rain fell alike on the just and the unjust.* No one was exempt. It wasn't a matter of "*if* trials come," it was "*when* trials come ..." Instead of filling her heart with fear and bitterness, that one painful truth about life flooded her soul with gratefulness and peace. How could she have survived her past or face an unsure future without the only unchanging One, the One who was knitting together the tapestry of her life? Some days it felt as though her life was merely a tangled jumble of colored threads, but she had placed her trust in the only One who could see the other side of the tapestry.

Berdine helped Mac fill out the paperwork and guided him toward the right people to help him make the necessary arrangements for his move that summer after graduation. Mac's grandmother lamented loudly about his "leaving her," but Berdine wondered if the feisty older woman wasn't more than just a little bit relieved they'd made it relatively unscathed to this milestone in her young grandson's life.

Berdine continued her work at the high school and maintained a vested interest in the Outward Bound program. She and Nell enjoyed their friendship and began the tradition of their annual trip in September out to the Isle of the Palms to commemorate the memory of Michael Caraway.

Berdine maintained contact with her young friend, Mac Richmond, and followed the success of his career with beaming pride. Because of his growing renown in the art world, it came as quite a surprise to learn that Mac was leaving the flurry and excitement of New York to return to the quieter life in Mount Holly. He had grown tired and a little disillusioned with the fast, sophisticated pace of the big city. He wanted nothing more than a quaint little office near town square and restful walks in the park. He reasoned he was close enough to Charleston if he needed a place to display his collections. Berdine tried not to pry into the reasons for this sudden change of location, but she often wondered if it didn't have something to do with a woman. Mac had never hinted at a relationship, but she'd seen something different in his eyes when he'd returned, and she respected his need to keep his reasons private.

She fell into an easy routine of dropping off a home-cooked meal now and then. It wasn't difficult to discover that Mac had an obsessive habit of locking himself in his basement workshop when he was engrossed in a project. He was always a little sheepish about his feverish pace, but he was effusive in his gratitude for a hot meal.

It was a cold, rainy November afternoon when Berdine came by with all the trimmings of a bountiful, delicious Thanksgiving dinner for Mac. She knocked loudly on his front door, trying to hold the umbrella in one hand and the roasting pan in the other. She waited a few minutes then pounded again. She was about to turn the knob on the front door when the door suddenly swung open. There stood an unshaven Mac, black hair wildly askew and longer than normal. His shirt was spattered with wet clay, and his jeans had holes in the knees. His feet were bare, and he didn't seem to feel the gust of cold wind blowing in on him. He grinned broadly, beckoning her in with the wave of a peanut butter and jelly sandwich.

"Why, Miss Berdine! What brings you out on this cold, wet day? Come in, come in … Would you like to join me in a peanut butter and jelly sandwich?" He chuckled, ushering in the bewildered little woman and placing a big kiss on her cheek. Berdine sighed heavily, shaking her head at her own hopeless devotion to this guileless young man.

"Mac ... *it's Thanksgiving!*" She held up the black-lidded roasting pan with two oven-clad mitts.

"You don't say! Is it really?" Mac laughed heartily at his lapse in calendar awareness. Berdine didn't even reply. She just smiled, pulling him into a hug and then pointed at his feet.

"Put some shoes on and help me carry in our feast. We'll celebrate together." Berdine nearly laughed at the delight in Mac's eyes. He was helpless to resist one of Berdine's home-cooked meals, and there wasn't another person in Mount Holly he'd rather share it with.

As they put things on the table and got out the dishes, Mac described his latest sculpture with animated enthusiasm. He was nearly beside himself with excitement, and Berdine listened with attentive indulgence. The meal was a delightful exchange of conversation and food. Mac leaned back in his chair, content. He laughed at the pleased expression on Berdine's face.

"Berdie, why don't you quit that dull job at the school and come take care of me? I can top that salary by a mile and promise you a kitchen that exceeds your culinary dreams!"

At first, he was merely teasing when the thought popped into his mind, but when the words spilled out, he realized there was nothing he wanted more than to take care of this beloved woman who'd been a mentor, a mother, a friend to him. The only way she'd ever allow that was if she thought it was *she* taking care of *him*.

Berdine eyed the laughing young man suspiciously, as though searching for a hidden motive, but all she saw twinkling back at her was the affectionate gaze of the boy she'd grown to love. "Now that's certainly a thought to chew on. Are you seriously offering?" She dare not let the leap of joy carry her away. Instead, she sat very still, a solemn expression on her face.

At first, her sudden seriousness made him chuckle, and then, in a sudden moment of perception, he felt the weight of sadness that she'd not had the opportunity to care for a husband or children. He had never truly understood that incongruity of life. Here was a woman born to nurture, protect, support, and care for loved ones ... yet with no one in her life to receive it! He knew she had lost someone significant in her life, but she never offered much information and he was not one to delve.

"*Of course,* I'm seriously offering. You've seen how I live! I barely remember to shower when I'm working with my clay, much less worry about clean clothes or eating!" Michael grinned lopsidedly, and then he uttered the magic words—the ones that would seal the deal. "I *need* you, Berdine!" His expression was boyish and pleading, and Berdine knew she was lost.

She hid her pleasure in playful gruffness. "Why I can never resist a hopeless cause is beyond me!" She shook her head, smiling, and then stuck her hand across the table to seal it with a handshake. "All right, it's a deal!"

Mac whooped and came around the table to give the little woman a big hug. "Let's go into the den and work out the details. You go on, and I'll bring in the coffee and pie!"

Berdine leveled a slow, stern look at her young friend. "If this is gonna work, we're gonna start out on the right foot. *You* go into the den, and *I'll* bring in the coffee and pie."

Mac laughed loudly and acquiesced graciously to the older woman. That night began a wonderful eleven-year working relationship between the two.

XXXIX

Nell looked across the table at her treasured friend, content to wait silently as she watched the expressions of Berdine's memories flitting across her face. She could tell by the slight smile on the other woman's face that she was remembering the early years of her friendship with Mac. Just as Nell knew with assurance what would follow, Berdine's face slowly crumpled, and she fumbled for a tissue in her purse. Nell beat her to it and handed her one, lightly grasping Berdine's free hand.

"I know. I know..." she murmured. "It's one thing when the loss is your own, but it's another when it happens to one of your children."

Berdine paused, looking at her friend in surprise. Suddenly, Nell's meaning sunk in, and the warm comfort of perfect understanding flowed over her.

"That's it, Nell. My own loss was painful enough, but for Mac to finally find the perfect love of his life only to lose both her and their unborn child nearly destroyed me. And you're right. No child of my flesh could have been more of a son to me than Mac!" Berdine blew her nose softly into the tissue while Nell dabbed at her own eyes. Both of them still felt the acute pain of Mac losing his young wife and child, though it had been two years now.

Berdine continued, "And Madeline was the daughter I always wanted, Nell. You know that. For weeks after we lost her, I railed at God. I questioned Him with a frightful anger and boldness … and then … I turned away." Berdine hung her head regretfully.

Nell murmured words of understanding and comfort, encouraging Berdine to continue. In all the time they had been coming to the Lighthouse Inn, they had not yet talked about the recent couple of dark years following the loss of Mac's young wife and unborn daughter. It was as if the wound was still too fresh, too raw to touch. But Nell was God's provision of a safe harbor in Berdine's life. And she was *nothing* if not persistent when she sensed healing was near.

"I worried about you, Berdie. But I didn't know how to reach you. When Mac decided to take an extended trip after it happened, *you* were the one I most feared for. Mac grieved openly. He wanted to talk to anyone who had a memory of Madeline. He wanted to visit the campus where she attended college and go to the town where she lived growing up. He wanted to learn about her extended family and meet the people who could tell him the story of her early years … but you … *You,* Berdine … began to shut yourself off." Nell's voice quivered.

Berdine started to protest, defending her slide into a slow isolation. But looking into the sad, gentle eyes of her friend, she knew she was faced with the truth. She *had* turned away. She had turned away from the people who cared, from the community who wanted to comfort her and from the God who had promised to never leave nor forsake her. She lowered her eyes, nodding her head slowly in agreement.

"It was too much, Nell. Too much pain. I could bear my own loss but not my Mac's loss too. Don't you see? I couldn't see God any more. If He truly loved me, why did He keep taking away the people I loved?" Berdine lifted tear-filled eyes to meet the exact expression gazing back at her.

"I don't know … " Nell whispered. "All I know is He promises He loves us. That's all we have. Whether life makes a lick of sense or not, the question is *can we still trust Him when all we see on the tapestry are tangled knots?*"

Berdine's head lifted, startled to hear her analogy tossed back to her. Slowly, she turned to look out the giant window at the dusky sunset casting a rosy glow over the ocean's surface. She pondered Nell's words and a nearly forgotten sense of peace settled like a balm in her heart.

What's the alternative? What choice do I have? He's either my God and He's trustworthy, or I can turn my back on Him and have . . . nothing.

Berdine turned back to her wise friend, searching the lined face she trusted and loved. The silence was unhurried. Finally, a sad, weary smile appeared as Berdine nodded her head. "Yes," she whispered. "I still trust Him."

The two women smiled at each other, the years falling away. Each saw the other as a young woman on the precipice of life's adventure.

Suddenly, Berdine started to chuckle. Then the gurgle became a laugh. Nell joined in, not even knowing what they were laughing about. Soon Berdine got so tickled, she began to cough. Nell started to rise, wondering if she should signal for a waiter, but Berdine waved her back. Her face was red, and she fanned herself with the napkin. She picked up her glass of water and took a few calming sips before trying to speak to her friend.

"The way I figure it, my friend, is this: what we got here are a couple of late bloomers! It's always been that way for me, and you're just the same. Your dreams got sidelined too. But look at you now. Here you are, sixty-four years old, about to finish your master's in business and engaged to the most handsome elderly Irishman I've ever seen! If that's not a late bloomer, I don't know what is!" Berdine began to laugh again, but this time her heart was light and full of joy.

Nell couldn't help but join in the laughter, enjoying Berdine's description of the two of them. She gasped for breath, trying to form the words that tumbled from her lips. "But what about *you*, Berdie? How are you a late bloomer *now?*"

The look of peace and contentment on Berdine's face stirred Nell's heart as nothing else could. Berdine winked mischievously at her lifelong friend and quipped lightly, "Well, that chapter hasn't been written yet!" She turned once again to gaze out at the ocean waves that seemed to call to her.

She smiled, and Nell blinked once, wondering if her old eyes were playing tricks on her. For a moment, she thought she'd seen the eighteen-year-old Berdine smiling back at her, the one who'd grabbed life by the tail, who'd take on any challenge.

Berdine leaned forward, whispering, "It's a magical night, Nell. Just look at that setting sun! Don't you just imagine it sizzling when it touches the water?"

Nell raised her eyebrows, smiling slightly at this younger, playful version of the Berdine she'd known all her life.

"What do *you* think, Berdie?" Nell queried, puzzled and amused.

"Oh, it sizzles. It *definitely* sizzles." Berdine winked slowly at her friend. She grinned and turned to gaze once more out the window. They sat in silence for a moment, watching the sinking orange orb on the distant horizon.

Finally, their waiter came, interrupting their private thoughts. "Ladies, will there be anything else?" The young man smiled charmingly, familiar with the annual ritual of these two older women … and the ensuing healthy tip.

Berdine turned to smile at the young man, waving her hand. "No, that's all, Will. Thank you again for an absolutely charming evening. You've outdone yourself… again. You've treated us like royalty!"

The young waiter beamed. "Well then, I'll be back shortly with your check. I'll be your cashier. Feel free to stay as long as you like." He smiled affectionately at the two women.

When he left, Berdine leaned conspiratorially toward Nell. "Is it *us* he loves … or is it our money?" She chuckled.

Nell entered the playful spirit of Berdine's teasing. "Are you kidding me? How can you even question his devotion?"

Berdine laughed in response, looking at her watch. Nell noticed and began to gather her purse and jacket. "Do you want to go on up to our room and watch movies?"

Berdine shook her head, a curious light in her eyes. "No, I don't feel ready to settle quite yet. I think I'll go for a sunset walk on the beach! Want to join me?"

Nell shook her head vehemently. "After that heavy meal? All I want to do is soak in a hot bubble bath, wrap myself in one of those fluffy robes, and watch movies in bed!"

Berdine laughed. "I hope that great, hulking son of an Irishman knows your propensity for retiring early!"

Nell blushed. "Don't you worry about my Irishman! We've got a schedule worked out!"

Berdine grinned teasingly. "You *would!*" She quipped.

The women left the restaurant arm in arm, relishing the familiar companionship and the beautiful, cool evening. They walked slowly down the sidewalk, their laughter echoing softly. In the distance, the mournful cry of a gull could be heard over the rhythmic swell of the sea. A soft southern breeze played across their faces.

The two friends stopped at the boardwalk leading down to the beach. Berdine leaned over and kissed Nell's cheek. "Are you sure you'll be okay going up to the room alone?"

Nell laughed, shaking her head. "*You're* the one with the twinkle in her eye. If I didn't know better, I'd think you were trying to get rid of your chaperone so you could meet a fella down there!" Nell gestured toward the beckoning waves. Berdine turned to look at the panorama before her. Her heart swelled, and she couldn't even begin to put words to the feelings coursing through her. She opened her mouth to answer, but suddenly a sob rose in her throat. Tears rushed to fill her eyes, and all she could do was shake her head, her fingers pressed tightly to her lips.

Nell hugged Berdine swiftly, then turned her toward the waves, now highlighted with an orange glow at their crest.

"Just go ..." she whispered fiercely, gently nudging Berdine.

Nell watched as Berdine took a few hesitant steps down the boardwalk, then a few more. Nell held her hands together tightly, trying to hold back her own tears. She smiled as she watched her dear friend square her shoulders, lift her head, and begin a deliberate walk toward the water.

Nell lifted her head to the stars just beginning to dot the evening sky. "I can't begin to understand Your ways, Father ... but I do know you love my friend even more than I do. Take care of her."

Nell blew an unseen kiss to Berdine and continued slowly down the sidewalk to the hotel.

XL

Berdine stood just beyond the teasing kiss of the salty foam. She watched as it playfully approached her shoes then shyly retreated. It drew her gaze toward the vast body of water churning and rolling like a giant gray beast awakening from slumber. The ebb and flow of the waves mesmerized her. Peace settled over her as she watched the sun sink lower in the horizon. As always, the scene before her pulled her back to another time. The years slipped silently away, and she heard the faint echoes of laughter riding softly on the wind. In her mind's eye, she could see a golden-haired girl laughing, twirling, splashing in the waves. She saw her call out playfully to the boy, squealing in delight as he reached out and lifted her high in his arms. He stopped, gazing at her, and slowly, oh so slowly, he let her body slide down his until they stood a breath apart. His strong hands cupped her elbows, steadying her against the push and tug of the waves. He smiled down at the girl, a private expression of undiscovered intimacy.

Berdine strained to hold onto the image, but it flickered and faded. Tears gathered in the corners of her eyes, and a familiar pressure in her chest gripped her heart and gently squeezed. She reached up for the delicate chain around her neck, fingers fumbling for the familiar pendant. Without thinking, she traced the tiny markings forever preserved on the sand dollar. It felt the same to her touch as it did years ago in the pocket of her dress. It was a promise . . . a promise of peace, of hope, and a love that transcended time.

Berdine smiled, remembering the day she wrote to Michael, telling him about having the little sand dollar they had found overlaid in silver and placed on a necklace. She could hear his delighted chuckles through the written words of his reply. *"Most girls get a ring when they get engaged. Not my girl. Way too ordinary. My girl wears a sand dollar!"*

Berdine began to laugh. Even as tears trickled down her cheeks, joy swelled up through her heart. She reached down and slipped her shoes from her feet, delighted at the cool, sucking pull of the sand under her toes. The water rushed over her feet, swirling at her ankles and tickling her with the tiny shells brushing past. A tiny white disc caught the light and winked as it tumbled across her foot. Berdine inhaled sharply as she watched a perfect sand dollar dance and spin its way back toward the ocean. She reached down and caught it in her hand. She lifted it, turning slowly to spotlight it in the last silver rays of dusk. She focused so intently upon it that she didn't see the lone figure of a man approaching slowly across the sand at the water's edge. He spoke softly before she noticed him.

"Berdine."

Slowly she lowered her hand, and his face came into view. Silver hair framed a deeply tanned face. Eyes sparkled and gleamed, belying his years. But it was his mouth that captured her gaze . . . lips that curled into a slight, lopsided grin, punctuated by a dimple unmarred by age. He leaned heavily on a cane and adjusted his weight slowly, gingerly . . . as if pain were his familiar companion. A deep scar marked his face, from the corner of his left eye weaving down to his jawbone, yet he bore the wound without shame. Berdine's eyes traveled over his face and form at a frantic pace, her mouth working to shape words. As she struggled to speak, the man reached out a tentative hand that trembled ever so slightly.

"Berdine."

This time, he spoke her name in a husky whisper. Berdine stood frozen, water swirling around her ankles. He saw the moment the shocked recognition dawned in her eyes. He let out a breath he'd been holding, a crooked smile beginning slowly to light up his face. She made an attempt to raise her hand toward his, but the effort seemed monumental. In understanding, he leaned forward and captured her icy fingers in his strong, weathered palm. He waited, his heart pounding a steady rhythm in his neck. She could see that familiar pulse at the opening of his collar that told of passion beneath a calm exterior. Berdine breathed in a long, shaky breath and exhaled his name on a sigh.

"Michael."

For a long moment, no words were spoken. None were needed. Only the faint echoes of the seagulls' cries announced the joining of the sun at the ocean's edge.

"I'm dreaming." Berdine could only whisper.

"No." Unshed tears glistened in Michael's eyes.

"How? You … I … I thought you … but … when?" Bewilderment and shock chased any coherent thought from her mind. She could only tremble. Michael shook his head slowly, smiling sadly, the tears beginning to fall down the lines of his face. He too shook as he drew her gently closer. He lowered his forehead to hers, trying to compose his words. Berdine saw the tremendous pain and anguish in his eyes, and she lifted a hand to cup his scarred face. He jerked suddenly as if her touch had burned him, but instead of turning away, he buried his face in her hand, pressing his lips to her palm. It was her undoing. Berdine sobbed and flung her arms around the man, burying her face against his chest. He lifted her face and began to cover it with kisses. She tried to return the kisses, but between tears and laughter and disjointed words, she wasn't sure she ever hit the mark. It was all they could do to keep from tumbling into the water. Gasping for breath, between choked laughter and sobs, Michael finally lifted his head and managed hoarse words. "Are … are you married, Berdine? I have to know … "

Berdine shook her head frantically, not letting go of her grip around his waist. With one hand, she fumbled for the necklace at her neck and lifted the little sand dollar for Michael to see.

"No … no, I'm not … *But I'm engaged.*" She laughed with joy.

Michael's eyes widened as he took in the little silver sand dollar. A slow grin split his face, causing the years to fall away. As his smile faded, his expression became tender. He looked deeply into her eyes, finding the familiar look of love he sought. He took a deep breath, exhaling as if he'd just run for miles.

"W-would you have a … a cup of coffee with me?" His nervous stammer was boyish and endearing. She could see the young man peering from behind blue eyes only slightly faded by the years.

"I'd love to." So many questions hovered at her lips, but as she slipped her hand into the crook of Michael's arm, she no longer felt the panicked urgency to have them answered.

Berdine bent to pick up her shoes, still holding Michael's arm. She looked up to meet that smile she knew so well. At that moment, she could almost swear she heard the sizzle of the sun touching the water as they made their way back up the beach.

EPILOGUE

Berdine lay snuggled next to Michael's side as they swung lazily in the hammock. It was another perfect morning. Palm trees swayed indolently overhead. The gentle breeze carried with it the faint scent of magnolias.

"I'm getting used to this, you know. And I'm not feeling guilty. Not a bit." Berdine smiled up at her husband of two weeks. She scooted even closer, wondering if this girlish infatuation would fade. His arm was wrapped around her, holding her tightly to his side. He reached down to collect a kiss from her upturned lips.

"Well, *I'm* not getting used to it. I hope I never do. We have a lot of years to make up for, young lady." Michael chuckled softly, squeezing her close. Berdine grimaced slightly.

She quipped, "If I'd known you were going to show up, I would have at least tried to go on a diet!"

Michael's expression grew serious. "Don't you dare. I want you the way I saw you on the beach that first night. No changes. You're beautiful and soft, and I may never get enough of you."

Berdine laughed softly, loving the sense of womanliness he inspired in her. It had been a surreal several weeks following the magical night on the beach when he walked back into her life. They could hardly bear to separate; they had so much to say, so many gaps to fill in. Only sheer exhaustion had them parting to seek a few hours respite each night. And then there were the hasty wedding arrangements to be made. Berdine truly had the ceremony and reception of her dreams, albeit forty years later—barefoot on the beach at sunset with a few close friends surrounding them—just as she'd always wanted. He had whisked her off to a posh condo on Hilton Head, South Carolina, for a long, luxurious honeymoon, where they continued to put together the missing pieces of their separate lives. He was so hungry to hear every detail of the decades they'd spent apart... so many questions he asked her. And if there weren't enough details to suit him, he'd push for more. On more than one occasion, she laughingly raised both hands in surrender, begging for relief. Yet when she turned the questions to *his* past, answers came slowly and wearily. She had sensed from the moment she had seen him that it might be years before she understood what had happened to him. Berdine never pushed. She knew he would peel back the layers as he was able. And if she never completely had all the answers, well, that would be all right with her too.

Many nights he startled her awake, thrashing and fighting against the bedcovers. It only took her cool touch and low, soothing voice to end his panicked struggles. Slowly, haltingly, over time, he began to reveal the terrible scarring of his mind. She had often traced with loving fingers the old wounds as he talked. But she knew that emotional healing might never be fully complete. The bits and pieces he'd shared were horrible to hear. She couldn't imagine how he had managed to survive his experience. Finally, after another tortured episode that had them both crying and on their knees beside the bed, Michael choked out the missing pieces of his nightmare.

"It was a simple reconnaissance mission through what was supposed to be a deserted village. We had our coordinates and the visual reports confirmed the village was empty. Our assignment was to locate a place to hide some much-needed artillery. I was leading a group of six men through a heavy jungle. Somehow we lost radio contact as we reached the edge of the trees and had the village in our sights. It was my decision to proceed, even though contact had not been re-established." Michael stopped abruptly, his eyes darting back and forth nervously, as if he were actually there. His breathing increased, and Berdine could see the nightmare playing out through his mind. She laid a firm hand on his arm, and he jumped slightly as though surprised to see her. As frightened as she was to hear what was ahead, she urged him on. She prayed silently for the finished work of healing in his soul.

"I gave the command, and we spread out, cautiously approaching the open area. No sounds, no evidence of life. Suddenly, there was a horrible explosion halfway around the perimeter, and one of my men went down. The two next to him panicked, thinking we were under fire. I yelled at them to freeze; we were in a hidden mine field ... but they ran. They *ran,* Berdine. And I couldn't stop them. Their eyes mirrored the horror I felt as I watched those men—boys, really, blown to bits. I wanted to throw *myself* on a mine. If I could have traded my life for theirs, I would have ... God knows, I *would* have." His expression was anguished as he grasped both of Berdine's hands.

Tears coursed down Berdine's cheeks, falling unnoticed onto their joined hands. She prayed silently, even as she murmured words of comfort to the broken man in front of her. She urged him to continue, although the pain of his words crushed her heart.

"Within seconds, the rest of us were surrounded, bayonets thrust inches from our throats. I was so proud of my boys. None of them spoke nor even moved. I was quickly identified as the leader, and a swift kick to my kneecap had me crumpled facedown in the mud. Yet neither of my men wavered. It's one thing for a person to hold out when *he* is the one tortured ... It's quite another thing to hold out when his leader is tortured in his place. I'd trained my men to expect that, and they made me proud. We were blindfolded and dragged off to the enemy camp and later transported to a prison camp."

At that, Michael lowered his head to Berdine's lap, trying to hold back a strangled sob. She smoothed her fingers across his forehead, pushing the silver strands to the side. She soothed and whispered words of love and healing to him. He looked up at her, begging her to understand, "Please don't ask me to tell you the things that happened in that prison camp. I ... I ... can't ever ..."

"Shhh ..." Berdine whispered, laying her fingers across his lips. "It's okay. You don't have to go on ..."

Michael shook his head, sitting up. He was like a man driven by an invisible force. "I don't know how much time passed. I thought we'd surely be rescued, so much time had elapsed. They kept us each separated and told us individually that the others were dead. I found out much later, the other two really were dead—tortured beyond recognition and left to die a lonely, painful death." Michael's voice broke, and he rubbed his hands over his face, as if to erase the images in his mind. He was silent for so long, Berdine was not sure he intended to finish. She simply knelt beside him and continued to hold him, praying fervently.

"They *broke* me ... completely ... to the point I *wanted* them to kill me. I taunted them, hoping they'd do it. But they wouldn't ... because they figured out it was what I wanted. Berdine, it was years before I got out of that hellhole. When the war was over, I didn't know who or where I was. And the tragic thing was ... I didn't care. Some British soldiers found me and transported me to a medical facility in Seoul and left me there. I was so out of my mind, the only thing they could ascertain was that I wasn't Korean and was so close to death, I probably wouldn't make it."

Michael leaned heavily against the side of the bed, his head resting against the mattress. He closed his eyes, exhausted and bewildered that the telling of his story from so many years ago still held such power over him.

"But I *did* make it ... though I'd lost my identity. The people there were kind to me. I was released into the care of a Korean family. As miraculous as my survival was, it was even *more so* to find that my caretakers were new Christians. I'm not sure they weren't angels of God. We couldn't speak a word to each other, but we understood that immediate bond between believers. It was such a long period of recovery and regaining of my senses, they became all I had in this world. They showed me a scrap of paper they had found in a small leather pouch tied around my ankle. It was the only thing that was familiar to me. And, at first, I didn't even know why." He paused, remembering.

Berdine leaned forward. "What did it say?"

"It was a portion of the Psalms. From the first word, I realized I could quote it. 'Your steps I have established and I delight in your way. When you fall, you will not be hurled headlong because I AM the one who holds your hand. As the Scripture played over and over in my mind, I saw a face . . . a beautiful face . . . and I remembered *you,* Berdine! It all rushed back . . . The day we parted and you gave me the best gift ever, you told me you had given your heart to the Lord!'" Michael closed his eyes. A frown furrowed his brows. He appeared to wrestle with other missing gaps in his memory. After a moment, he shook his head, frustrated. He turned and looked at Berdine. "That vision of your face and God's promise to me were the two things I never lost. They were always in my mind, and I clung to them like a lifeline."

The shadows fell away from his face for the first time that evening. She saw peace settle over him. She wasn't sure he was even aware of the change that came about as he had quoted that verse to her. But she saw it and recognized it as the power of God's living word. In her heart, she praised her faithful God. It didn't even occur to her to ask Him why. She had lived long enough and walked through enough valleys to know that this life didn't give her all the answers. Yet where would they be without Him?

Then Michael smiled, but she could see a cloud of sadness in his eyes. He turned toward her, clutching her hands in his. "From that moment on, my purpose was to heal enough so that I could find my way back to you. I made it back as far as the states . . . and then I had serious doubts. What if your feelings had changed? What if your grief had finally eased and my sudden return into your life caused more pain for you? My God, Berdine, what if you were *married?* How could I face that? I wasn't even emotionally or physically whole! I just couldn't make myself go home."

Berdine ached for the loss: lost comrades, lost time, lost hope. But she marveled at how God's grace protected their hearts from bitterness. Instead, acceptance and even gratefulness prevailed. They continued to talk softly, filling in gaps and giving comfort to each other. Berdine was not surprised that Michael had found fulfillment during those lost years serving as a chaplain for troubled soldiers. As they talked about their years apart, they recognized that God had taken two shattered hearts, restored them, and used them to uniquely touch other broken lives.

Berdine whispered, "Nothing was wasted, Michael. God used these cracked, broken vessels, didn't He?" Michael nodded, smiling softly. She leaned over, cupping his strong, war-scarred face and kissed him gently. He turned, pulling her to him. There was healing in that embrace. Michael sighed, resting his head against Berdine's. They sat quietly for a moment. Then Berdine tilted her face to meet Michael's gaze. Michael could read the unspoken question in her eyes.

"Berdie . . . finally . . . one day, God told me to trust Him and that it was time. It has been such an incredibly long walk home. But God kept that promise He gave to me. He has held my hand every step of the way." His mouth curled into that old, crooked smile that never failed to cause Berdine's heart to skip a beat. She nodded against his chest, joy causing a lump in to lodge in her throat. She couldn't have spoken a word if she'd tried.

Michael yawned, feeling cleansed and finally at peace with his past. He turned, smiling at his wife. "Let's get some sleep, my love! We've got a *lot* of livin' to do . . ."

"Yes, we do, Michael. We certainly do."

e|LIVE

---

listen|imagine|view|experience

AUDIO BOOK DOWNLOAD INCLUDED WITH THIS BOOK!

In your hands you hold a complete digital entertainment package. In addition to the paper version, you receive a free download of the audio version of this book. Simply use the code listed below when visiting our website. Once downloaded to your computer, you can listen to the book through your computer's speakers, burn it to an audio CD or save the file to your portable music device (such as Apple's popular iPod) and listen on the go!

How to get your free audio book digital download:

1. Visit www.tatepublishing.com and click on the e|LIVE logo on the home page.
2. Enter the following coupon code: f1f7-45f2-f2c2-3cf7-ee27-899a-4797-ed4f
3. Download the audio book from your e|LIVE digital locker and begin enjoying your new digital entertainment package today!